THEY TOOK IT INLAND

JAMES DAWSON

SIX POINT PRESS

Copyright © 2026 James Dawson

All rights reserved.

No part of this book may be reproduced, stored in a retrieval system, or transmitted in any form or by any means, electronic, mechanical, photocopying, recording, or otherwise—including AI or automated systems—without the prior written permission of the author, except for brief quotations used in reviews or scholarly works.

This is a work of fiction. Names, characters, places, and incidents are either products of the author's imagination or used fictitiously. Any resemblance to actual events, locales, or persons, living or dead, is entirely coincidental.

ISBN 979-8-9945977-0-5

Six Point Press

For my grandfather,
who wanted to write a novel but ran out of time.

CHAPTER 1

San Bernardino, CA—The Streets

All-terrain Goodyear tires screeched along the asphalt of the 210 freeway with the eerie howl of a high-speed pursuit. The dark blue Honda Accord did its best to pull away, but Detective Zane Bruce worked the steering wheel of his undercover truck like a seasoned rally car driver.

His hands, calm. Nerves, quiet. Eyes focused.

His partner, Paul Duncan, carried enough frenetic energy that mirrored an empty Diet Coke can that rattled away in the center console. "You're losing him, man."

"I'm on his ass," Zane said. He threw a quick punch at the can, smashing it down into the cup holder to cease the vibration. "Any closer, we'd be in the back seat. Update our twenty." His body temperature continued to rise under his uniform. A trickle of sweat rolled down the valley of his spine. He pushed his back into the seat to suppress the condensation. *Stay calm.*

"Seriously, you're driving like my grandmother." Duncan pulled the dispatch radio to his mouth. "Control, Unit 97. Vehicle pursuit in progress. Dark blue Honda Accord. Plate, six-November-Oscar-Whiskey-three-two-eight. Occupied one time. Northbound on Waterman, passed Baseline. Speed about sixty, failure to yield. Requesting backup and an airship. Notify CHP." Duncan re-cradled the radio.

Zane picked the radio back up. "Suspect is Raymond Tenoso." He returned the radio. "Good job on the radio. I'm impressed you didn't call dispatch, dude or bro." He wouldn't have felt surprised if Duncan had cinched his ass tighter than a snare drum. Duncan had a white-knuckled grip on the oh-shit handle. "Gotta breathe, brother. Does the grab bar owe you money? Why are you grabbing it so tight? Hate to see you take a piss."

Streams of headlights streaked by like lasers. The steering wheel heated under the pressure of his grip. Driving and defensive tactics were his favorite part of the job. Had been since he first started driving, and his father put him through the wringer. He had a natural ability to stay calm while his adrenaline spiked like a seismograph.

Duncan released his grip and rubbed his palms on his pant legs. "Your prying eyes would love to see it. Promise you wouldn't be able to keep your eyes off it. Where you think he's heading?"

"Back to the neighborhood. Thinks he'll have a fighting chance on home turf." Wildwood Park was nearing, and with that, the added obstacles of homeless encampments and streetwalkers. Just after 2300, the nightlife took shape.

"Shouldn't his neighborhood be closer to the casino?" Duncan asked.

Before Zane could answer, a compact sedan shot out from the intersection, oblivious to the red and blue lights flashing from the truck's grill. He yanked the wheel hard to the left to avoid the collision.

Duncan threw his middle finger at the window.

Zane steadied the truck and pressed onward, closing the distance between them and the fleeing Honda. "Clueless fuck. Your middle finger did wonders. I'm sure they saw it as we sped by."

"It did me. Feel better now."

"Thank God it's night. Any earlier and we'd be fielding another complaint. Get assigned to *Coffee with a Cop* for the next six months."

"Don't suppose telling them we're in pursuit of a fentanyl trafficker with a history of sexual exploitation of minors?"

"Never," Zane said.

They continued eastbound and drove by the Wooden Nickel, a local dive bar known for a rough crowd of motorcycle club affiliates. Tonight was no exception, as a group of bikers leaned against the front porch railing outside the bar and spat as they drove by. One stood out amongst the crowd with his long white goatee and steel-eyed stare.

"Was he out there?" Duncan said.

Zane extended his arms, ignoring the question, and pushing his back into the seat. "Give dispatch an update on our position. I'm going to close in and force him home. He'll run, thinking he knows the neighborhood better than us." He did. Probably had safe houses and pre-planned hiding spots. "Can't give him any room or we'll lose him. Neighborhoods like this protect their own."

"Even knowing his crimes?"

"Oh, they don't. It'll be a fight to prove, so be ready. This neighborhood is predominantly tribal members who stole from the tribe. So, they assume they all got caught trying to skim. Guy like Raymond must keep his mouth shut, and the rest will assume he's just like them."

Raymond was worse, much worse. Made Zane's skin crawl and his body incinerate like a furnace of rage and anger. Raymond needed to go down. Cuffed, detained, prosecuted, and then the natural selection of prison life takes its turn at punishment.

A voice crackled through the radio that wasn't dispatch. It was their lieutenant. "Know our jurisdiction," Lieutenant Carmen Cruz said. "Anything on the Kizh property isn't ours. We have notified the tribe."

Zane beat Duncan to the radio. "Roger that," he said, tossing the radio over to Duncan. "You need to sharpen your quick-draw skills."

"I have other skills that don't include a jerked motion toward the radio," Duncan said. "Makes me think you've been doing a lot of jerking with that hand."

Zane smiled and shook his head, eyes ahead on the Honda while shifting to any movement in the periphery. "We should be turning into the neighborhood once we cross Kendall, but before the university."

Duncan snapped into focus as if he remembered to turn off the stove. "I know the neighborhood. Been a minute since I've been over this area."

"Truck stop bathrooms have been your preferred beat." Despite the banter, Zane's hands remained calm on the steering wheel. Smooth hand-over-hand turns. Soft manipulation between the brake and accelerator pedals. His core temperature raged like an inferno, but that didn't damage the calm nature of his extremities.

Duncan unbuckled his seatbelt, and Zane shook his head.

Duncan pleaded his case. "What? I gotta be ready to run."

"Too soon," Zane said. "We're not even in the neighborhood yet. Other than the direction, there's no sign he's turning in. Could try to lull us—"

Before he could finish, the Honda did just that and blew by the turn into his excommunicated neighborhood.

"He didn't turn in," Duncan said.

"No shit. Put your damn seatbelt back on."

Duncan clicked in. "You think he's making a run for the Rez?"

"Yes. Fuck. Update our twenty."

Duncan followed his request, and before he could return the radio, Lt. Cruz was back on the speaker.

"Do not cross over the Kizh boundary," Lt. Cruz said. A forced back repeat. A command that was not to be dismissed.

Zane's eyebrows raised, and he forced out a hard breath. "He's gonna run at some point, and we'd better be quick." Duncan reached to eject his seatbelt. "Don't even think about it until we're in a neighborhood."

The speed of the pursuit had quietly slowed from sixties to fifties, forties, and so on until they turned into a neighborhood outside the boundary of the Kizh tribal land. The casino was another mile away, but this is where the housing began and stretched up into the hills with smog-filled views of the valley. When the Santa Ana winds are blowing, the view clears, and on a good day, the distant outline of Catalina Island appears some twenty-two miles off the coast of California.

At night, as the hours crossed over into the next day, this neighborhood was quiet. Chain-link fences surrounded the front lawns and driveways of most homes. Every other one seemed to be peppered with "Beware of Dog" or "Private Property" signage.

Zane re-gripped the wheel. His knuckles turned white as the blood squeezed out of his hands and fingertips. "We're coming up on the guard shack. He turns in, we're fucked."

The Honda slowed, but didn't turn in. A Kizh security vehicle angled itself to block the entrance. A tall man with a large presence leaned against the rear fender, looking on. He wore an official uniform, and he pulled his hair back into a ponytail. Time seemed to have slowed down as they rolled by.

"Just our luck," Zane said. "We need to bring that behemoth a gift card to the steakhouse." The passenger seatbelt clicked free, and he shot Duncan another glare. "I have that feeling too." He clicked free. His palms hot, he slipped the belt free of his shoulder. Eyes glued to the Honda. Foot ready to lock in the brake and then throw the truck into park. It didn't take long for the thought to pass before he was in action.

Duncan was out the door before the truck came to a complete stop. Zane slammed down on the brakes and shoved the gearshift into park. His shoulder got caught on the seatbelt as he attempted to free himself from the last bit of slack.

Door open. Boots on the pavement. Shoulders out. He was free. Music echoed off the surrounding hills, but before he could pinpoint the song, a force like a miniature missile slammed into his ankle. He lost his balance but didn't fall thanks to the brace on the truck door. The dog held onto the bottom of his pant leg and fought like he owed the small beast money.

Where the hell is Duncan?

He shook the dog loose and scanned the street. Suburban tract homes that repeated their facade every fourth house. How charming. The homeless encampment at Wildwood Park had more character. Where did Duncan go?

Duncan came through the radio. "Control, Unit 97 — foot pursuit. Male suspect running northbound on Lakeview Drive, 1800 block. Male wearing a tracksuit."

Ray-Ray wasn't. Zane shook his head. Duncan looked gassed and not in the shape he needed to be. Zane scanned his whereabouts and took off northbound.

The music's bass thumped as each of his strides connected with the pavement. His heart pumped blood into his limbs, and his fingers tingled. Duncan was talking shit to Ray-Ray up ahead, as Zane closed the gap. He envied Duncan's ability to be winded and trash-talk at the same time. He had to reserve the extra energy for the fight at the culmination of the pursuit. There was always a fight, even if it was short-lived, which it had to be. The longer the fight, the higher the likelihood of cameras and a lawsuit. Even if they were following their training and not doing anything excessive. When everyone carried a camera in their pocket, there was always a possibility.

He saw Duncan turn between two houses, and he followed him. Up and over the fence, Duncan went. Zane merely flipped open the latch on the gate and stepped through. Too easy. Duncan was still steadying himself, and Zane blew by him like he was a parking cone.

Ray-Ray jumped the back fence, and this time Zane had to do the same. His boot was wet from the grass, and he almost slipped off, but his grip held tight to the top, and he muscled over.

Ray-Ray kept moving ahead. Duncan lumbered over the fence behind him. Zane called out to his partner, "He's heading for the property line."

Duncan offered something in return, but Zane couldn't hear it. He had to reach Ray-Ray before he crossed the Kizh line. If he crossed over, this pursuit was over, and Ray-Ray would live free to do more harm. Justice not served.

He ignored the call of exhaustion. Mind over matter. It was time to push. Stop Ray-Ray now. Dogs barked in a chorus of displeasure at the neighborhood's intruders, a violent disruption of their normal evening sniffing around the yard.

Zane was ten yards behind Ray-Ray. One first down in football terms. The guy was in surprisingly decent shape for his preferred crimes. Zane pushed harder, pumping his arms and legs. The burning in his muscles drove him. He closed the gap to five yards. Then three. He could almost reach Ray-Ray as they hit the street between the last row of houses before tribal land began.

Ray-Ray hit the street first. Zane reached his hand out, but got clipped at high speed. A swarm of teenagers on e-bikes cut him off. Unable to slow his momentum in time, he slammed into one kid. He soared through the air like a superhero with training wheels. The teen wobbled for a few seconds but held strong. The bikes buzzed by like a swarm of bees. Dozens of e-bikes cut Zane off from Duncan.

Get up. Ray-Ray is getting away.

He pushed himself upright. Gravel stuck to his palms. He located Ray-Ray ducking between two houses that backed up against a hill. If Ray-Ray made it up the hill and got over the property line fence before him, the pursuit would be over.

Instead of following in Ray-Ray's path, Zane opted for the hill. Take the slope over whatever was unforeseen in the shadows of the houses. His quads burned. Lungs squeezed air out harder and heavier the steeper he climbed. The music beat pulsed and boomed.

A Kizh house on the other side must be throwing a party. Great. Was Ray-Ray looking for safety? A friendly house that doesn't know Raymond's past indiscretions. Just a victim of an unwarranted police pursuit.

Ray-Ray popped out from behind the neighborhood houses. Zane was already on the hill. Ray-Ray only looked back and ahead, focusing on what was behind and in front of him. Zane had the element of surprise, but still needed to make up ground. He came at an angle.

Zane's foot slipped on a loose bed of rocks, and he slid down a few feet before catching himself. The commotion alerted Ray-Ray, and he picked up his charge up the hill.

"Fuck," Zane said. Duncan breached the same fence Ray-Ray did and started his own ascent. Zane got back into the chase. To keep his balance and avoid another slide, he stayed low. He fought, one hand on the ground for support, clawing ahead.

Get to Ray-Ray first.

It was going to be close. The music got louder as the property line to the house party was the direct path Ray-Ray was on. Out of the corner of Zane's eye, he saw fellow red and blue lights arrive on the scene. Two younger officers would join the pursuit. The others would stay with the vehicles.

Get to Ray-Ray.

Zane had the angle of a defensive back tracking down the lone ball carrier on a breakaway. His balance held. He darted forward. Ten yards.

Push Zane. Five yards. Go. Everything you have.

Ray-Ray lunged for the fence. He made it halfway up the chain-link fence, announcing the Kizh property line. A cinder block wall a foot on the other side, where the house party was. The savory scent of food mingled with the aroma of smoked wood, spun in the air.

Zane reached up, but Ray-Ray kicked his hand away. He slipped on the loose rocks and repositioned himself. Ray-Ray got closer to the top. Zane sprang upward like a spider monkey. His muscles screamed for relief, but he ignored their cries. He had recovery methods for that. Ray-Ray reached the top of the fence. Zane was on Ray-Ray's heels.

Ray-Ray steadied himself on top of the chain-link fence and extended a leg onto the top of the cinderblock wall. He went to step across, but Zane grabbed his ankle like a vice. All the shaking Ray-Ray could muster as he balanced between the two fences wasn't enough. Zane used leverage and pulled himself up to meet Ray-Ray.

Zane caught his breath. "You're not going over," he said. "Nice and easy, back down."

Ray-Ray tried to tug away but was weak. "Fuck you," Ray-Ray said.

The crowd from the party noticed the unscheduled performance and gathered at the base of the cinderblock wall.

"Those aren't friendly words, Ray," Zane said. "The Kizh expelled you already. They aren't taking you back. Not with what we know." Ray-Ray spat, but missed. Thank God. "You're pissing me off. I don't want to hurt you in front of a bunch of people."

"Just when the cameras are off. Fuck you." Ray-Ray pulled again, but to no avail. He looked down into the backyard. A sea of similar faces with uncertain looks. Ray-Ray tugged harder to get away from him. Zane's grip tightened like a boa constrictor.

The chain link rattled. Duncan was climbing up. A look of menace and drive on his red, sweaty face. He motored ahead. Drawn to Ray-Ray like a tractor beam pulling him closer. His speed was frightening. Zane's reaction time couldn't keep up, and before he could warn him, Duncan slammed into them like a freight train, and three grown men tumbled over the block wall and into the party's backyard.

Zane's firearm and non-lethal compressed into his hips as the ground and bodies impacted in a heap. LT was going to have their asses for this. Not good. The pulse of the music slowly faded, and the house party guests approached the scene. Not good.

He sprang to his feet as if the ground were a high-voltage electric current. His hips begged for mercy, and he was certain blood was coming from his elbow. Not now. Where was Raymond Tenoso?

The partygoers were calm and silent, but it wouldn't last forever. Zane found his target.

Ray-Ray was in a pathetic heap, with low, audible sounds coming from his mouth. "Help me," Raymond said. "Help." He coughed and spat on the grass.

Zane mounted him like a rodeo calf and secured Raymond's hands behind his back with a set of handcuffs. He stood Raymond up. Through labored breaths, Duncan radioed in their status behind him.

The crowd closed in. Zane pulled Raymond closer and tightened his grip. Someone would likely recognize Ray-Ray and want to know why he was in handcuffs and why he was with outside authorities.

"Not a word, Raymond," Zane huffed into his ear. "Let's get out of here nice and easy." Raymond attempted to wiggle free, but Zane only firmed his position.

The crowd continued to gather. More bodies filled the gaps, and rows in the back turned into breathing shadows. The food smelled incredible. If only they had invited Zane and his company as guests under more pleasant circumstances.

Bystanders began whispering. Then a voice shouted, "Ray-Ray, is that you?"

Ray-Ray seized the moment. "Help me. They're profiling. I did nothing wrong. Please."

Duncan stepped forward with intent. Zane put a hand up to slow Duncan's progress. It worked. Adrenaline in Zane's body shot bolts of energy to his limbs, and his eyes tightened into refined beads of focus. He scanned the crowd for threats. Shiny objects in hand. Obvious signs of altered mental states. Anything that screamed of danger.

Where was the air support? An aerial spotlight would do wonders.

Ray-Ray continued his plea. Zane and Duncan stood back-to-back and shuffled in circles, keeping their fronts toward the crowd. The backyard party surrounded them. At least five adults deep, the circle around Zane and his partner tightened, the back row growing like a snake coiling to strike.

On the other side of the block wall, the fence rattled. Reinforcements that were destined for their perch without crossing over the line.

More constriction from the crowd, Zane's veins moved blood throughout his body to keep his extremities at the ready. He'd have no choice but to release his grip on Ray-Ray to protect himself and Duncan.

Don't let it come to that.

Ray-Ray wiggled and tried to pull forward, but like a dog on a short leash, he stayed tucked into Zane.

Frenetic energy buzzed through the onlookers. Zane's skin hugged his muscles; his jaw clenched. "Stay tight," he said. The heels of Duncan's boots turned in lockstep with his quick steps. Knees bent. Balance secured.

A sprint of movement caught Zane's attention. He pivoted. A boy had run from the crowd. He was in the gap, a few feet between the safety of the party and a suspect in custody by two uninvited guests. Before the boy reached Zane, someone picked him up and took him back into the sea of bodies. This elicited further murmurs of dissatisfaction.

Zane made eye contact with a member in the front row. "Please remain calm. We're sorry for bursting into your party with the interruption. If you'll show us the exit, we have no problem leaving you to get back to your celebration."

Another body shot out from the crowd. This time, not a boy. A man. A blur of speed and aggression. Zane swung around but got barreled into by the charge before he could set himself. He hung on to Ray-Ray, and they went to the ground together. A mess of limbs and mayhem, for the second time.

Duncan came to his aid. "Bruce, you good?" Duncan didn't hear Zane's response before another body blindsided him. He held his balance and turned on the balls of his feet. A balled fist in the air like a torpedo that left his shoulder. Target, whoever was dumb enough to start this.

Zane pulled himself and Ray-Ray back upright just as Duncan's punch connected with his attacker. *Thwap.* The sound of Duncan's knuckles sank into a cheek and facial bones. *Fuck. Duncan hit a woman.* He couldn't have known before contact. Perhaps a split second before contact, he could have let up. He'd have to ask Duncan later.

The woman remained upright. A hand to her cheek. She spat blood onto the grass. "Is that all you got, white boy?"

Zane stifled a laugh.

Duncan's eyes were wide. He looked around. Nobody else was rushing in. "As a matter of fact," Duncan said. "It is."

Zane slid over in front of Duncan. His hand was numb from the grip he had on Ray-Ray. He desperately needed a switch without giving Raymond an opportunity. The woman still stood there, laughing at Duncan. She was fearless, or

Duncan knocked something loose in her, but she wasn't letting on. Zane decided she was the scariest of the bystanders. He didn't blame her actions. He and Duncan were the intruders.

"Look," Zane said. "Your boy, Raymond, has done some bad things. He did them over on our side. That's all." Would they believe him? It was the truth. Should he have come up with something better? Maybe, but he was past that.

"Bullshit," a random voice shouted. More joined in.

Yeah, he should have come up with something better.

Duncan leaned over to speak closer to Zane. "May have to let Ray-Ray go."

"No chance," Zane said.

"Do you have a death wish? I don't," Duncan was cracking.

Zane wasn't. "No. But where the fuck is air support? Would be nice for the eye in the sky to add an assist. Be happy to give them the credit."

Profanity-laced jabs spewed toward Zane. The mob was going dark. The woman Duncan hit still hadn't moved. She had become locked in a standoff with Duncan.

Zane's hand throbbed. Or maybe not. Without looking, he couldn't tell if his hand remained attached. Time was running out.

A loud horn disrupted the standoff. The sound was somewhere between a train whistle and a factory blower calling the end of the shift. Bodies parted like a choreographed production. Four large men with raven hair and sharp suits emerged from the opening. They got in front of Zane and split into pairs on either side.

A woman brought up the rear. She wore a tailored pantsuit with stitching that shone in every speck of lighting the backyard offered. The reflections gave her a smooth and angular appearance.

"Raymond, Ray-Ray, Tenoso," she said. Her voice carried an authority most men wished they had. "We exiled you, but somehow you returned. No surprise, local authorities now have you in their custody."

Who is this woman? Zane liked what he was hearing, but he needed to find out. Before he could speak, Ray-Ray chimed in.

"Lynn. Please. Please have me back."

Let's see this play out.

Lynn stood still. The crowd had given her a wide berth. More than respect, she embodied power. "Lynn?" she said. "No. It's Mrs. Sanmaura. We don't take back predators that prey on minors."

The crowd gasped. Their venom took a sharp turn from Zane and Duncan to meet its new target, Raymond Tenoso. Zane took the moment to switch hands. The release of blood into his hand that had been holding on to Raymond began tingling like electric ants were working into his fingertips.

"Thank you, ma'am," Zane said. He pushed Ray-Ray forward toward the opening, but Lynn raised her hand to stop him. Now what?

"You trespassed onto our property," Lynn said. "I'm sure you were under strict orders not to do so. I know Captain Green and will give him a personal call to go easy on you."

"I appreciate that," Zane said.

Lynn cut him off before he could say anything more. "Your partner struck one of my residents. Justified or not, I can't let that have the same level of treatment."

Zane looked back at Duncan, his head turned down like a scolded dog. "Understood, ma'am," Zane said.

Lynn stepped aside. "My team will escort you back to your vehicles."

The four large sentinels turned without a sound and began the escort out of the backyard. The familiar sound of helicopter blades whirring ahead grew louder, and in an instant, the whole backyard was lit up by the spotlight.

Of course. An emphasized illumination of disobedience. What could go wrong? An ass chewing from Lt. Cruz was coming. Zane's only hope was that Lynn's call to the station provided context, and the chewing would be Charmin soft.

CHAPTER 2

San Francisco, CA – Oracle Park

Tyler Truman Junior wasn't another hotshot executive in San Francisco. He was heir to a real estate empire, TruProperties, a firm built from San Francisco's foggy ground up by his father, Tyler Truman Senior. Everyone, including Tyler, just called his father, Senior.

Often, Tyler wondered what everyone called Senior before he was born. Being the son of Senior, naturally, everyone called him Junior. A moniker ranked in the void between slamming his shin into the corner of a coffee table and having his testicles crushed by the stiletto heel of a dominatrix. With the latter, there should at least be an exhilarating climax.

Tonight was rivalry night. The San Francisco Giants were hosting the hated boys in blue from down south. A team he'd rather not name, but to mask any confusion and give credit where credit is due, the Los Angeles Dodgers. The defending World Series champions. Gross. At least with LA's ballooning homelessness crisis, sorry, *unhoused*, the cities mirrored one another. Call the tragedy on the streets whatever you want; it won't change the fact that those in charge of city government aren't interested in truly tackling it.

His guest for tonight's game was David Johnson. David was the son of a local mayor down in San Bernardino, a suburb roughly 60 miles east of Los Angeles. David was getting the royal treatment. First, a drink on the patio at MoMo's with a sea of black and orange-clad Giants fans that mainly had tickets for the upper levels.

"Smart not to wear your Dodgers gear," Tyler said. "It's not as bad as wearing Giants gear to Dodger Stadium, but one too many Fernet shots and gums start flapping. You won't get the Bryan Stow treatment from us."

David nodded in agreement. "Despicable what happened over a baseball game. I'll claim to be an Angels fan if anybody asks."

"Good move. Guy is still in a wheelchair a dozen years later." Tyler got bumped from behind. "Fuck this place. Too crowded for my liking. What do you say we class it up a bit?"

David polished off the rest of his vodka soda. "Works for me. What did you have in mind?"

"Two doors down. Rooftop bar at Hotel Via. Better-looking people. High-end cocktails. Then we'll walk over to our suite for the game. Meet up with Senior and Russo."

"Had me at rooftop bar."

As they walked into the lobby of Hotel Via, a sign greeted them.

ROOFTOP FOR HOTEL GUESTS OR PRIVATE PARTIES ONLY

David slowed down.

Tyler gave him a gentle push from behind. "Don't worry. I helped build this place. I'm always on the list."

A smooth elevator ride up, and the doors slid open to a scene of elegance. The high-end tables, decorated with sustainable materials, offered a full view of the city. Oracle Park's brick facade stood directly in front of them. The double-decker masterpiece straight out of Gotham City, that's the Bay Bridge to their left. To their right, the SoMa District stretches toward the South Bay and Silicon Valley. Opposite the ballpark, skyscrapers that made him forget all about the economic battles taking place on the streets.

A block of cabanas with maroon drapes flapping in the evening breeze took center stage. Surrounded by an energetic buzz of well-dressed members of society toasting with fake smiles. The men wore smart glasses, sport coats, pants a size too small, and loafers. The women had a bohemian style, looking as if they had just come back from a photo shoot in the VIP section of Burning Man. They wore flowing dresses, large-brimmed hats, ankle-high boots, and knitted shawls that looked more fitted for collecting oysters than for keeping them warm. Style over function.

"Do you have a cabana waiting?" David asked. His eyes were wide in search of direction.

"No time for that tonight," Tyler said. "This is a quick stop. We'll have one, enjoy the ambiance, and then head over. Check out the view. I'll grab us a drink and find you. They make fantastic Singapore Slings."

He elbowed his way into the bar and ordered a couple of drinks. He ogled the bartender, and she didn't mind. At least he didn't care whether she did. Wasn't his problem. He'd earned his place. He found David leaning toward the glass along the edge of the rooftop.

Giving David his glass, he said, "One of my favorite drinks. Had them put it on their menu as an homage to Hunter S. Thompson. He's drinking them at the hotel pool at the beginning of *Fear and Loathing*." David nodded along as if he knew the reference, but Tyler was certain it flew right over his head. "Ever seen the movie or read the book?"

"I think that was before my time." David took a drink and swished the libation around in his mouth before swallowing. "Tasty drink."

"The rule is, only one of them. You push it to two, or fuck, send it with three, and you will pay the fucking price. I promise you that."

"Thanks for the advice." There was a moment of stillness between them. Two red-blooded professionals eyed women like prey, a conquest if time allowed. "So, why'd you fly me up here?"

"Thought you'd like to watch a game." Tyler smiled, knowing his line was bullshit. "Senior wanted to meet you. Shake your hand and show some gratitude for the work you've been doing for us. Expanding the Tru empire into a new market isn't easy. It's why I travel back and forth to oversee the operations. Told him how much you've been a part of establishing TruCapital as a serious player."

David held up his glass. "It'll be an honor to meet him."

Tyler toasted and sucked down the remains of his drink. "Finish up. We don't want to be late."

After crossing over King Street like every other general ticket holder, he guided David to the side of the Willie Mays gate to the suite entrance door. This door opens directly into a food hall. Not one you'll see at the local mall with Hot Dog on a Stick and Sbarro's. No. This is gourmet. Thin hand-carved brisket sandwiches, Kobe beef smash burgers, and made-to-order sushi.

He leaned over to David. "Only thing you'll find here that the rest of the ballpark has, garlic fries. They've been a staple since the Bonds era and a must-have for first-timers."

David's eyes jumped from one food station to the next, and he followed some patrons who walked away with their dishes. "How's your breath afterwards?"

"Garlic, as expected. You'll want to find a girl who's also enjoyed some if you plan on any action tonight. Don't worry about waiting in the lines down here. Same menu up in the suite, plus some."

"That works for me."

A private elevator ride took them to the Interior Diamond Suite level. Meticulously positioned two-thirds up the stadium behind home plate, the view offered the entire field from foul pole to foul pole.

David stopped to take in the initial view, but Tyler grabbed him by the arm to pull him along. "Same view from our suite. Don't want Senior beating us there."

"Why's that?"

"I just don't. He'll give me some guilt trip about skirt-chasing and being handed everything in life. It's bullshit. I've made my way." Tyler's guest remained silent. He wasn't sure if that meant David agreed with him or with Senior. Better be him, with the white-glove treatment he's dishing out. "Third door on our left."

The last remaining taste of sunlight illuminated the windows of the suite and out the open door like a beckoning call. His heart thumped in his chest, and he fought the urge to throw up. Nerves about dealing with Senior in professional settings, despite being handed everything, were regular occurrences. Like an unrelenting onslaught of silver-spoon guilt. He bit down on the inside of his cheek. Not enough to draw blood, but enough to feel. Biting his thumbnail was unprofessional. Don't let Senior down.

He entered the suite first. Fuck. Senior was already there, standing on the other side of the glass that looked out at the field. Two rows of seats for that stadium feel. Senior's preferred starting point: watching batting practice.

Al Russo was inside, overseeing who entered the suite like the good soldier he was. Russo was Senior's right hand. There since the beginning.

Russo shook his head in disapproval. His red, bulbous nose shaking back and forth like an usher's flashlight, "Come on, Junior. You let the old man beat you here."

Tyler hated being called Junior, but once Senior approved the nickname, he was stuck. He shook it off. "Please. I'm hosting our guest. Russo, this is David Johnson. David, Al Russo."

David stepped forward to shake Russo's hand. Russo stayed locked in his position and outstretched his bearlike paw. Russo caught David's fingers and squeezed.

"Not much of a handshake," Russo said. "Guessing you'll be dropping him off in the Castro after the game."

"Don't be a dick," Tyler said. David looked back at him for clarification. David's fingers were still the victim of Russo's grip. "Famous gay district. Russo's old stomping grounds."

With that comment, Russo relinquished his welcome. "Hundred bucks and you can watch."

Tyler peered out to see if Senior had noticed him. Nope. "Hundred? It used to be fifty."

"Inflation. Prices have gone up."

"We're in a rent-controlled city."

"Not for new builds."

Tyler laughed. "There's nothing new about your old ass." The air in the room shifted. Senior had opened the door to enter the suite from the exterior seats. His skin crawled. He didn't need to see him to know the man's presence. "Senior." He paused as he turned to face him. The room was suddenly empty of others. "How are the Giants looking during BP?"

Senior eyed him. Then Russo. Last, he eyed David. Ignoring Tyler's question, he focused on David. "You must be our guest from down south."

David, his eyes uncertain as they bounced around the room. "Yes. I am."

Senior didn't blink. "So, you're to blame for Junior being late. Making me get set up in the suite."

By me, he meant Russo. Tyler knew that. Likely, so did Russo. David needed to absorb it. Don't break. Weather the initial onslaught of Senior. Play to Senior's ego.

Senior finally addressed Junior. "Where are the girls?"

"Russo was just telling me he got lost in the Castro during his search."

Russo laughed, but quickly stifled it as Senior shot him a nasty glare.

"Is it boys you want, Dave?" Senior took liberties to shorten David's name. "If that's the case, you'll have to wait for me to exit. It'll be boring for you with all the tits and slits."

Aggressive phrasing. Tyler's skin tingled. Senior was pushing David's boundaries. He wanted to see if the newest addition was tough enough or would curl into a ball and beg for mercy.

Tyler jumped in to cut off Senior's momentum. "The girls will be here. Told them batting practice was your private time." Russo covered his mouth. A vain attempt to suppress a laugh. He continued, "Lunch shift ended at four. They have eliminated the pungent odor of dragon rolls and soy sauce. Even if it's high-end from Au."

Senior folded his hands in front of him. "Ah. Yes. Another one of your endeavors, I helped set you up with. Despite my warnings. Sixty percent—"

"Of all restaurants fail in the first year." Tyler finished his sentence. "We're past that, so I guess we're going to be the eighty percent that fail within their first five years."

Senior's eyebrows raised. An expression of part anger, part impressed. "Maybe you do listen to me after all, Junior." Senior held onto the nickname for extra emphasis.

Tyler bit down on the inside of his cheek again. "Of course I do. I want to be my own man. Now, let's not bog David down with our relationship quirks." Senior nodded, so he carried on. "He has inside knowledge of the Kizh tribe and their interest in The Verge." He stepped over to David for a pat on the back, a vote of confidence. Also, to be near the food as it was certain to arrive shortly.

Senior took real estate on a tall barstool under a picture of Will Clark playing first base with his iconic eye black streaked across his cheeks. "Well, spit it out. Make the investment in your visit worth it."

David's mouth moved without words expelling from it like a career politician short-circuiting. Tyler resisted the urge to kick him in the back of the leg to get going. David had better not be like this with the girls. Christ, how long was this going to last? Maybe he needed to kick him. The moment he lifted his foot, David finally spoke.

"Lynn Sanmaura is the head of the Kizh," David said. "She may not be at the top of the totem pole, but she's the face of the tribe."

Tyler watched Senior's reaction. Senior awarded David a nod of approval for the cultural reference. He mirrored Senior. His fists were like balls of clammy meat in his pockets. "David is going to push Lynn to purchase The Verge. Knows her from community events."

David jumped in. "Gina knows her mostly."

Uh oh. Senior didn't know he sent Gina down south to run The Verge. Tyler needed someone he could trust to be the eyes and ears. Who better than an old fling?

Senior made a sucking sound with his tongue, which distracted Tyler from the trays of food coming in. Garlic fries, brisket sliders, and fresh sushi took their stations on the buffet table. His mouth watered, and he released the tension in his hands.

"We'll table my thoughts on Gina for another time," Senior said. "When one girl leaves, another must arrive." He checked his gold Vacheron Constantin watch. "Game's getting ready to start, Junior."

Tyler stood erect with confidence. "They'll be here," he said. As if on command, a chorus of feminine laughter and banter reverberated down the hall outside the suite. He flashed his perfect teeth at Senior. "Never a doubt." There was little doubt. The inside of his cheek was proof. Evidence Senior wouldn't be privy to.

He moved to the entrance and greeted each woman's arrival with a half hug and kiss on the cheek. Each woman leaned into him and spun out with enthusiasm. The five women all matched. The base layer was crucial: a black bodysuit tucked into form-hugging jeans and paired with knee-high black boots. This was a ballgame, not a fashion show; somehow, they managed both.

Tyler went through the paces of introductions; they knew Senior and Russo from their weekly lunches and occasional dinners at Au Sushi. "Senior, Russo. You remember Li, Holly, Emily, Mieko, and Chanel. Ladies, you're not strangers to Senior and Russo, but let me introduce our special guest, David Johnson. Son of a mayor down in SoCal."

The quintet of women made their rounds, giving welcoming hugs, and settled into the room. They ordered and received drinks, and the atmosphere in the room shifted from stifling business posturing to enjoying the company of the girls. There were no financial ties present. No quid pro quo, not yet. Like David, they received luxury suite treatment; only this group had their phones out to film influencer content. Senior and Russo were off-limits. Tyler and David were fair game.

Senior whispered something to Russo and then exited to the seats to watch the game. Russo waved Tyler using only a finger. Tyler didn't like that. His skin pulled tight against his bones, and his palms perspired. He bit down on his cheek instead of a thumbnail. The girls couldn't see that. Nobody could. It was his pain and anxiety to deal with.

He tried to remain cool. "What's up?" Russo examined him as if he were trying to read a poker player. Stay calm. "Enjoying the view?"

"Nothing I haven't seen before."

"Yeah, but it's different when they aren't serving you a seventy-two-piece sashimi platter where the lights are dim. Full view here. I've dialed in the hiring practices."

"Senior's worried about your hiring of David. Doesn't think that the hiring practice is too good. Needs some work."

Tyler looked over at David. One girl had pinned a *BEAT LA* pin onto his jacket, and he was being pulled in to join two of the girls for a TikTok dance. Laughter spilled out. "Come on, he's helping them enjoy themselves. Without him, the girls would be bored. You and Senior are as lively as a cardboard box on Market Street. I'm old news. Not that I wouldn't if opportunity fell into my lap." Russo threw an eye roll at him. "Despite my reputation, I've learned my lesson about mixing business with pleasure."

"Is that why you have Gina working at The Verge?"

The roar of 41,000 fans came to life. Senior was on his feet, clapping. The iconic Coca-Cola bottle above the left-field bleachers lit up and flashed in all its glory. Surprised it didn't come with a seizure warning. This was San Francisco after all, as litigious a population as could be.

Tyler anchored into the chair next to Russo and watched the rest of the game unfold. He laughed to himself that Senior made a big stink about having girls around, only to stay in the seats watching the game. Senior had put on a show for David, but he was more of a Giants fan at heart. Beating the Dodgers was always the night's preferred outcome for Senior.

The tension in his hands and cheeks finally broke as he watched David continue his attempts to rush the sorority. David was out of his league and didn't even know it. Together, he and Russo laughed as they watched his guest's posture.

He leaned over to Russo, not to be overheard. "He's so deep in the friend zone he doesn't even know it."

Russo nodded, his bulbous red nose itching for a drink. "Poor bastard."

A loud foghorn blasted, and the familiar tune of Journey's *Lights* played from the speakers. Giants fans sang along to the classic hit played after home game wins. Senior sprang into the suite as if he were ten years younger.

Senior clapped his hands together. Everyone snapped to attention. "Fuck the Dodgers. Love the pitch clock. Beating those scumbags in under two and a half hours is a beautiful thing. Where to next?"

Tyler and the rest sent high fives in every direction to appease Senior's spirit. "I have a cabana booked back at Hotel Via."

"Perfect," Senior said. "Why don't David and the girls run over? We'll catch up."

The girls of Au Sushi grabbed their pledge by the wrists and pulled David out the door. The suite fell quiet, as if it were a sensory deprivation room. A low hum of vibration filled Tyler's ears. An uneasy tension shifted to reality.

He looked at Senior, then at Russo. Reassurance was the missing link. "What do you have?"

"He's not our guy," Senior said.

The curtness caught Tyler off guard. He chewed on his cheek, hoping to squeeze out the right response. "He's perfect. Does what I ask. Has the tribe lined up on The Verge? What more is there?"

Senior reached for his coat from Russo. "He's sloppy and knows too much."

"Knows too much?" Tyler's surprise sparked in his voice. "He hardly said three sentences to you."

"Call it instinct. He'd spill my life's work to get a sniff of Lin or any of the girls. Fuck, he'd probably do it for a troll under the Bay Bridge. Get Gina in position to take over tribal relations."

Tyler worked his hands into fists and stretched them out repeatedly. Less than ideal circumstances. Gina was a throwaway card, not the ace in the hole. What to do, what to do?

He submitted. "Fine. It's your call. If it doesn't work out, this is on you."

Senior smirked at his challenge. "Been doing this a long time, kid. Have strategies you only wish you knew about. Go catch up with the group and ensure that the group sets up the cabana correctly. Get that black waitress with the Southern accent. Combination just right."

Tyler bowed out with pace in his steps. He didn't want to leave David unattended for too long. David would be a minnow in a pool of sharks. Before Tyler reached the elevator, he pivoted to head back. Don't let Senior settle the suite tab. A task left for Tyler. Earning his place in the pecking order.

He got to the edge of the door. Russo's voice was first.

"What's the plan?" Russo asked.

There was a pause. Tyler listened for footsteps heading in his direction. Nothing.

"He's got to be neutralized," Senior said. "Remember the job at six sixty Clipper? Take Junior with you this time. Make him earn it."

Russo's voice was low and cold. "Wellness check, party of two."

"Exactly."

Tyler didn't need to hear anymore. He wanted to get to the Hotel Via. He needed a few more Singapore Slings to witness the world going dark for David Johnson. If this was going to be the last night of David's life, he had to ensure that David went out with a bang of glory, no matter what, for the family business.

CHAPTER 3

Tyler couldn't see a damn thing in the dark. Someone yanked him violently out of bed from a sea of incapacitated limbs. His clothes were somewhere. He bulged his eyes to expedite the change and allow him to make out shapes.

A giant paw of Al Russo goon-handed the crook of his elbow and led him away from his bedroom. That's where he was, right? Still too dark to confirm. Was this his place? The farther removed from the pungent post-orgy scent, the better.

Bedroom door. Hallway. Kitchen. Breakfast nook. Living room. Fourteen hundred square feet for an apartment in the Cow Hollow district didn't sound like much, but the tight turns expanded its square footage. The darkness broke through the light, revealing the TV circulating offerings of streaming media.

Relief at being on home soil cracked like an egg as his head wailed inside his skull. Three Singapore Slings definitely pushed it. Who was in his bed? Hopefully, not hired staff from Au Sushi. Conflict of interest.

"The fuck, Russo?" Tyler said. He covered his eyes with his hands to shield himself from the TV's light and faced Russo.

Russo smacked him with a light backhand. "Keep your voice down. Those broads don't need to wake up now. Let's go. We have a job tonight."

Tyler stood naked and shrugged. "What are you talking about?" Shit, this was about David. The wellness check that his father and Russo discussed. "I need to get dressed." He made his way forward, but a heap of clothing met him in the chest.

"No time. Put these on. I got another change for afterwards." Russo looked back down the hallway. "How long they going to be out for?"

"Long enough."

"Good answer."

Tyler liked David. He liked the family business more. If this was his moment to prove to Senior that he was ready for more, then so be it for David's demise. David brought it upon himself. The sliding doors of fate. Tyler quietly slipped into the dark canvas pants and button-down shirt. He felt like a mechanic. Only part missing was the reflective stripes around the cuffs.

Russo checked him out. "Okay then. My car is downstairs." Russo had two cars: one for business, leased by TruProperties, and another for after-hours.

Russo led Tyler to his early 1990s model Subaru Outback. In the dense darkness of the night, Tyler couldn't tell if the car was forest green or navy.

"You wrestle a bull dyke for this car and then drive it off the campground?" Tyler said.

Russo shook his head. "Funny. Just get in. You gotta pull the door closed tight. Gets a little sticky."

Tyler got in and struggled with the door before figuring out the trick.

"Told you," Russo said.

"Had to lift as I pulled," Tyler said. "I'm surprised this thing has leather seats."

"Leather adjacent. Easier to wipe down."

Tyler didn't want to hear it. Which made his mind race with the options. Blood. Brain matter. Other bodily fluids. "Hope you used Scotch Guard." Was David's the next life to be wiped off the seats? That's not what Tyler wanted, but he wanted to be accepted by his father. So, whatever it takes not to disappoint. Be a big boy and get invited to the table of power.

Russo aimed the Subaru east on Bay Street until it ran into Embarcadero, where he made a right heading south along the piers. They passed the exquisite Ferry Building before ducking under the two-tiered Bay Bridge.

There was a steady diet of transients and street life meandering about the sidewalks. Like shadows of life and reality, an ignored section of humanity.

Russo took the curve around Oracle Park. The scene was a shell of itself from hours earlier when the stadium let out, and Tyler led the party at Hotel Via for David's unknown send-off. Russo made a left onto King Street and drove into the Dogpatch. The Dogpatch was a neighborhood that comprised a combination of industrial warehouses and shipping-receiving facilities. The buildings were a cement gray and resembled tombstones against the backdrop of the city's skyscrapers.

Tyler's heart rate picked up. The *thump-thump* played the soundtrack to his nerves. Palms sweaty, he chewed on the inside of his cheek. What was he about to witness, or even worse, do? Poor David.

Tyler's thoughts began the violent agreement. *No. Fuck David. It's him or you.*

A light screech of the brakes, and the Subaru came to a stop. A chain-link fence greeted Tyler as he looked out his window. Barbed wire wrapped around the top in curls of razors. NO TRESPASSING and FOR SALE signs hung in faded red and white metal along the perimeter.

Thump thump.

Thump thump.

Thump thump.

Tyler remained frozen in his seat.

"Get out," Russo said. "We're here."

Here? Here, where? Tyler thought.

He stepped out of the car. Instinct told him to be quiet. He eased the door shut and leaned in with his hip to ensure the door latched. Russo gave him a nod.

"We looking at buying this?" Tyler asked.

"Already own it," Russo said.

Tyler gave a confused look at the for-sale signs.

Russo tapped him on the shoulder and walked up to the padlock. He pulled out a key and popped open the lock. He swung the gate open and made way for Tyler. "Senior says it's time you learned more about the business. After-hours operations."

Tyler took the gap provided by Russo and stepped through the gate. His eyes followed the building from the foundation up toward the night sky.

Thump thump.

Thump thump.

Russo closed the gate and reapplied the padlock. "Congratulations. You made it through door number one. Now, let's move to door number two."

Tyler followed Russo a couple of steps behind. He was ready to bolt. Wanted to bolt. But couldn't. Whatever was inside this building, he had to face. *Merit. Worth. Respect.*

The night air was still. The only sound from the outside world was the faint alert of a foghorn. Russo stopped at a door the size of a castle drawbridge. He unlocked the door and eased it open before leaning his back on it to once again make room for Tyler to step through.

Tyler hesitated, but he entered. A lump in his throat the size of Alcatraz pinched off his breathing.

Russo smacked his back, "Now, you've made it through door number two."

Tyler pushed through a smile. "The prize better be good."

"Just on the other side of door number three." Russo retook the lead, and the two began walking down an open corridor.

Cement and metal were the only two materials Tyler could make out. A far cry from capital gains improvements for residents in Pac Heights. The lights clicked on as they made their way. Each section would come to light before shutting off once they exited.

"Can't you just flip a switch so we can see the whole place?" Tyler asked.

Russo remained on stride. "Where's the fun in that?"

Fun wasn't a word Tyler had in his current lexicon. "Is this where they filmed the *Saw* movies?"

Lights on.

Lights off.

Lights on.

"Never seen them." Russo's voice was dry and cold.

Lights off.

Lights on.

Russo stopped at a door.

"Let me guess," Tyler said. "Door number three."

"Bingo." Russo pressed down on the lever door handle and slid open the door. The building reverberated with a rumbling groan as the metal door slid along its track.

Tyler struggled to move through the door. "What kind of building is this?" he asked. Warm air from inside the room seeped into the hallway. A slick of sweat formed on the back of his neck.

Russo's mouth twisted into a weak smile. "Get inside, kid."

Tyler's feet trembled as he took his steps inside. His legs were weak and numb. He wiggled his fingers in search of feeling. There was only a tingle. He bit down on his thumbnail before shoving his hands into his pockets and gnawing on his cheek instead.

The first thing that came into Tyler's line of sight was the two men in yellow suits. They looked like latex bananas, one tall and narrow. The other, closer to the ground, was the shape of one of those balls pregnant women sit on to open their hips. These men, certified crayon eaters, had underground faces unsuitable for public places. Respirator masks hung around their necks like jewelry from 3M.

Set off to the side of those two was a claw-foot tub. It looked like someone plucked it out of a Victorian apartment in Pac Heights. This one didn't come with upscale features such as a rain showerhead with a marble tile surround. The tub had chips of paint missing from the edges, and inside was a naked man.

Blood had already dried around his nose and mouth. His eyes had swollen shut, and it was difficult to determine if he was still alive.

Tyler's nuts were in his throat. He turned to Russo. "The fuck is this? Who the fuck is this?"

Russo's eyes resembled empty pits of darkness. "This is our after-hours business. Righting the wrongs we can't make good on during normal business hours. Free from courts and judges and cops."

After hours, Tyler's mind was a circus of thoughts and concerns. His morbid curiosity pulled him toward the tub. He stepped forward.

The man's feet were bound at the ankles. His gnarled toes suggested he was an avid runner, or the yellow Bash Brothers worked from the bottom up. Whatever leg hair the man had was stuck to his skin by a combination of blood, sweat, and piss.

Tyler could use one of those respirator masks. He covered his nose with the inside of his shirt. It didn't help. He skipped the man's junk and went to his torso.

More blood and sweat covered tattoos of the San Francisco 49ers logo and a list of names only relevant to the man in the tub. His hands were bound at the wrists and draped neatly in front of him as if he were in prayer. A little too late for help from the Almighty.

Tyler pushed closer to the man's face, trying to see through the violent damage that left the man swollen and split open. A set of pink lips tattooed on the man's neck, along with an inked diamond on his cheek, gave Tyler a suspicion.

Tyler stepped back. "Is this Josue? 735 O'Farrell?" His shirt muffled his voice.

The two figures in yellow remained still as if frozen in place, awaiting to be thawed out by Russo's command.

"Josue has been double-dipping," Russo said. "We've set the market value, but he's been holding bidding wars. Driving the price up and pocketing the difference."

Tyler looked between Russo and Josue's pulverized face. "It's a Tenderloin building. How much money we talking? Only a couple apartments become available each month. Few hundred bucks, maybe a grand? He's lying naked in a tub full of his own bodily fluid for the price of a box seat at the Giants game?"

"We gave him a warning at a few hundred. He didn't listen."

Torn between disbelief and *holy shit,* Tyler thought about the dozens of building managers who had come and gone over the years. Free apartments to sweep the entryways, vacuum the halls, and handle routine maintenance in San Francisco was a pretty good gig for some. Add in the $500 commission on renting out vacant units, and being a building manager was a livable reality. Even in the 'Loin. Was this how Senior and Russo handled turnovers?

Tyler pushed down the lump in his throat. "How much are we talking? No bullshit. What does it cost to turn someone into hamburger meat?"

Russo looked over at the guys near the tub and then back at Tyler. "Forty. That we can trace."

Forty wasn't a few hundred. It wasn't box seats. It was season tickets. A furious rage built from Tyler's toes up his legs like the first shot of Clase Azul tequila. Warm and inviting. His fingers tingled, but instead of the nerves from earlier, they were electric with rage.

"What's next?" he said.

Russo snapped at his two guys, and they finally broke free from their trance.

The shorter one grabbed Josue's bound hands and raised them as high as he could force them.

The taller one reached up and grabbed a hook at the end of a cable. Tyler's earlier shock prevented him from taking in the entire scene, and he missed what hung above the tub.

A large steel cable dangled down from a pulley some thirty feet above. The hook was sturdy, like something a tugboat would use to latch onto a cruise ship. Seemed like overkill for the circumstances.

The hook attached to Josue's ankles, and they raised him until his head was just above the lip of the tub. His arms lay limp on the tub's base. Popping noises like firecrackers came from his hips as his legs held the weight of his bloody torso. The body shudders. Josue's lights were damn near extinguished.

Tyler bit down once more on the inside of his cheek. *Pain is weakness leaving the body.* Witnessing this side of the family business was unreal. Would he even be able to talk to Senior about it? He would not be the one to bring it up. An untold secret of murder for the bottom line of the balance sheet.

The stockier man in yellow steadied Josue's body, which hung like a grotesque piñata. The taller one came around from latching the hook and exposed a knife in his hand. He approached Josue and placed the blade under Josue's ear along his already bloody neck.

Russo cut in. "Wait. Have Junior do it."

CHAPTER 4

Rim of the World, CA

The cold water ran over Zane's head. He focused on controlled breathing to regulate his heart rate. The water rode his chilled skin before running along the chain of a necklace from which a Saint Christopher pendant dangled free. The silver was worn. An inscription on the back had faded through the decades. The necklace once belonged to his old man. An academy graduation gift once he finally followed his father's footsteps into law enforcement. The connection to his dad was more important to him than the religious symbolism.

Icy water from the mountain pipes jolted his body and mind awake. Cold showers always did the trick. He held onto an empty bottle of Jack Daniel's, the label completely gone. He let the water revive him. Minimal sleep after a late-night pursuit equaled the fog. This was a more effective wake-up than anything else: increased recovery, alertness, improved circulation, enhanced mood, and, more importantly, stopped the throbbing between his ears.

His eyes opened. Socks still on. He chuckled. He stepped out of his socks and swept the waterlogged clump to the corner of the fiberglass shower. Bruises were in the early stages of forming on his hips. Swollen yellow rings from the fall he sustained off the block wall into the Kizh backyard.

He checked his Panerai watch. Five minutes in, he cut the water off.

In his towel, he took inventory of his bedroom. A set of feminine-toned shoulders peeked out from the disheveled sheets. Right where he left her. *Check*. His Glock 17 was still in its holster in the nightstand's top drawer. *Check*. Alarm clock. *No check*.

He placed the water-soaked Jack bottle near the broken plastic clock pieces. Opting for a cheap digital clock powered by two AA batteries, he decided against searching for his phone in the middle of the night. He replaced them often: the clocks, not the batteries. Once the ear-splitting beeps cracked through his sleep-deprived head, they came to a stop when his fist came down upon the clock like a sledgehammer.

Could probably afford better sleep tools if I didn't have to keep buying clocks.

He picked the whiskey bottle back up. A memory of prying it from his father's hands flooded him, and for a moment, the sensation of drowning washed over him. Just another cliché, jaded cop. Not him. The pair of bare shoulders in his bed wrestled and rolled over. Dark hair covered half the woman's face.

He greeted the waking beauty, "Good morning, *Lieutenant*."

Lieutenant Carmen Cruz brushed the hair from her face. One eye found him while the other fought to absorb the light. "You can't be saying that. Especially being your superior officer."

He sat on the bed next to her. "You're right. But you know I kind of like it."

"You can *kind of like it* by pouring me some coffee."

"Yes, ma'am," he said. He winked, and she rolled her eyes in return. "Shower up. There should be plenty of hot water."

He chose his *Pat Tillman Foundation* mug and poured dark roast coffee. He took it piping hot and black, always black. The shower started up, and he poured a cup for Carmen. He dumped a handful of mixed nuts into a bowl and stepped out onto the back deck.

The crisp San Bernardino Mountain air demanded his attention. He loved these mornings. The fresh pine swirled amongst the limbs before being cast away. The steam danced above his mug as if it were performing ballet. Better drink up. His phone buzzed from inside the kitchen.

"They're just gonna have to wait," he said to the squirrels. He did not intend to deal with the day ahead until he finished his coffee. The squirrels frolicked through the trees. "It's why we live in the mountains. Less bullshit." Quiet, clean air, peaceful - at least for the surroundings. What took place between his ears was far from it. Stay grounded.

A few squirrels jumped from tree to tree like a SWAT team moving in on the house. He had seen their moves before. Raising his mug in a toast, he finished the remaining half of his coffee. He plucked a peanut, cashew, and an almond from the bowl and placed them in a line atop the deck rail. The row led to the bowl. The squirrels inched closer. "Until tomorrow morning. Enjoy, my friends."

Carmen's voice cut in. "Hey, squirrel whisperer. Captain wants us to report. ASAP."

The squirrels scattered for cover from the uninitiated.

"Is that what that call was?" He wanted to watch the squirrels, but Carmen was more enticing. "I'll give you a fifteen-minute head start. Showing up at the same time would look suspicious."

She smiled. "Phrase it however you want. I know you want to hang out with your little critter friends."

He smiled back. "See you at work, *Lieutenant*."

CHAPTER 5

San Bernardino, CA—Police Headquarters

Zane was ready for the captain's urgent shift brief. The morning calm of his mountain abode felt like a distant memory. The warm body of Carmen, more so.

He timed his drive to perfection. He had manipulated the steering wheel down the mountain's edge. Hands steady, he took the curves next to jagged rock faces and cliffs with painstaking precision. One moment of distraction could lead to a head-on collision. No opportunity for highway hypnosis to slip in.

Carmen was well into the weeds by the time he pulled his late-90s Ford Ranger into the secure San Bernardino department parking lot. He could afford a newer car. One with power windows and door locks, but the Ranger still survived the commute. Fewer bells and whistles meant a deeper connection to the road. Particularly when navigating the windy roads of Highway 18 daily.

He scanned the briefing room, full of familiar faces, searching for one in particular. He played it cool when he saw Lieutenant Carmen in their professional setting; she wasn't his priority for now.

Like water off a duck, please don't make it obvious.

He didn't find his target before the authoritative voice of Captain Steven Green cut in. "A call came in for a body over at The Verge, a luxury, high-end apartment property. CSI and coroners are already on scene."

The name of the property caught Zane by surprise. The Verge stood out against the neglected city of San Bernardino like a jade stone in the middle of a sandpit.

He slid through the bodies until he shouldered up near Carmen. "You know this is your job next, right?" She didn't take the bait. "I hope you're as colorful."

The police captain heard him and called out, "You got something to add, Bruce?"

"No, sir."

"Good, cause I'm not finished."

Never is.

"If the identity of the resident checks out, this is high-profile. We'll know more soon."

"Couldn't the guy just write a fucking note?" A voice shot out from the front. It was the man Zane was looking for, his partner, Detective Paul Duncan. The only person dumb enough to interrupt the captain.

"Don't you think I would have led with that, Duncan?"

"Fucking Duncan," Zane said. His voice hushed for Carmen's ears only.

The captain carried on, "I'm putting together a team to head over to interview neighbors and staff of the property. Heading up this unit is Lieutenant Cruz, and she'll lead Bruce and Duncan in conducting these."

Duncan looked back at him. He blew a kiss back.

"Cruz, you have my permission to beat the holy hell out of these two and make them carry the load. Take no shit from them."

"Yes sir," Carmen said.

Zane caught a subtle elbow from her that was hidden enough to avoid detection. The bruises on his hips weren't eager for more company. He didn't need to answer questions about their newfound bed-sharing.

"The rest of you are on standby to assist with the investigation on an as-needed basis. For any questions, please direct them to Lieutenant Cruz. All right, dismissed."

The captain lingered behind the podium. Pretending to gather vital information that helped him address his department.

"Cruz. Bruce. Duncan. My office."

Zane followed the LT and Duncan into Captain Green's office. Duncan jockeyed with him to be the first through the door.

"You two dipshits knock it off," Captain Green said. "This case is serious. Fall in."

Zane enjoyed being in the captain's office, even if it wasn't warm hugs and compliments. Photos that dated back to the department's inception adorned the walls like a yearbook. He always went to the black frame where two uniformed, grinning officers stood in front of a pair of Harley-Davidson Electra Glide police bikes. Their knee-high boots looked ridiculous, but he wouldn't dare say that to either man in the photo: his old man and a much younger version of the captain who sat in front of him. Zane locked in on his father's image, from respected motorman to outlaw.

Green was a well-decorated police captain. People heavily credited Zane's father for his early success. Green ushered in a new era of younger police captains, but his age did not equate to a lack of experience. Twenty-five productive years on the job, climbing the ranks from focused academy cadet to head of the gang unit, to detective, to sergeant, lieutenant, and captain, could mean that one day Captain Green would be the next chief.

Green's office, filled with plaques, certificates, newspaper clippings, medals, and event photos featuring local politicians and leaders, was a testament to all his accomplishments. He'd molded his life to fit the law and protect his community. His department respected him greatly for it. Even the ass-chewing hadn't diminished Zane's respect.

"Cruz," Green said. "I trust you'll keep them in line. I don't want another call from the Kizh PR."

"Of course, sir," Carmen eyed Zane. Duncan stiffened in his chair. Her expression could be more threatening than words. Even with a romantic relationship underneath the department's surface, Zane wouldn't test their limits. Not here.

"David Johnson is our deceased."

"Johnson, sir?" Zane interrupted. "As in-"

"That's right. As in, the son of Mayor Mike Johnson."

Green's office doors and seams sucked out the air.

"You said we were still waiting to confirm the identity," Zane said.

"Correct. That was in the briefing, but here and now, I'm telling you he's our victim."

Zane glanced at Duncan. They worked hard cases together, but nothing of this magnitude. Best to be engaged, not fuck around, while the captain carried on. For them. For Carmen.

"Any leads yet?" Carmen asked. "Suspects. Enemies of the mayor. Disgruntled coworkers or employees?"

"We'll get there, but not yet," Green sifted through the papers on his desk. "I've seen images of the scene, and it's grim. Found him in the bathtub."

Zane had seen a lot in his years on the force, but the son of a local politician was straight out of the movies. "Once news breaks, leads will come in far and wide."

Green straightened up once he found the right piece of paper with his all-caps handwriting notes neatly organized. "I have a name, Gina Kramer. She's the property manager of The Verge. See if she has information."

"Copy that, sir."

Carmen took the note and held it out.

Zane snatched it before Duncan had a chance, risking that they'd look like siblings squabbling over a juice box. "We'll head there right away. New construction should lead to new security systems. High tech. Facial recognition." He'd have this case closed by tomorrow. Wouldn't hurt to have that feather in his cap. Especially after the pursuit with Ray-Ray ended over the Kizh property line. Less than ideal.

"Good," Green said. "Dismissed."

"Yes, sir," Zane, Duncan, and Carmen said in unison.

Zane was on the move, but someone hooked the back of his belt. He stopped. The tug pushed the pain in his hips into a frenzy. He owed Duncan payback for that one. He turned to face Carmen. The longing glow of her face that greeted him in the morning was nowhere to be found.

"You disobeyed my command," Carmen said. She stood firm. This wasn't a light reprimand. A slight quaver in her voice. She took a half-step closer. "Don't let what happens outside these walls obscure your judgment of what needs to happen in between them."

He remained silent. The heat between them warmed the front of his neck. "Yes, ma'am. But I wasn't defying your orders. It was–"

Carmen cut him off. "I don't want to hear your excuses about Duncan. To ensure you're in line with department protocols. They want more over watch."

"Doesn't sound too bad."

She lifted an eyebrow and cocked her head.

"Maybe not the time?" he said.

Without a word, Carmen pivoted and left him standing in his own thoughts. *Great.*

The sting from a slap on the back of his neck shocked him out of his daze. Duncan had pulled up behind him and taken liberties with the small section of exposed skin. Prick.

"What was that about?" Duncan asked.

Zane took a moment. Caught between a desire to enforce payback on Duncan and his growing feelings for Carmen. He placed his hand on Duncan's shoulder. "Life. It's about to get a lot more complicated."

A glazed expression washed over Duncan's face. With that distraction, he unleashed a returning slap to Duncan's neck and walked off.

CHAPTER 6

Zane pulled up to The Verge luxury apartment community in an unmarked black Ford F-150 - no sirens, no attention. Gina Kramer, the resident manager, was the person they needed to find.

Carmen rode shotgun, while Duncan squirmed and fidgeted in the back seat. Zane watched him in the rear-view mirror as he backed the truck into a stall.

"Department already owns the truck," Zane said. "Unless you're planning on your next position being investigating Lemon Law cases, I think you can stop pressing every button."

"I like buttons," Duncan said. "Not every day I'm in the backseat. LT took my spot." He tried to open the door, but nothing happened when he yanked on the lever. "Child locks. Really?"

Zane laughed. "Act like a child. Get treated like a child."

Duncan flipped him the bird.

Carmen stepped in. "Now I can see why captain wanted me along."

Zane released the doors, and they exited the vehicle in unison. The sun burned hot in mid-August, so the trio made quick work of the parking lot and into the lobby.

The Verge was set back off the Interstate-210 and up along the foothills. Its landscape reflected the suburban desert, a combination of palm trees, drought-resistant plants, and water-recapture fountains. No chance of sneaking around these grounds without the loud crunch of rocks and stones underfoot.

All was quiet. The parking was oddly underused.

Once they tucked into the building, Zane's eyes adjusted to the light transition.

"Thank Christ for air conditioning," Duncan said. "I have sweat in places I didn't know I could sweat. Willis Carrier deserved all the blowjobs."

"We walked thirty feet," Zane said. "Maybe less hoagies and a few more laps around the track. You used to look respectable. And who the hell is Willis Carrier?"

Duncan puffed out his chest and checked his biceps. "Please. I can still fit in my academy uniform. Any time, any place. I'll blow by you like you were a parking cone. Mr. Willis Carrier is the father of the air conditioner. We'd all be walking around with swamp ass if it weren't for him. Even you, LT."

Zane laughed. Carmen gave Duncan's comments zero attention.

The lobby had mosaic tile flooring that transitioned to posh retro wallpaper. Illuminated metallic beams with orbs hung from the high ceilings and gave off an outer-space vibe. A citrus aroma of bergamot mixed with sandalwood filled the space. The temperature was perfect. Something you'd miss if you weren't trying to absorb every ounce of relief from the external elements.

An empty glass desk was off to the side with a lone Apple MacBook closed, sitting on top. A high-backed orange leather chair was tucked neatly behind the desk.

Zane walked over to the desk and tapped on the glass top. "Think they'd at least have a bell to ring with this kind of welcome party."

Carmen motioned toward the windows overlooking the pool. "Somebody is out by the pool. Can't make out the face, but looks to be wearing a name tag."

Zane turned to look out at the pristine poolside. Lounge chairs, umbrellas, cabanas with outdoor couches enclosed by white linen drapes.

Duncan held up a baseball-sized metal heart he had picked up from the desk. "If I throw this through the window, think she'll come say hi?"

"Put that down," Carmen ordered.

A voice from down the hallway interrupted their shuffling around the desk.

"Welcome to The Verge. How may I help you?" The voice wanted to be more authoritative than it came across. Politeness through an annoyed tone.

"Business major," Duncan whispered.

"Nursing," Carmen whispered.

Zane shook his head. "Nah, it's clearly theater."

Carmen and Duncan approved of his assessment.

The woman's presence was straight out of central casting. She walked smoothly despite her tan heels looking stiff and tall. Her matching tan pencil skirt was wrinkle-free and met up with the perfectly paired white linen blouse. Comfortable, but still showed off her athletic frame.

As she approached, Zane read the name on the chrome badge that was placed a couple of inches below her left clavicle: *Gina*. She extended her hand to Duncan first, as he was the nearest. His jaw dangled like one of the orb lights that hung from the ceiling.

"Hello, I'm Gina," she said.

Duncan froze. The only part of his body moving was his hand in a monotonous up and down motion as he continued the handshake.

Carmen gave him a toe poke to his calf.

"Duncan," he said. "Uh, yeah, Duncan."

Gina didn't seem to be in a hurry to release her hand from his. "So, is that first or last name?"

"I do."

Zane chimed in. "These aren't wedding vows, man." He shook his head in embarrassment.

Gina kept her eyes on Duncan. "And…"

"Paul," Duncan said. "My name's Paul Duncan."

"Well, Paul Duncan, it's nice to meet you. Welcome to The Verge. I'm guessing you're here to see unit three-two-eight?" She released the hold on Duncan to turn toward Zane and Carmen.

Carmen introduced herself and then Zane to finish up the formalities. "Detectives Bruce and Duncan are heading up the investigation. If you'd be so kind as to lead us to the unit. That would be great."

"Sure thing," Gina said. "Right this way." She spun on her heels and began walking back down the hall she had come from. Her hips swayed in a manner that held Duncan in a trance.

Zane gave him a motivational shove. "Don't tell her you still live in your mom's basement."

Duncan stepped forward. "That joke is getting old. I've been on my own since I was eighteen. Not all of us are groomed to follow daddy's lead and become a cop."

"Dick."

Duncan picked up his pace to catch up with Gina. Zane slowed to be closer to Carmen. Their hands brushed against one another as they walked.

Unlike Zane, the landscaping was climate-adaptive. Stone, steel, and plants that smelled of rosemary, lavender, and sage when the heat pressed down upon them. A noticeable lack of security cameras in such a high-end community.

"When's the last time you saw him?" Carmen said.

"Who?" Zane said. A response he knew wouldn't slide. Carmen raised an eyebrow but didn't say a word. "I see him everywhere. He's tough to miss. Now, when's the last time I've spoken with him or spent any amount of time with my dad? Been awhile. I don't keep a running tally."

"Do you miss him?"

"Of course. But he made his choices and showed his true colors. Those colors aren't ours anymore."

They wound their way down another pathway and pulled up shy of apartment 328. Police tape ran from the handle to the door frame. A thin yellow warning that the evidence inside was silently doing its work.

Gina used an app on her phone to unlock the door.

"Enough technology for door controls, but not cameras?" Zane said.

"We've had some vendor turnover. Tough economy has led to businesses shutting down. We lease the cameras while under contract, so once that goes away, breach or not, they take their equipment and sell off what they can."

Zane pulled on a pair of disposable nitrile gloves and removed one side of the police tape.

Duncan followed, snapping his on at the wrist. "Time for your exam Detective Bruce."

Gina took a step back. "On that, I'll be at the pool. Timecards need to be entered. Please let me know if you need anything."

Duncan's eyes remained on the property manager. Zane smacked him in the chest to break him from it.

"Eyes up, buttercup," Zane said. "Solve this case, and I'm sure you can ask her over to your mom's basement."

"It was old the last time you said it," Duncan protested. "And the time before that. And the time before that."

"Yet you still won't move into a place of your own."

"Gentlemen," Carmen said. "You boys go inside. I'll keep an eye out here."

Zane pushed the door open and looked back at Duncan. "Time to rock and roll."

CHAPTER 7

An odor Zane couldn't quite place permeated the air of unit 328 like a night of regret after a night out. He held up the crook of his arm and shoved his nose into it. "How long did it take to discover the body?" he said.

Duncan coughed. "Always forget it takes a few Mississippi to get used to. Guy appears to be living the good life."

"Lived," Zane corrected.

Duncan looked back at Zane. "My mistake."

The Touch of Modern app must have supplied everything in the apartment. A black leather couch was the principal attraction in the living room. A sleek, minimalistic coffee table sat in front of the couch. The sleek design was sterile enough for open-heart surgery.

Zane's feet sank into the plush carpet, leaving an indent of his size eleven boots as he carefully walked the room.

Black and white photography of Joshua Tree National Park hung on the walls in silver frames. Above the couch, movie posters for *Kill Bill Vol. 1 and 2* allowed Uma Thurman and her sword to watch over their actions. What did she witness in this apartment?

Gray smudge marks where CSI dusted for prints: edges of door jambs, remote controls, countertops, glassware. Each mark represented a ghost hunt.

"Where'd they find the body?" Duncan said from the kitchen. He flashed a high-lumen pocket-clip flashlight at Zane and then back at the cabinets.

"Tub, according to the report."

Zane moved down the hall and passed the first half-bath. He entered the master-suite. Duncan pulled in behind him. A bed twice the size of the room greeted them.

"Queen size probably would have been just fine," Zane said.

"Can't live like a king in anything smaller than a Cal King," Duncan said.

"Jealous? Or did your mom finally let you upgrade the futon in her basement?"

"I'm going to call you Recycle Bin with how much you reuse jokes."

Zane scoffed. "When they're good, why stop? Play the hits and give the people what they want."

A black dresser was against the wall before they reached the bathroom. On top was a collection tray, empty except for one item. An orange and black lapel pin that said, BEAT LA.

"Apparently, we need to be looking at Dodger fans," Zane said.

"What else is new?"

Black hexagon tile flooring made up the bathroom, which created a stark contrast to the porcelain toilet and fiberglass tub. A glass-enclosed shower was at the foot of the tub, which allowed one's partner to have a good view while they soaked.

If it weren't for the pink-stained shadows around the tub's drain, this bathroom was ready for move-in. Too sterile. CSI did their best impression to show off their work.

The remnants of black and gray fingerprint dust were in all the usual places: medicine cabinet, kitchen utensils, drinkware, remote controls, light switches, and faucets. Bits of red evidence tape stuck to the towel bar and bathroom cabinet, announcing CSI had bagged and removed the towels and whatever else.

A sterile hint of bleach cut through the room as a haunting reminder of the cleanup someone attempted before they fled the scene.

Zane remarked, "It's awfully bland given the state in which the body was discovered."

Duncan looked over the tub and then stepped out of the bathroom. "What do you mean?" he said.

"I mean, someone brought the body back here." Zane paused. "Heavy wet work done off-site and then brought back to his apartment to stage the man taking his own life."

"How'd you come up with that, Sherlock?"

"Too clean. Pink shadows around the drain tell the desired story, but if it were real, the streaks would run up to where his wrists came to rest."

"Fair enough, but you'll need more than that," Duncan said. "Known enemies?"

"Guy's dad is the mayor. Indirectly, probably had plenty he never knew about until it was too late."

Zane pushed past Duncan and back out of the bedroom. He peeled off his gloves by rolling them into a ball and then shoved them into his pocket. A disposal later when they're back at the department.

Sunlight smacked him in the face as if he owed it money, and his lungs welcomed in the herbal scent of the low-water landscaping. One was better than the other.

Duncan followed, his gloves still on, and his eyes toward the pool area.

"Another time, lover boy." Zane slapped the side of Duncan's cheek. "We have work to do."

Carmen stood to the side of the walkway with her arms directing them back out. "Anything good in there?" she said.

"Ask Sherlock," Duncan said.

Zane lifted his eyebrows. "Too clean. Need to see what CSI lifted. My hunch tells me it wasn't much."

He threw an arm around Duncan's shoulder and did his best to keep his eyes from drifting back toward Gina. "She's too high-class for your mom's basement. We can put a game plan together when we get back."

"Whatever you say, Recycle Bin."

Carmen threw Zane a confused look. He mouthed words to her; he'd explain later. Carmen jumped into the front passenger seat of the truck, Duncan into the back. Zane started up the truck, threw it into drive, and pulled out of the empty parking lot.

His body steered them back to the department, but his mind was on David Johnson's apartment. The cleanliness. The lack of danger. A lapel pin from a baseball team over four hundred miles away was the only thing that stood out. It wasn't much, but the wheels of justice were churning.

CHAPTER 8

San Bernardino, CA—TruCapital Office

Tyler Truman Jr. had a headache on his hands and between his ears with the expiration of David Johnson. He peered around his 360-degree glass-enclosed office. It was no San Francisco office building, for sure, but at least he had decor to match his favorite surf destination down in Costa Rica.

His office in the TruCapital investment firm occupied the center of the second floor. This office was an offshoot of his father's San Francisco real estate empire, TruProperties. Being half a state away from Senior was a good thing on days like this.

Within the breast pocket of his suit jacket, his iPhone vibrated. His heart leaped an extra beat. His fingers silenced the buzz before he could see the phone screen and the caller's name, which brought him more relief.

"Gina, to what do I owe the pleasure?" He stepped out of his office so his staff could witness how polite and accommodating he was. Theatrics. He nodded pleasantly at those passing by, an act for the phone conversation. "Give the cops what they want. Make it easy on yourself."

That was a lie; he wanted her to make it easy for him. He stopped caring for her on a personal level long ago.

"Just trying to be protective of you and Senior," she said. "I know how he preferred to do business. At least before we arrived here."

"They moved you down here. I relocated to start a new venture." He bit his thumbnail and moved back inside the private confines of his office. The temperature rose against his delicate ego. "Senior isn't running things down here; I am. He has no jurisdiction."

He ended the call with Gina and occupied his desk. A digital frame next to his black computer monitor flashed through images of the beach in Tamarindo. Surfboards and local women. A destination he would much rather be at than his sterile office with so many eyes on him. Senior and Russo followed through with their intentions. Tyler's input was not wanted. Seek, destroy, and protect the family legacy, TruProperties.

The acidic flavor of vomit coated his tongue and throat. The thought of calling his father was rising to the surface. A call he couldn't avoid much longer. Neither would his body's reaction to it. He pulled the metal wastebasket from under his desk and released the bile from his insides.

Once he was back to baseline, he shook his computer to life. He found the calendar he shared with Senior and scheduled an appointment. Rumors of malpractice to maintain leverage in San Francisco could always be filed as just that—rumors. Now, death was on his doorstep, and the police would soon be knocking.

CHAPTER 9

San Bernardino, CA—Police Headquarters

Zane's desk was as if nobody occupied it. His computer monitor collected dust and lacked power. He set the status of his office desk phone to busy. He hadn't pulled the chair out in over a year. Because funding to fix the air conditioning was delayed for weeks, the vinyl seat glued itself to the metal desk frame. He flat-out refused to use it.

Paul Duncan's desk sat on the other side of his own, and it looked like local fraternities from the 1980s had rented it out. Duncan was stuck in the decade. The monitor screensaver on Duncan's desk bounced around a montage of pictures from Sylvester Stallone movies: *Rambo, Cobra, Over the Top, Rocky I - IV*, but mainly *IV*.

Zane was confused, looking at the papers scattered on Duncan's desk in a field of organized chaos. Certainly, anxiety-inducing for those outside Duncan's brain.

Duncan spun in his chair, looking at the ceiling like a toddler bored at Bring Your Child to Work Day. Zane grabbed his chair.

"Hey, Sly." He referenced Duncan's clear man crush on the action star. "The ceiling tiles stop spinning yet? You gonna call her or what?" He tapped Duncan's hand, which had a tight grip around the phone number Gina had given him. His reflection in Duncan's eyes told him his partner was still spinning. "We're feeling a Cobra Day today. Sweet toothpick, bruh."

"No," Duncan said. He pulled a match out of his mouth. "Stallone chewed on a matchstick. Way more badass than a toothpick. If, and when I call her, it's official business. And I'm all business." Duncan put the matchstick back between his lips and straightened up in his chair. "Why don't you sit down at your desk and let's call the victim's office. Make ourselves an appointment to speak with his boss over there." He held out his arms to present Zane with his desk.

"Pass." Disgust sank in thinking of sitting at his desk. "I'd rather you break down the finer aspects of why the movie Rambo was the reason for the fall of the actual Soviet Union than sit at a fucking stationary desk to hell."

Duncan popped up in his chair as if he were on a well-oiled spring. "John Rambo terrified the Soviet people so much, and in such a kick ass bad ass way, the Soviet Union was the single biggest purchaser of bootleg copies of the film. And it is a film. Don't give me that movie bullshit again. Show some respect for Christ's sake. Soviet citizens tied fucking headbands on as they stood up to the Communists."

Carmen's voice cracked over the pointless debate. "Zane. Duncan. You two better not be arguing over Stallone films again. Unless they remake *Cobra* starring Glen Powell, nobody under the age of fifty will have a clue what you're talking about. We have an investigation to run. In my office now."

Carmen used Zane's first name. That was new. He was the first to enter Carmen's office, like high schoolers sent to the principal's office.

She tied her hair back into a tight bun, exposing her sharp brown eyes and angular face. She radiated confidence. "You're not in trouble. But don't think I give a shit about whether Rambo was the fall of the Soviet empire."

Zane flipped Duncan the bird.

"A lead has come in. Worked with Dave Johnson," Carmen continued. "Wants to talk. Few details were given. Said something about not being safe over the phone. The guy sounded sketchy. You'll meet this guy at the YummyMum Donuts on 40th."

"Copy that," Zane said. "Do we have a name, or just assume the guy slinging maple bars is our lead?"

"Vernon, no last name given."

"Roger that."

"Vernon, not Roger," Duncan said. No reaction. "Oh, come on. That was a good one."

"Maybe five years ago, when you used it the first time," Zane said.

"Oh, and one more thing." Carmen held their attention. "No donuts."

Duncan walked out, but Zane couldn't resist. He stopped just before exiting Carmen's office and turned back. "I have an idea on how to work off the calories." He winked at his blushing LT and caught up with Duncan.

CHAPTER 10

"You ever train legs, or no?" Zane prodded his partner.

He threw the unmarked F-150 into park outside their destination at YummyMum Donuts.

"Bro, I'll out squat you any day of the week," Duncan replied.

Zane laughed at his partner's absurdity. "Living in the mountains is ten times the workout climbing out of your mom's basement is. Coffee?"

The display menu taped to the inside window of the donut shop showed the food range as it transitioned from maple bars and bear claws to Chinese food and fortune cookies.

"No, I'm good. Any idea which one is our Vernon?"

With no interior for customers, the YummyMum was a walk-up only establishment. The scent of fried dough and sugary frosting filled the sidewalk and corner where a handful of people stood. The patrons patiently waited for a sugar rush and an impending late-morning crash.

Zane returned from the order window and took a full drink of coffee without as much as a gust of wind blowing the steam off the top of his paper cup. "Just keep your eyes open and head swiveling."

"All the smoke with that coffee?" Duncan asked. "Scold your insides and just keep going. Insane."

"You want me to wait around for it to get cold? That's for soccer moms in yoga pants spending time between school drop-offs and pickups. If I let this cool down, then I might as well not bother ordering it. We're not here on a social call. You can save that for the apartment lady. I'm sure she'll sit with you while your coffee gets cold. You can stare, she can talk, and your coffee can get cold. Helluva first date."

"She's getting us access to this guy's apartment. I think I'm doing just fine."

The friendly conversation paused when a beat-up late-80s Acura Integra pulled up. One pop-up headlight appeared to wink while the other remained tucked away. Faded red paint, battered with sunspots, showed its history of baking in the Southern California sun.

"Check this beater pulling up," Zane tapped Duncan on the shoulder. The car slowed to the curb. He waited for the passenger window to roll down. It didn't. The man's head popped out of the sunroof, and he took a half-step back to reassess.

"I'm Vernon," the squeaky voice said. "Get in and we'll talk."

He looked at Duncan and then back at the car, which was idling on the curb. He didn't move.

"Well?" Vernon pleaded. The man's head popped up and down like an arcade Whack-A-Mole.

He moved to the car and looked down through the sunroof. His stature was above the compact sports car. His right hand moved to his hip. Sig was where it should be. All was clear of threats, the stench of spent napkins and fast-food bags notwithstanding.

"No."

"No?" Vernon's head popped up and back down.

"For one, hell no. And for two, there's no chance in hell we'd fit."

"I need somewhere safe, and this is all I can think of."

"Oh, I know that's all you can think of. Otherwise, you wouldn't have suggested it. Drive around back and we'll take a walk. My partner, the guy back there with the 80s baseball player sunglasses. He looks like a clown, but he's the best at spotting tails. He'll make sure you're safe. Hell, you don't think I want to be safe as well?"

Head popped up, "The guy from the 80s movies is going to protect me?" Head popped down.

He suppressed his laugh, "Yeah, we both will. Come on." He looked back, Duncan in all his vintage glory. Vernon drove around the back. He gave Duncan a rundown.

"So, I'm just a lookout?" Duncan complained. "I can be in the conversation too."

"I know you can, buddy, but this dude is meerkat sketchy and likes the comfort of a tough guy looking after his safety." He patted Duncan on the shoulder and squeezed his trap like a coach supporting his star pitcher. "This is where you're needed. I promise I'll get you a new pack of toothpicks to chew on."

"Promise? This is my last one."

"There you go. Now, we aren't going far. Just need him to tell us what he knows and we can report back to LT."

Duncan watched over him and Vernon like a hawk. He gave Duncan a nod of approval.

"I'm part of the night crew at TruCapital. Clean out trash baskets, break down cardboard boxes, scrub the shitters. Lately, I've noticed that people have been cleaning out their own. Nobody does that."

"Does what?" Zane asked.

"Trash. Nobody cares about the shitters. So now it's noticeable when there is something in there. Before, I'd grab the can and dump it into a larger bag I keep on my cart and not think anything of it. But when there's nothing, you look. One paper. Handful of paper clips. That's nothing. A USB stick, though? That's something," Vernon held up a metallic USB thumb drive that was in the shape of a key. "I took it just on a hunch, and when I heard that morning the place was closed down and why, the back of my hair stood up."

"You mean the hairs on the back of your neck?"

"Yeah. That's what I said. Well, here. I don't want this anymore." Vernon pulled out the silver USB thumb drive and handed it over. "Scary shit, man."

"You're sure this is from that trash can and not something you invented yourself? I run this back to the station, plug this in, and our entire network shuts down because you handed me some computer virus."

"Check out my car. I clean shitters, dude. I don't sit in my mom's basement like that cop back there."

He protected his laughter, but enjoyed the rib on his friend.

"I'd look into the final boss over there," Vernon's squeaky voice continued. "Yeah man. The boss. Pervy dude. He stands up top and watches the women. He once threatened to fire me because I removed the plastic film from his mouse. Who keeps that on? Been in a lot of offices, and nobody keeps the plastic film on the mouse."

"Anything else, um, Vernon?"

"That's it. Can't think clearly beyond that thumb drive. I need a vacation."

"You take that vacation, and we'll take it from here. Thanks for the tip." He shook Vernon's sweaty hand and dried it on his pants. He gave Duncan the details on the walk back to their vehicle.

CHAPTER 11

San Francisco, CA—TruProperties

"These newbies to city life are in for an awakening," Tyler Truman Jr bit on a thumbnail. A bad habit he couldn't shake. A scheduled meeting with Senior had him rattled.

TruProperties was impressive from the sidewalk, with its all-white facade and gold leaf trim. White columns sucked energy from the corner of Market Street and brought in seekers of overpriced living spaces. On the border of the Castro District, it is renowned for being one of the first gay communities in the country.

To the northwest of the office, Haight-Ashbury. The 1960s destination for all things counterculture. Now, resembled a lost souls vibe of teenage runaways.

Al Russo was Senior's right hand. He splayed out on a black leather sofa across from Tyler. "Out of their protective bubble of college campuses and into the real world." Russo's words spilled out from under a push-broom mustache. The thick lip of hair stood out like a fairway divot against his bald head. He wore a dated black suit, but it still fit him well. Despite the long hours and vices, it didn't affect his waistline. Not bad for the dirty old man.

The TruProperties building was grand, with glass doors atop marble steps. Inside, the hustle and bustle of the apartment leasing world bombarded you upon entry. Cubicles and desks stretched out to each side until they reached spiral stairs that led up to the second floor. Glass-walled offices overlooked the action.

"They just don't make buildings like this one anymore." Tyler straightened his tie. A meter maid drew chalk lines on car tires parked below the bay windows of his office. It was good to be back in the city, even if it meant a meeting with his father, plus two dollars and fifty cents for an hour on the curb.

"Senior's happy you came up for the meeting. He hates Zoom calls." Russo's white mustache puffed with each word. His bulbous nose had streaks of red, and the skin looked cracked like a peppermint under the weight of a boot heel.

Tyler shrugged it off. "Then why am I still waiting to meet with him? Shouldn't be this hard to meet with my father."

"I gave him intel on your minor problem down south. He's chewing it over."

Great. The longer Tyler waited, the more his insides churned.

Russo was a former police officer turned security guard for Bay Area sports stars throughout the nineties and into the 2000s. Once those guys retired, he saddled up next to Senior. Russo would rather take hand-me-down real estate and go on deep-sea fishing trips with former ballplayers than ante up with the younger generation unless they were female, of course.

"What's your title now?" Tyler asked. "Not that it matters."

"I got moved away from the Leasing Manager. I guess my hiring practices aren't up to HR standards."

Tyler crossed the hardwood floor of the office. "Can't only hire twenty-year-olds fresh off sorority row. Couldn't have mixed in one or two guys? Maybe even gay."

Russo sat, legs spread as if he were airing out. "You didn't seem to mind. I believe you were being paid in pussy when you first started here."

Tyler couldn't resist a smile. His freshly shaven cheeks stretched tight. "So, what's the new title?"

Russo took a long inhale through his plump nose. "I'm the Chief of Staff for the President."

"Bullshit. Let me see your business card." Tyler held his palm up and waved his fingertips.

Russo feigned reaching for it and stopped. "Alright, Executive Assistant."

Tyler's hands slapped together. "I knew it. Might as well put secretary on there. Senior will never stop demeaning you."

"As long as the cash is right. Senior can call me whatever he wants." Russo leaned over to check the time. "Senior is taking his sweet time. Isn't he?"

Tyler flopped down into the high-backed leather chair. He pulled himself tight against the desk. The computer screen opened to the company's portfolio of properties. The address, purchase price, and current market value accompanied a thumbnail image of each of the properties.

"He's got more to worry about than my problems." He spun the monitor toward Russo. A column displayed a list of properties. All in the red. "The old man's been outbidding himself on these. It's killing us."

Russo feigned ignorance.

Tyler continued. "Loser after loser. He shipped me down south to run TruCapital. Only to sink the ship up here." He spun the monitor back around and closed the screen. "What happened to the system? Acquire at under market.

Identify the rent-controlled tenants. Buy them out or *otherwise*. Jack up the rent. We all drive around in Bentleys."

"Your old man still drives around in a Bentley." The voice caught him off guard. It wasn't Russo's.

Senior occupied the door frame. He wore pressed black slacks and a white dress shirt starched with French cuffs. Gold thread monogrammed Senior's initials above the sterling cufflinks. Black shoes polished like mirrors. His barrel gut pushed into the office space first, and the air inside got tighter. Squeezing around Tyler's throat like a python. Senior's Cane Corso, Lombard, behind the old man. Senior was never without his dog, Lombard.

"There's the big guy," Tyler forced out the words. Hopefully, his enthusiasm looked better than Russo's ignorance.

Senior ignored Russo on the couch. "You're focusing on the wrong numbers. As usual."

Tyler anchored into his shoes. *Shake it off.*

Senior continued. "They match all the numbers of importance we've used since I've been around building my empire. Long-term tenants under rent control, number of renovated units, commercial gains, parking, laundry, price per square foot, and so on."

Would Tyler ever earn Senior's trust to run the empire? Times have changed. His father was out of touch with the reality of the new business world. A discussion for later.

"Nice of you to carve out some time for me." He motioned for Senior to join Russo on the couch.

Senior turned and patted Lombard on the top of his rigid head. Halfway down the hall, Senior called over his shoulder, "My office."

Lombard looked at Tyler. He looked at Lombard. Saliva foamed at the corner of the canine's wide mouth. The dog's tongue swiped its jowls, knocking the saliva free onto the floor. Then trotted after its owner.

"Always demeaning, Russo. Always." Tyler pressed up from behind his desk and joined Russo in the center of the office.

He checked his skinny navy tie in the reflection of the bay window. His tailored suit was crisp and ready. Was he?

Russo gave him a push from behind, "Now let's see who Senior is going to demean."

The meaty hand still had plenty of strength for the aging enforcer. Ready or not, Tyler needed this meeting with Senior to go smoothly. He bit his thumbnail and stepped forward.

CHAPTER 12

Tyler arrived in his father's office with Russo right behind him. Senior sat in his high-backed leather chair like a king on his throne. Lombard lay on the cool marble floor next to his dog bed. The dog bed cost more than a studio in the Tenderloin, and Lombard wouldn't sniff either.

"Why the song and dance for this meeting?" Tyler found a leather chair and sat down. It was noticeably smaller than Senior's. He made sure his tie and jacket weren't twisted and tucked in.

Russo stood tucked inside the double-wide glass doors. Arms crossed. More of a nightclub bouncer than a message-taking secretary. He had known the aging enforcer long enough not to be intimidated by the posture.

"Russo informed me he dispatched his guys to reel in our problem." Senior's tone was firm. Volume suppressed.

He raised his eyebrows and glanced over. Russo stayed locked on Senior. His father continued.

"I'm afraid you don't have the appetite for what it takes to get things done."

He had heard this line before. Was Senior unaware of his involvement in the wellness check on Josue? He gave Russo a disappointed look. His father used it as the barrier to entry for employment at TruProperties. Home for the summer during his college years. Four summers spent working the tourist trap of Pier 39 and not learning the business alongside Senior.

"I have a distinct style of doing things," Tyler responded. "Can't hit everyone over the head with a hammer when things don't go your way." He sat tall in the cool leather chair.

Senior ignored him. "After we handle our problem, I'll move to phase two of this mess you created."

He went back to chewing on a thumbnail. "What's that?"

Senior leaned back in his chair. The old man's weight pushed the design to its limit. "We're going to offload The Verge to the Indians."

The insensitive tone didn't bother him. He'd heard worse. Been called worse and used worse. He leaned over, elbows on the tops of his knees. His silk navy tie dangled between his legs. "This isn't like the negotiations of the Great Plains. Let me work on this?"

His old man remained pushed back in his chair. Listening for the first time.

He continued, "The Kizh tribe is prominent in the community." Big-ticket donors to every cancer walk and school program in the area. They do not restrict themselves to their allotted land.

Senior's seat offered authority. "I know. That's why they're perfect for The Verge. We need to drive up the value to maximize our earnings. Finally, someone else can overpay."

"The public head of the tribe is a woman," Tyler said. "I have Gina running The Verge. Should be a proper pairing."

"You're not thinking with your little head again?"

Senior was one to talk. How long ago did his mother leave? The old man was selective in his hiring practices as the company grew. A resume with a loose moral code and discretion went a long way. He remained stoic to his father's question.

"I'm as clear as I've ever been. This is the smart play. I'll clean up the other mess."

"Russo is already on it."

The revelation caught him off guard. He jumped to his feet and looked over at Russo, who stood like a sentinel by the glass doors. "You were in my office for an hour plus and said nothing?"

Russo looked down at his worn-in shoes and then back at him. No words came—only the stare of a man loyal to his handler.

He puffed in disappointment and then went back to his father. "This crew better be clean and vanish like a hired escort. Nothing blows back on me, or it blows back on all of us."

Senior's face turned red and swollen like a balloon that had taken in too much hot air. The old man popped, "You don't throw threats around here. You've never known your place. I call the shots and I make the deals and you get to be grateful for every breath you breathe, every dollar you have, and every pussy you sniff."

He hated how right his old man anchored in. The words echoed in his soul. Reverberating off every bone and landing in his heart. He sat back in his chair. Senior stood and motioned for him to stand back up.

Senior moved to the edge of the glass office that overlooked the downstairs desks of busybodies. Dead spots under the wood flooring groaned at the weight of Senior's steps.

"Join me, Junior," Senior said. An outstretched arm welcomed him into Senior's view. He submitted and slid in like the child he was. "Earn this. I built this all on my own."

Tyler looked back over his shoulder at Russo. The man who helped Senior muscle his way into the real estate game in the early days. The enforcer who intimidated and greased palms as TruProperties rose in power and influence. Russo's face remained expressionless. He, too, had given in and submitted to Senior.

"As long as I'm breathing air, the Tru empire will be under my command," Senior said.

The old man squeezed his shoulder tightly. The acidic taste of vomit coated his tongue. He spun free of Senior's grasp and stumbled toward the desk. His hands and eyes reached and searched. *There*. He grabbed the wastebasket. The smell of the plastic lining only lasted for a second before his insides emptied into it.

"Dear God, Junior," Senior slid a few steps sideways. Putting distance between him and his son. The old man's face twisted and grunted.

He unfolded himself. He pulled a blank sheet of stationery off Senior's desk. Wiped his mouth with the thick paper before tossing it in with the acidic remnants of anxiety.

"I'm going to repeat this," Tyler said. His head throbbed, but it gave him an out-of-body feeling. He sucked in a breath. "This isn't eighties and nineties Frisco." *Frisco*, a term anyone from the area hated, but he needed to prove a point. "You can't simply grease palms and use muscle." He eyed Russo and continued, "Currency exchanges have gone digital. Cryptos. NFTs. With finesse."

Senior stood silently. In disbelief, his son was from the same gene pool. "You'll be involved when I say you are involved. My name will stand on the building long after I'm gone. Not because of your make-believe currencies."

The hubris of his old man was on full display. He shook at his father's inability to adapt. Stuck in the Stone Age of real estate.

Senior checked his Montblanc 18k solid gold chronograph watch. "I have another meeting of importance. Russo, escort Junior out." Senior moved past Tyler as if he were no longer there and sat back behind his desk. He slid the wastebasket out. "Don't forget your lunch."

He leaned down and grabbed the receptacle. "Always a pleasure, Dad." He walked by Russo. "Don't bother. I know my way." He took one more step and paused. Russo kept his eyes fixed on Senior. "You're more of a dog than Lombard. How old do you want to be before you die without dignity?"

Russo's head took a half turn. Eyes straining in thought. In reality. Death before dignity.

Tyler worked his way downstairs. He was departing, yet he wasn't backing down. His takeover of TruProperties needed to begin. He knew exactly where to go.

CHAPTER 13

The uneasy feeling in the pit of Tyler's stomach was a constant reminder of the hell his father had put him through. Nobody outside his father treated him this way. Enough was enough.

He checked the time on his Apple Watch. Too early for where he needed to go. Who he needed to meet. He took an Uber up to Chestnut Street in the high-end Cow Hollow district. Rents for a one-bedroom unit exceeded $3000 a month. That was for a dump. He had a greater need for a libation than a place of residence. With no appetite for food, the alcohol hit him quickly. His toes tingled. Chest full. Headspace free.

He was always out to make a name for himself away from Senior and assume the lead of TruProperties. TruCapital was a nice consolation, but with Senior in charge, he'd always be the boy in his dad's shadow.

He spent hours exploring the outskirts of San Francisco. He killed time down by Oracle Park, home of the San Francisco Giants. Then he worked his way up the Embarcadero and slowly paced through a small farmer's market outside the Ferry Building before he moved on to the high tourist traffic of Pier 39. A place he was all too familiar with. He stood at the end of the pier, looking across the cold bay waters at Alcatraz. Maybe he had time for a tour. The annoying bark of a dozen sea lions sunbathing along the docks put an end to his daydreams.

What he was looking for wasn't to be found in these areas. He found a nondescript bar on Polk Street, sat down, and ordered a rum and Coke. His feet ached from the walk. He tried rubbing the sticky gunk off his shoes using the bar foot rail. Why were bars in this town so sticky? At least the scratched wooden bar top was clean enough.

After a couple of refilled highball glasses, he hit the head. It had been some time since he was last here, and the mirror above the trough-style urinal caught him off guard. The mirror ran overhead the entire length of the pisser. Angled to reveal what every man standing was slinging. Guys are guys regardless of whether they're attracted to women, men, or both. Tyler was relieved to be alone. His own sexuality was secure, but what would he do if confronted with it?

One stall flushed, and he positioned himself at the hand sink. A woman. At least in appearance. Her body frame was slender. She straightened the flowing hair - or wig- before taking it all the way off, revealing a shaved head with scars and tattoos. He froze at the hand-sink. *What am I seeing?* The water continued to flow over his hands. He washed and washed. His eyes focused back at himself in the mirror, but he strained his peripheral vision for a better view.

"Save some for the rest of us," the wigged woman said.

He kept washing. Stopping would make it too obvious.

"Thirty-one times," he said. "That's the number I have to hit before I can stop. Is that why you wear the wig?" He nodded upward with his head and eyes, showing the scars.

"Only for a couple weeks until the hair grows back in."

"Chemo?"

"Just cutting right through the bullshit and into the personal questions?"

"Sorry. Thought I was alone. Twenty-nine, thirty, thirty-one." He pulled his hands away from the sensor and shook them dry.

"You are in a bathroom. In a bar. The whole concept of these places is so that we don't have to be alone, especially in the middle of a weekday. Demons don't sleep. But we do work."

"So, is that what you're doing? Suppressing your demons?"

"Something like that. Maybe opposite for me. I suppress my humanity so the demon can live." She revealed her hands. Stained red.

Paint or blood? Could go either way.

She ran her hands under the water and gave them a light scrub. "See something you like?"

Tyler nodded. Was this real? His unintended pub crawl was taking its toll.

"Daddy must be misbehaving. I'm coming off a job. I'll need to clean up first." She walked up and blew softly into his ear.

Tyler's skin tightened, and his neck ran cold. She walked out and left him staring up at himself in the angled mirror.

He swayed in the poorly lit bathroom for longer than he wanted. Alone again. He made a beeline for the door. The bar was empty. How far could she have gone? He left his half-full rum and Coke and shot out the door onto Polk Street. A bus unloaded tired office workers. He ran north up to Broadway. Nothing. He reversed course toward California. More letdown. He needed her services. The time had come. Would she be back?

Back in the bar, the stern glare of the bartender met him. In a city welcoming people of all piercings, tattoos, hairstyles, sexual proclivities, and anything else, he was stunned at the relatively normal appearance of the bartender: tall, short beard, backwards hat, and a southern drawl.

"Glad you're back," the bartender said. "Thought you'd ditched out on me, and I wasn't too pleased about having to dump a perfect rum and Coke."

"Yeah, sorry about that," Tyler said. He caught his breath and settled onto the bar stool. "You by chance didn't see the woman come out of the bathroom? See where she headed, did you?"

"A woman?" The bartender looked around. "Just you and me in here today, bub."

His ears perked up like hot irons. How many drinks had he had? Or was he simply losing it?

"I appreciate it." Tyler paid his tab and left a hundred-dollar tip for the service.

He spent the next few hours back along the Embarcadero. His problem and the solution that awaited were getting closer. He felt a connection to the small but mighty tugboats towing and moving the large cruise ships around the bay. Their navigation and knowledge of the tight waters were true expertise. The tugboats brought unrecognized value and made possible the entire operation of tourism and shipping. The little weathered boats were the lifeline of industries that will never heap their praise upon them.

He would make the moves necessary to receive his praise. His father would know just how capable and powerful he could be. If Senior had Russo deploying his hit team, he would have to do the same.

CHAPTER 14

San Bernardino, CA

Zane spoke on the phone while Duncan drove

"Skittish is right," Zane said. "I think we need to head to TruCapital. Vernon has strong feelings about the man running things."

Carmen sighed on the other end. "After the Kizh mishap. Your fault or not. You need to bring this case home. I trust you'll make the right decision."

Zane put his *Ray-Ban* aviators on. The glare caught Duncan's wrap-around fluorescent sunglasses and reminded him who his partner was. "Roger that." He ended the call and lightly tossed his phone into the center console.

"What did LT say?" Duncan asked.

"Hard to remember with the glare those wraparounds are giving off. Follow my instincts. Keep letting you hold onto my coattails. You know? The usual."

"Bitch. I've saved your ass more times than I can count."

"That's just cause you can't count. Correct statement would be that I've recovered from your attempts to save me more times than you can count."

The drive to TruCapital took less than twenty minutes. A glass office building in the corner of an outdoor strip mall, built thirty years earlier, was easy to spot. Big-box stores held the plaza up and littered in between with the frequent turnover of grand openings and clearance blowout sales. *Spirit Halloween* was always lurking around the corner.

"Always crushes me a little to see going out of business signs," Zane said. Duncan drove them down a stretch of the parking lot that had more than a few. "Big chains propped open while mom and pop claw and scratch for every penny."

Duncan nodded in agreement and eased the unmarked F-150 toward TruCapital. The radio exploded with action that perked Zane's attention and tightened his jawline. Reports of shots fired near their previous location at the donut shop caught him by surprise. No words required. Zane knew who the target was: Vernon.

He didn't even get eyes on the entrance to TruCapital before he sped up the truck toward the crime scene. Thoughts of why it happened tortured him. The janitor was skittish for a reason. Maybe that reason was in his pocket now.

How'd they know? Who were they? Did they see him and Duncan? Are there more targets?

Duncan played with his sunglasses. A stark reality set in for the 80s superfan that he wasn't quite prepared for.

Zane knew it as well. They were in for a fight. More bodies would appear. The death of Dave Johnson was not an accident. There were players involved. The who, what, and why. He needed Duncan. He needed Carmen. They needed him.

Stop being melodramatic, Zane thought. *Prove them all wrong.*

Lieutenant Cruz was already at the scene when he and Duncan arrived. Despite the grim scene outlined by yellow police tape, he got a kick out of watching Duncan hop down from the driver's seat of the lifted police truck.

"You're such an asshole," Duncan said. "We're at a crime scene for fuck's sake. Show some damn respect."

He knew Duncan wasn't serious. "I'll be all business once we cross that yellow tape. Until then, I'll admire how perfect a lifted bro police truck is for our very own vertically challenged 80s bro. Maybe the department can make you a flat-billed hat to complete the look."

The playfulness vanished like a hunter's wind check the moment Zane ducked under the tape. The sandblasted red Acura Integra now looked like a bullet-riddled shooting target left out in the middle of a dry lake bed. Vernon's motionless leg stuck out of the driver's door. Most likely trying to make a desperate escape before his killer ended him with the last bullet.

"Ugly scene, detectives," Lieutenant Cruz said. She caught up to her men. "I thought you two were looking out for our lead. Did little good. I guess he was onto something someone didn't want us to find out about."

"You sure they're connected?" Duncan asked. "Alright, dumb question. Bruce talked with him and I kept a lookout. Nothing stood out as a potential threat."

"Certainly not of this caliber," a crime scene investigator held up a gloved hand and displayed a shell casing before putting it into a paper bag for evidence. The trio acknowledged his poorly timed pun and got back to their conversation.

"The guy had the paranoia of a meerkat, but I kind of liked him," Zane said. He looked over the fallen body and bullet-riddled Acura. Morbid sixth sense for simply finding an office item. What did he miss? He could feel the thumb drive burning in his pocket like a new sensory input. A reminder to right the wrongs of his old man. Bring back respect to the Bruce name. His name.

The crowd swelled with curious bystanders, along with the small-town community news, and nearby residents and business owners. Zane's eyes moved along those outside the yellow tape for anything that stood out as more than curious.

Them.

Two large men, overdressed for this occasion, in pressed suits, no ties, crisp white dress shirts. Even the mayor was likely to be seen in checkered Vans rather than a pressed suit and loafers. The men sank back from the front of the crowd. Their slicked black hair caught the sun's glare as they walked away. He followed.

The best part of being a low-key detective was casually following people who wouldn't think twice of the guy in jeans and a tee shirt. He was a pro. Not too aggressive in his pursuits. Trust human instinct to panic and let them make that mistake. He didn't need an error for these two guys. They were lazy. Maybe worse than being lazy - arrogant. They never looked back to see if they were being followed. They walked to their black-on-black Cadillac XT6, which featured limo-tinted windows. Murdered out. The mid-size SUV pulled out in a hurry, cutting off several cars that were slowing down. No plates. Trouble.

He hustled back to Duncan.

"Where'd you go?" Duncan asked.

"I think I've got eyes on our suspects."

"Is that right? LT? You hear this? Bruce here, got eyes on suspects." Duncan's voice was low, so the crowd couldn't listen in.

Was still too loud for Zane's liking.

Carmen perked up next to him. "Zane, what have you got?"

He enjoyed having her next to him. But there it was, his first name again. Certainly, Duncan would catch on. Later.

With dead bodies piling up, Zane's protective instincts were kicking in. Duncan looked at his proximity to Carmen.

Does Duncan know?

Zane nudged Carmen's arm. She smiled.

Did Duncan see that? Focus.

"Those who commit crimes aren't often far from the scenes they create," Zane said.

Carmen took half a step back from him. "Who'd you see?"

"Matching suits. Matching slicked-back hair. Matching sunglasses. Matching spray tans. Like they were checking off boxes on a list. Not a care in the world." Zane's hands emphasized the violent nature of the crime scene around them. "I followed. They jumped into a blacked-out Caddy SUV and whipped down the road. If Cobra here hadn't parked on the other side, I could have tailed them."

He pointed at Duncan. Duncan shook his head at the slight.

"You run plates?" Carmen asked.

"There were no plates or even dealer papers."

"That's not much to go on."

"I know, LT. It's my gut feeling." Zane's tone was that of a respected colleague and an intimate partner. "These guys work for whoever is behind Meerkat Vernon and Johnson. We'll see them again, and it won't be without confrontation."

Duncan jumped in, "What should we do? Go back to TruCapital?"

He looked at Duncan and then back to Carmen. His eyes were soft. He felt Duncan's stare as he looked at her.

"No," Carmen said. "Well, not like you originally were. Just go cruise the parking lot and eyes up for that SUV. If your hunch is right, they'll end up back there."

Zane slapped Duncan in the chest and moved. Carmen grabbed his forearm. Holding him back from leaving.

"If they are, call me and we'll call in support. No cowboy shit."

CHAPTER 15

"Dammit," Zane said. He reached into his pocket and fished out the USB drive Vernon had given him. "Seeing those goons distracted me from handing this in."

Duncan shamed him with a headshake.

Zane shook back. He pulled out an evidence bag and slid the USB drive into it before tossing it into the glove box. "Better off my body. Bad juju keeping it on me."

He exaggerated the bumps of the suspension as Duncan drove the unmarked truck back onto the TruCapital parking lot. The air conditioning ran at full blast. He tweaked the vents for maximum contact with his body.

Duncan backed the truck into a stall with a good vantage point of the entrance. "With any luck, these clouds will bring rain," Duncan said.

Outside was still blazing hot. A summer storm threatened the heat. Clouds hung over the mountains and were pushing their way across the valley.

"So, how's the love life?" Duncan asked.

A jolt of adrenaline spiked in Zane. He shifted in his seat and did his best nonchalant impression. "Not much. You know. Married to the job. You?" *That's it, deflect and put it back on Duncan.* He saw his own reflection in Duncan's wraparound shades. He definitely wasn't buying his own story.

"Yeah. Same." A smile curled up at the edge of Duncan's mouth. "I'm thinking about asking Carmen out."

Zane unbuckled his seatbelt. The A/C wasn't cooling him down fast enough. Play it cool. "Yeah, you should. I mean. You're risking it with a coworker. Let alone your superior. Just make sure I'm there so I can witness the rejection in real time."

Duncan spat out a laugh. "Are you high? I'm a secure man, but there's no way I'd be able to handle that side of her."

The side Zane had become familiar with. Naked. Smiling. Relaxed. Connecting. He pushed back into the seat. "It's gonna take more than another warm body to fill that spot. For both of us. I need a deeper connection, not just a soft spot to land."

"By deeper, do you mean waking up to cold showers and chugging scalding hot coffee?"

Damn, Duncan's close.

"Wouldn't expect you to understand. You can keep chasing your female Stallones. That isn't going to work for me."

"Don't sleep on the female Stallones. They didn't turn out looking like Sly."

He continued to exchange jabs to avoid being told about Carmen. He trusted Duncan with his life, but somehow this information was hard to spit out. Masculine vulnerability and all.

Nothing stood out in the half-vacated strip mall. Each empty storefront came with a pile of dirty blankets and scraps of trash. The cars that came and went from the parking lot varied. From a Toyota Prius to a Tesla, and from a beater pickup truck to a six-figure Ford Raptor.

TruCapital was easy to monitor.

Zane's ease and enjoyment came to a halt. A freshly waxed BMW M-series whipped into the parking lot. He slapped Duncan in the chest with the back of his hand. "What kind of asshole would speed through a parking lot with this many speed bumps?"

The BMW hit one, and he and Duncan winced. How was it still on the road? The BMW pulled into the handicap stall closest to the entrance of TruCapital.

"See a blue placard?" Zane didn't need the answer. The driver's door of the car popped open, and a pair of hot pink sneakers shot out. *Interesting.* More so was the hot pink wig that accompanied the man's head. "I think this guy stole your look. If he's banging a Stallone, hang it up and call it a career."

"Not cool. Shall we go ask him about the wig?"

"We definitely need to talk with this guy. Parking there tells me, douchebag. The pink shoes and wig send a different impression. Guy is definitely overcompensating for something."

"Height?"

"No, that's what you drive this truck for. That and your small—"

"Don't even say it. I've seen you staring in the locker room. Can't take your eyes off it."

"Never seen one that small before."

"Pretty telling statement on the number you've seen. May need HR to look into your prying eyes. Get the internal investigation team on this."

"Shut up and look." He pointed at the incoming black Cadillac. Same one from earlier pulled up behind Mr. Pink's Beamer.

The pink wig moved to the passenger window with a look of comfort. Mr. Pink knew the guys inside. The SUV drove off as quickly as it had pulled up. It left in its wake a man in a pink wig whose confident face from moments ago had melted into one of agony and frustration.

Zane clicked his seatbelt back in. "Looks like we have our guys."

"You don't want to stay with Mr. Pink?"

"He's not going anywhere. These are the guys who killed Vernon."

CHAPTER 16

Zane and Duncan arrived at The Verge luxury apartment community a few minutes after the murdered-out SUV. He was convinced Duncan didn't follow too closely to avoid suspicion. Thankfully, it wasn't another stop-and-go strategy like back at TruCapital. His hunch proved correct.

Directly before the lobby and leasing office entrance, the Cadillac XT6 was situated. The golf cart, left abandoned, hadn't budged from its spot since their previous time on the property. The SUV was not running and was empty. He and Duncan faded back and began their surveillance. Time crawled slower than a desert tortoise. The clouds continued to move in.

Duncan broke the silence. "Man, this place is dead."

"No shit. Dead body gets found in an apartment and people scatter like cockroaches," Zane said. He looked up at the beefy black clouds rolling off the mountain. "Bit too ominous for my taste."

"Spooky. Like these rain clouds."

"Thank you for dumbing it down for me. But hey, if a little rain breaks up this heat, I'm all for it. Nasty-looking, though."

There was no sign of the slicked-back duo.

"What kind of man you think Carmen goes for?" Duncan asked.

"I'm guessing someone who understands what we do. Hard life to build from the outside." His gut twisted. He needed to tell Duncan. His partner for over a decade. Not now. "Surprising question. You typically enjoy reserving these talks for Stallone movies and terrible sports cars from the 80s."

Good subject change. The clouds fattened. Thunder banged in the distance.

"We all need to ask ourselves why Ford was so willing to crush the Mustang brand during that time. Those cars were hideous. Ferrari was banging out the Testarossa. There's a reason Vice had Johnson and that car on the posters."

"It was a 1972 Ferrari 365 GTS/4 Daytona Spyder."

"No sir, it was a C3 Corvette they had to make like a Ferrari. Lawsuits brought all that out."

The back and forth halted. Zane noticed the two men at Vernon's murder scene who were on the move.

His head replayed the day's scenarios. "Those are definitely the two I saw walking away from the crime scene."

"You sure?"

"Yes. They were at TruCapital. Now, they're here. They sure get around. That makes it three for three on our day."

"I'm on it." Duncan slid the gear into drive and eased the truck onto the road. Raindrops, fat and heavy, pounded away at the windshield.

"Guessing they're heading to the 210. Whichever way they turn, go the opposite way. Circle through the neighborhood. Should be able to blend in with a few of your bro trucks and can tail them better."

Duncan scoffed at his remark. "They're going right. I'm going left," he said. Duncan piloted the unmarked truck through the neighborhoods with the precision of a shark through water. Effortless, but bulky. The clouds broke open, and the streets thickened with water.

The suburban tract homes all looked the same. Houses built in the 1960s in a once-thriving community now feature overgrown lawns, chain-link fenced yards, and the occasional bullet hole in front windows.

Duncan pulled the truck up to the stop sign a block before the 210 freeway on-ramp that would send commuters 60 miles west toward Los Angeles. The sea of trucks and sedans had them in a solid position to see the SUV. Zane needed his suspicion that the Cadillac was heading out of town to be correct. It was.

One traffic signal cycle and he spotted their mark onto the freeway.

Duncan waited longer before punching the accelerator and merging onto the freeway. The rear-wheel-drive truck sprayed water behind it. The tires yearned for traction. Duncan was patient behind the wheel. Fast enough to catch up, but methodical. Duncan knew not to draw attention in their target's rear-view mirror.

It didn't take long for them to catch up. The SUV was driving like a couple out on a weekend drive, soaking up every minute away from the kids and taking time for themselves.

"What's he doing?" Zane said. He adjusted in the passenger seat. His knuckles went white as he gripped the handle above the door.

Duncan lifted his foot off the gas pedal. "Chippy traffic breaks go faster than this." Duncan was still a few vehicles back. The rain helped them blend in with the other freeway dwellers. The SUV kept slowing down.

"Have they never driven in the rain before?" The thought of telling Duncan about Carmen popped into his head. *Ignore it. Not now.*

"No clue, but if I slow with them, they'll know something is up." Duncan moved one lane over from the SUV. Almost side by side. "Stare or not to stare, that is the question."

"Oh, it's stare, like every other asshole would."

The water sprayed high and wide from the freeway. Drops continued to pound away. The windshield wipers swooshed and whipped from side to side.

He turned his head to ID the driver. Rain streaked across the window. The droplets vibrated violently. The impact threw him sideways, and he whipped back into the passenger window. His seatbelt anchored across his chest. His shoulder and knee shot into the in-line center of his body. Bones and muscles squeezed together with force.

The SUV had made them. Greeting his side of the truck with angry intent. Duncan wrestled with the steering wheel.

The SUV tucked in behind the truck. Duncan was still fighting to keep them on the road.

Zane kept a death grip on the handle, confirming its nickname. Adrenaline spiked. His world spun hard and fast. The SUV pitted his side of the rear bumper. His partner couldn't hold on. The truck somersaulted like an Olympic gymnast. His brain turned off the sensory of sound. Screeches, crunches, and shattering of glass all muted into the void.

The sound of flowing water. The *whoosh* of cars and wind.

Footsteps approached. Shards of glass snapped and cracked between weight and asphalt. An empty passenger seat flashed. Then darkness.

Fight dammit. Fight.

Was the truck sideways, or just him?

Duncan.

Zane fought to sit up. He was stuck. Pain ravaged his body.

Where's Duncan?

Words were trapped inside Zane's mouth. The chaotic scene around him smelled of burned rubber and exhaust.

The footsteps stopped. Couldn't have been over twenty feet from Zane's twisted-up body. There were audible sounds of voices, but he couldn't make out the words. Then the suppressed sound of a gun. Two rapid ones, a pause, then a third.

Footsteps crunched toward Zane's position. He was next - a sitting duck waiting for his execution to join Duncan in the afterlife.

Zane's world went black. The footsteps retreated, and he lost consciousness.

CHAPTER 17

San Bernardino, CA—TruCapital

"Good afternoon, Junior," the TruCapital concierge greeted him as he arrived. He nodded and tried his best not to look frazzled. Russo's hit squad rolling up on him before he entered the building threw him off. It had to be the day he wore the pink ensemble. A photo shoot for one of the local magazines. A necessary move to ingratiate himself as one with the community. Not simply an outsider looking for a financial score.

The concierge was in her late twenties, peppy. She had a well-proportioned tray of strawberries and hard cheese. Trying her best to combat the long-term impact of sitting in an office chair all day. "It's photo shoot day. Are you ready for your close-up?"

"Cancel it. Schedule it another time," he said. His irritated brown eyes pushed her away.

"What day is best?"

"You're the one with my calendar; shouldn't you know the answer to the question?" He wasn't looking for a reply, and didn't allow her one. "Find an open date and stick it in." His hot pink sneakers squeaked on the tile floor. The pink wig was stiff as a board. Cheap plastic thing.

He didn't bother with his routine fake smiles and hellos as he walked past his employees. His employees. The threat from Senior and now Russo's guys made him territorial over TruCapital.

Once he reached his office, he squeezed the bridge of his nose with two fingers. Tired from the recent trials at TruProperties' main office in San Francisco. He plucked an old, framed picture off his desk. His first surf trip to Costa Rica. Local women and waves. Simpler times.

The glass design of his office should make his employees feel he was accessible to them. Really, it was so he could look down on them. Occasionally, he'd gaze long enough until he could see down some blouses. He knew the ones who did it intentionally. They'd slow their walk, stretch their arms before moving their hair out of the way. He'd exchange a smile with them as they walked away. It was another one of his fake smiles. Pathetic. Those women were too easy to please.

He liked challenges. The women would be disgusted if they knew he wasn't checking for busy work. He was getting his rocks off.

There was no time for this now. His plan needed to be expedited. His own insurance policy against the madness of Senior. If he couldn't rely on Russo to back him, at least not yet, then he had to rely on the resource he reserved for desperate times. He retrieved his phone from his coat pocket and placed it on his glass desk. Then pulled another phone from a locked drawer behind him and set it next to his phone.

His top-of-the-line iPhone sat next to a dusty-looking, scratched phone. His burner. *Time to get dirty.* He turned on the old phone and placed a call to the only contact it had.

When the phone picked up, there wasn't a warm greeting, just the faint sound of breathing. He pulled in a breath.

He closed his eyes. "Mom wants to have dinner tonight."

The call ended.

He wiped the sweat from his forehead and then vomited into the wastebasket under his desk. He wiped his mouth and went back to looking at the picture from Costa Rica. The intercom interrupted the serene memory of entangled tan skin and the sensation of warm salt water on his desk.

"Check your calendar and make sure the rescheduled date is good."

Why is she calling for this? "Couldn't this have been an email?"

He wiggled his wide gamer monitor to life. Three windows were already open: CoinGecko, Google Finance, and CNBC. Always open and in view. The fourth window he dedicated solely to his USB thumb drive. To the trained eye, it was far more than external memory. This was his crypto cold wallet. The ability to trade on MetaMask, Coinbase, Binance, or any other place that gave him the security and anonymity he demanded. Thank God he avoided the FTX collapse. He found his calendar and confirmed the date.

He longed to return to San Francisco. He'd stand in his office, looking out his window at the cable car passing below him. *Who rides these things?* Suckers. Tourists. He had disdain for the tourism industry, except for the tugboats.

Tourists who expected their California vacations to be filled with the famous California sun. What few tourists ever prepared for was San Francisco's summers.

The sun doesn't come out until September and will stretch into late October if you're lucky. He loved seeing the tourist suckers arrive in his city and fork over another $40 on a fleece pullover with "SF" emblazoned across the left breast. Multiply that $40 by the number of family members who need to stay warm. It was a cash cow. He liked that aspect of those days. There was always money to be made from someone else's misery.

    He had one piece of his plan in motion. Now, he needed to bring Russo on board. Convincing his father's enforcer to work against Senior wouldn't be easy. Russo was the ultimate piece. A final middle finger to his old man for never thinking he was good enough or smart enough to run the family empire. Another trip to San Francisco was in order.

CHAPTER 18

San Bernardino, CA—St. Bernardine Medical Center

Most people don't like hospitals. Zane was no different. The sterilization. The monitored beeps. The disease - the death. People often forget that out of all that also comes birth.

An entire wing dedicated to welcoming new life into the world. Human life, born in the same building as an emergency room that's filled with people in horrendous pain. From accidents to crimes against them, and sometimes, both.

This was his rebirth. His eyes fluttered. His body was fighting. Bright lights. Darkness. Bright lights. Darkness.

His muscles seized sporadically. Memories flashed and triggered events - both fresh and ones he'd buried deep. The decade of 911 response calls as a cop. He refused to mask with the bottle. Not like the other cops. Not like his father did. No, Zane would not step across the blue line. He would stay in the fight.

Where was Duncan? Same room? Same floor?

Fight dammit.

Who was in the room with him? His eyes refused to find their mark. Muscles twitched. A soft, feminine hand slid along his forearm.

Carmen. She was here.

The department could have sent many of the men and women in uniform to safeguard the bodies.

The bodies. Where was Duncan? Carmen was here. Who was watching Duncan? Carmen was here. With him. Where she had been since their days at the academy.

Both eager and young. Pushing each other. Carmen worked harder than everyone in their class. One of only a few women didn't leave her a choice. She proved it every day.

Out work.

Out train.

Out think.

Zane was born to be a cop. The son of the most respected lawman in the department, for a time. Raised to fill the role behind the shield. His old man should have retired as a sergeant.

He was reluctant to follow the same career path. To him, his father was his dad. To the rest of the department, his father was something more. A legend. A legacy. A disgrace. A cautionary tale.

It was that reluctance that led to Carmen's initial response being about Zane's entitlement. He gave her the initial impression that he didn't have to work as hard. Opportunities that others may or may not have received, he received. It wasn't entitlement. It was his act of defiance. He could never live up to the Sarge, and he wasn't sure he wanted to.

Once Carmen understood him, they quickly became study partners. Carmen welcomed the push. So did he. Flirtatious nights studying went no further. They were colleagues. He helped her study to excel in their class. She helped him take things more seriously.

They were the last two standing on the night of their class's graduation. A large group of classmates gathered at a local dive bar called Black Watch. Dingy dive bar with an old jukebox and a set of pool tables pushed into the corner. Nothing special, but it backed the blue and offered cheap drinks. Simple. A recipe for becoming a favorite of law enforcement.

They drank beer together and toasted to finishing the six-month grind.

Laughter filled the conversations between them. They shared subtle looks. Playful touching. A decade later, they'd finally act on those moments.

Duncan was in their class. *Where was Duncan?*

Did he erase Duncan from his memory?

Fight dammit.

Bright lights.

Darkness.

Bright lights. Bright lights.

Carmen. She was there, next to him.

A soft hand on his forearm. He could feel her. Envision her. Hear her - the beeps. Holy shit, the beeps. Make them stop. His mouth was dry like cat litter. Swallowing felt like a hot tumbleweed was trying to go down his esophagus.

Carmen looked at him as if she couldn't believe he was looking back at her. His muscles spasmed. His words stuck like a pinched hose. So many words. So many questions.

"Duncan," he said. His partner's name, Duncan, he muttered, as if sweeping it up in a dust storm. Carmen's eyes told him everything. She leaned over him.

Close to his face. She squeezed his hand. A tear streaked down her cheek and landed on his. He reached for the tear with his tongue. A desperate act for moisture. Her lips were against his ear.

"He's gone."

CHAPTER 19

Zane's mind was on fire. Ready to unleash hell on the guys that forced an End of Watch tag on his partner. His body would heal. Duncan was gone forever. He was ready to move, to leave.

Carmen had finally fallen asleep. He didn't know how long she had been in there with him. How long had it been since he and his partner truck cartwheeled on the 210 freeway?

The beeps continued.

Wires and hoses draped across him like angry boat lines, keeping him anchored to the monitors. To the beeps. The relentless beeping must have exhausted Carmen. She was curled up in the visitor's chair with a hospital blanket. From the angle of his head, Carmen looked as if she would fall off the chair at any moment.

A blur of red shoes stepped into his room sideways, as if they were walking up a wall. No, he was sideways. He knew those steps. He lifted his head to straighten the image of the old man: his old man, The Sarge.

Sarge stood like a statue. His gray goatee hung down to his chest, hair like a wizard's. Long and slicked back tight, flowing down his back like a rebellious waterfall. Sarge's hawkish eyes shifted between him and Carmen. Arthritic hands, half-clenched, hung off the sides of a patched-up leather vest. Few people would know he once stood on the right side of the shield.

His father fully crossed over to his defiant side after his exit from law enforcement. Some might argue even before he turned in his badge. They wouldn't be wrong. Sarge came from the old school. A time when they frowned upon expressing a softer side. Was it a better way of life? Not likely.

Zane needed that edge from his father.

Sarge looked like a gunslinger. A spirit of the border - a death wind. Ready for a showdown to defend and exact revenge. "I see you looking at these hands." He lifted them and studied the tight bones. "You think they're out of the fight?"

Zane shook his head. His mouth was too dry. His body was too tired to object.

Sarge spoke quietly, "I always got one more in me."

Zane must have heard a thousand stories of how things used to be. More fists. Less paperwork. Once someone placed black tape across the badge in honor of the fallen, jurisdiction no longer applied. He wasn't sure he had it in him.

He took his eyes off his old man to find Carmen. She was awake. He pushed as much moisture into his mouth as he could. His throat scratched. "This is my dad." His leg muscles spasmed in short, angry bursts.

Pain. Rebuilding.

Pain.

More beeps.

Carmen stood up and extended a hand to the sarge. "I've heard a lot about you, sir."

Sarge accepted Carmen's hand. "Thank you for looking after my son."

Zane's words dragged through his dry throat like an anvil through sand. "Duncan."

The meet-and-greet ended. Sarge cracked his knuckles.

More pain. More beeps.

Zane reached his limit. "Can someone stop the fucking beeping?" His throat turned to lava. He reached for his neck.

Carmen shot out of the room to find a nurse.

Sarge stood over him.

Zane's throat burned following the outburst. Pain pushed his desire to leave the hospital and begin his pursuit.

"I need to get out of here," he said.

Sarge walked up to the edge of the hospital bed. "I can't just sneak you out the front door. We have to do this part right. Make sure you're cleared of anything major."

"Since when did you care?" Zane reached for his ribs. His body ached as his insides fought desperately to repair themselves. Nothing felt out of place. Cuts and bruises. Lucky. More than lucky. "I need to find these men." He pushed himself upright. Abs burning. "Handcuffs or removal from this life."

His father looked down at him. Hawkish eyes narrowed and focused. "Do you know what you're saying, son?"

The beeps continued. Zane pulled the pulse oximeter off his finger, and the beeps increased. "Yes. Bury them all." His father nodded in approval. Silence sufficed.

Carmen came back through the door, accompanied by a white coat. Carmen sat back in the chair she slept in. The doctor saddled up on a rolling stool and began entering passwords to retrieve his medical information.

Sarge gave him a look that told him he was leaving, but wouldn't be far.

The doctor went over his results before she caught herself. The doctor looked over at Carmen and then back at him.

"She can stay," he said.

Carmen smiled. Her eyes were tired. "Okay. Then let's get you out of here."

Sweet words of relief. The beeps faded away. Revenge for Paul Duncan was on the horizon. Zane might have been the one. It should have been him. It wasn't. Those responsible needed to be held accountable.

CHAPTER 20

San Bernardino, CA—TruCapital

Tyler stood in a cloud of his CK Eternity cologne. The catwalk above his employees gave him another vantage point of them. More so of the women that didn't frequent the space underneath his office windows. An entirely new crop.

He was their caring boss. Their watchful boss, overlooking his crew fulfilling their dedicated tasks. He wasn't. Sneaking glances down women's blouses sent blood flowing into his crotch. After all, he wore pink for breast cancer awareness. *Protect the tatas*. It wasn't sexual arousal as much as it was about power. Authority.

He was in charge and could do as he pleased. Like a form of perverted meditation. He was resentful of the women who knew what he was doing. It took the power away from him and put them in control. Senior gave him no control. This, he could. Power is control.

A fruitless moment of closed blouses caused his mind to drift. The mayor's son died on one of his properties. He wasn't responsible for that. Was he? Did Senior have something to do with it? Russo? Maybe both. It wouldn't make sense, though. He needed backup. He knew who.

Motorcycle clubs were more prominent when he was younger. Between South San Francisco and Oakland, patched-up leather bikers were commonplace on the Bay Bridge and Embarcadero.

Then, there were the stories growing up. Altamont Free Concert of 1969, a suburb an hour outside of the city, when someone decided a renowned MC should provide security for the event. A tragic end to a movement that was supposed to be about *peace and love*.

Over half a century later, things would need a similar approach for Tyler. He was too polished to appear as a cop, so at least he had that going for him. But his yuppie lifestyle was also a deterrent.

Wooden Nickel would be his destination. A bar set in the northern part of town that was busy enough to keep a lively crowd, but remote enough to stay free from the eyes of law enforcement.

Dozens of motorcycles lined the curb outside the saloon. Leather-clad bikers aligned their steel horses against the curb by backing in. Their alignment was a work of art.

Inside the local bar were four billiard tables in a grid, followed by a row of dartboards along the back wall. An L-shaped bar pressed against the back wall, so Tyler had to work his way through the room before getting a drink.

The music damn near skipped when he walked in. Neither a biker nor a local. He was an outcast.

Hold steady. Nobody knows who you are.

He should have changed his clothes. Gone with something more subtle than his Breast Cancer Awareness shirt. He leaned against the wooden bar top people had scarred and carved over the years to resemble a love and lust letter to alcohol.

An on again off again buzzing sound emanated from a corner of the bar. Tyler looked for the source and found a seasoned woman with her left leg draped over a tabletop, and a man tattooing the inside of her thigh.

A bartender, twenty years too old to still be bartending, greeted him. "What'll you have, hun?"

He hesitated. This was no place for a Singapore Sling or a White Claw. This was a beer and bourbon place. "PBR and a shot of Fernet," he said. A combination that was as common in San Francisco as sourdough bread and clam chowder.

The bartender's eyebrows raised, and she flashed a smile that hadn't been a full set of teeth since Carter was in office. "Maybe you do belong here," she said.

He pulled out his credit card and slapped it on the bar.

The bartender returned with his beer and shot. "Sorry hun. Cash only." She pointed to a handwritten sign stating such and then pointed between the pool tables and dartboards to the nearest ATM.

This place smelled of wooden floorboards soaked in ninety-proof liquor. A hint of blood and regret soured from the makeshift tattoo station. A thin layer of smoke clung to the ceiling, which told Tyler this place didn't play by the rules.

After a seven-dollar out-of-network fee for his ATM withdrawal, he was back at the bar and ordering a second round. A friendly back and forth with the bartender ensued. He couldn't remember her name to save his life, but that wasn't who he was here for.

He made his way over to the billiard tables and watched some bikers cracking away at 9 Ball, and a wad of cash went undisturbed on the long rail. This was his way in. Lose money and buy drinks. One biker was tall and wiry, like a hanger from the dry cleaners paired with eyes from a forgotten alley. Something easily disposable, but give it the right twist in the right hands, and it's more than capable of causing damage.

Tyler ate another seven-dollar fee from the ATM to make a larger withdrawal of twenties and headed back to the tables.

"Hey, Johnny Ta-tas," the wiry biker said. "You want to run a game?"

Tyler pulled the print on his shirt forward and pushed his eyes over his nose to read. He smiled. "Yeah, I'm down."

"Good. You rack'em. I crack'em. First game starts at twenty bucks."

"Twenty?" Tyler pulled his cash out and slapped five bills onto the green felt. "Let's start at a hundred. Work our way up."

The biker's eyes narrowed into slits. "You try to run," he looked at the back door. "They'll find you in a heap out back."

"I'm not here to run," Tyler shaped the balls into a diamond using the rack, pulling them tight, before setting them for the break.

"What are you here for, then?"

"Break, and I'll see if you're interested."

Tyler stepped back. With a crack, the biker sent the cue ball like a missile. The ball found its mark just off-center. The first nine billiard balls caromed around the table in all directions. Only the five-ball came to rest at the bottom of a pocket.

Tyler started his pitch, and the night carried on.

CHAPTER 21

San Bernardino, CA—St. Bernardine Medical Center

"I want to see the body," Zane said.

He was more cognizant by the minute. The relentless beeping had stopped. Thank God. His head and body still throbbed in places he didn't know existed. He had kept food and liquids down. Wires and IV lines removed. Ready to avenge his partner's death and bring justice to those involved.

Carmen checked him over with her eyes before answering. "You sure you're ready for that?"

"Does it matter? I feel responsible." He caught Carmen before she could interject. "Don't tell me I shouldn't feel that way. He's gone. I'm here. Why?"

"It's called survivor's guilt."

"Well, it sucks. That's for sure." He sank deep into his hospital bed. "Any word on when I'm getting out of here? I feel fine-ish. Thinking clearly has to count for something."

"I know you're eager to get back. Track down those men. Maybe sleep on it for a couple days. Clear your head. Talk to someone."

He threw his legs over the side of the bed. He ignored the last comment. "I gotta take a piss." He walked by Carmen and intentionally flashed the back of his open hospital gown. "That's what I think about that plan."

Carmen rolled her eyes. "Good to see your sarcasm hasn't faded."

He closed the bathroom door. He had bruises, but he wasn't pissing blood. Red is bad. Orange, not ideal. Yellow, meh. He flushed and limped back out.

"You're here. Doesn't this qualify as talking to someone?"

Another eye-roll from Carmen. "That's what you came up with while you were in there."

The door opened. Carmen turned. Her hand was at the ready, atop her sidearm.

White coat. Stethoscope.

"You're definitely looking better, Mr. Bruce," the doctor said. "All the labs are clear. As long as you're not in any discomfort, you'll be free to go."

Zane checked in with Carmen. A giddy smile, like he'd won the fifty-fifty raffle at a high school football game.

"I'll notify the nurse of your discharge. I'll give you a mild prescription for the pain. After that," the doctor motioned to the door in a sweep of her hands. "Freedom."

The doctor left. Zane stood and began removing the hospital gown. "Don't suppose you brought me a spare set of clothes."

Carmen held up a backpack. "As a matter of fact, I did. Close the door, though."

He plucked the backpack from her hands and slid into the bathroom.

Once he was discharged, Carmen pushed him in a wheelchair down to the pharmacy.

"This is dumb," he said.

Carmen playfully flicked the back of his head. "No. You're trying to bravado your way out of here by walking would be dumb."

He rubbed the back of his head as if it were the most painful part of his body. Carmen brought the backpack, and he tossed the paper sack in. He kept shooting his weight forward in the wheelchair, eager to leave. Feel the sun. Breathe the air. Not to hear goddamn beeps.

The sun blasted both of them as they breached the automatic sliding doors. He welcomed the sun on his skin despite the summer temperatures that came with it. The freshly cut grass smelled like watermelon.

He clutched the sides of the thin tires. "Stop." He held his hand straight up. "You see that?" He pointed to the end of the rounded driveway. "That's them. That's the SUV that took Duncan."

Carmen shielded her eyes with her hand and scanned the direction of Zane's finger.

"I don't think so," she said. "Sticker in the window says *there's a baby up in this bitch*. And the SUV is green. It's not even an SUV. It's a minivan. Maybe I need to wheel you back inside."

Zane's head hung to his chest like his neck were on a loose hinge. Carmen turned the wheelchair as if she were heading back inside.

"Don't even think about it," he said. "Fuck."

"You gonna be alright getting in this car?"

"Depends. Who's driving?" He gave her a look like; Please don't let it be you.

"Don't give me that."

She smiled and positioned the wheelchair back around. Truck tires screeched on freshly laid pavement that made up the curved entrance to the hospital.

A quick jolt of adrenaline washed away once Zane recognized the silhouette of his Ford Ranger. "Well, that's my truck."

The sun glared off the truck's windshield as it stopped a few feet from Zane. The familiar tone of his father's voice called out.

"Lucky you, son. I'm still your emergency contact."

An hour-long car ride with his father, whom he hadn't spoken to in over a year, wasn't where his mind was. Maybe Carmen was the better option to drive him home.

Play it cool.

"Feels like I'm getting picked up from high school football practice." Zane looked back at Carmen. "You didn't happen to be a cheerleader, were you?" She ignored him. "This is lose lose between my chauffeur options."

Sarge and Carmen bonded over the slight. Zane carried on.

"With how much you two love tapping the brake and fluttering the accelerator. I'm sure glad I did all those neck-strengthening exercises in my youth. I'm gonna need them."

Zane made whiplash movements with his head and neck to exaggerate his point. Too far. A twinge shot down his spine, and he yelped like a dog—a poor choice.

Carmen and Sarge showed little sympathy.

"Don't get smart, son. I'm sure years on the bike have smoothed me out. Your mother used to fall asleep on the back of the Harley. I think I'm doing just fine."

Used to.

His mother had left two years before. Why would he bring her up?

Not now. Deal with that later.

"Think your crippled hands can reach the steering wheel?" Zane said. He still held on to the back of his neck with one hand. Gotta ease into it.

Carmen interjected. "Alright, you two. I'm sure there's plenty to rib each other about on the drive. About an hour from here?"

"Hour and a half in this beater," Sarge said.

"Forty-five minutes if you know what you're doing," Zane said.

Carmen wheeled Zane to the passenger side. He wanted to jump up, but his newfound stiff neck reminded him to stay put. Take the help.

She pulled open the door, which groaned as though it had never been opened. She offered her hand, and he accepted the spot. He slid into the seat and settled in.

"She going to buckle your belt for you, too?" Sarge said. His tight hands gripped the worn steering wheel and twisted it as if it were a throttle.

Zane returned an eye-roll. So did Carmen.

Carmen stepped back from the truck. "I'll call you in a few hours. Need to head back to the station and see where we are on arrangements for Duncan's memorial."

A dense fog of reality fell over the playful atmosphere. Zane's partner was dead. Murdered while he hung helplessly inside the truck. The road to recovery was going to be long. More than his broken ribs. More than a banged-up shoulder. And more than this stiff neck. His soul would need the most healing.

Sarge saw the change in his son. "I'll see him home safely, LT. Keep up the strong work."

Carmen gave two taps on the hood with an open palm. Sarge drove off and pointed the old Ford Ranger toward the mountains.

CHAPTER 22

San Bernardino, CA—TruCapital

"Be strong. They'll come around." Tyler paced his office intensely. He missed his regular view of the women walking below his glass office. Frantic to reach his new biker contacts. They didn't blow him off as much as they seemed indifferent. She'd come around. Had to. He needed it sooner rather than later. Russo's goons were closing in and creating problems that didn't need such force.

When will Russo's guys show back up, drag him out to a dark section of town to find an insubordinate in a bathtub?

An answer to his question came quickly. The glare of the afternoon sun reflected through the wide-open office space from the front entrance. A detail overlooked by the architect during design and construction. He peered down and spotted the heavies crossing the lobby. They ignored any pleas by the front desk greeter to check in.

He pulled the security phone out of the top drawer of his desk. Still nothing from the MC.

He found a reflective spot on his glass wall. "Be strong, Ty. Fuck these clowns. They will not come into my office and bully me around. Nobody bullies Tyler Truman Jr. around. Nobody."

He flipped a switch on the wall behind his desk. A silent hydraulic system kicked into gear. His desk rose off the floor half a foot. Power position.

He eased into his high-backed leather chair. He searched for the lever under the seat. There. He pulled it and felt it lift under him until it was as tall as it could go. No chance he'd last a full day with his feet off the ground. It'll do the trick while he handles Bert and Ernie.

The duo approached at a pace. They looked as if they wanted to make a scene. He was prepared for this. The tandem reached for the chrome bar on the glass door. He timed it perfectly. He pushed the automatic open button under his desk, and Tom and Jerry fell through his office.

"Careful. There's a lot of glass around here." He smiled down at the two men.

"What kind of bullshit was that?" The larger of the two said. He had a head like a bowling ball. Not a nice one either. One loaned that's full of scratches with chunks taken out of it.

Tyler pretended he didn't know what he was talking about. "Gentlemen, what do I owe the pleasure of your visit? My greeter wasn't able to capture that information when you graciously arrived."

The shorter man wanted to chime in. Tyler would not give either of them a chance to answer.

"You two don't act on your own. More obey and follow. No surprises here. My father and Russo seem to forget that I grew up watching their games. Only for Russo to invite me into your world."

The henchmen broke into fits of laughter.

Tyler bit down on the inside of his cheek to hide his annoyance. *Maintain position.*

"You have no power," Bert began.

Or was it, Ernie? Tyler didn't know or care.

The bigger one continued. "Cleaning up your puke that night was worse than cleaning the wellness check. Senior is making plays, and you need to stay out of our way. We'll keep it clean. Been doing this a long time."

Tyler smacked the desk. "I'm in the way? I'm keeping things afloat down here. Have been. He does not know how much shit I eat for him. He knows nothing about."

Bert and Ernie laughed.

His eyes widened with rage. "You don't know what's at play. What are the stakes? You're taking orders from Russo, who is taking orders from Senior."

"And who is taking orders from you?" Ernie said.

Confusion washed over Tyler. He blinked hard and resisted the urge to chew on a thumbnail. "Everybody here." His arms swung wide.

"We're not talking about that," Bert said. "We're talking about the tail you have following us."

The tail? The MC had started. They worked in the shadows. Messages received.

Bert pulled out a tracking device and tossed it up to him. He caught it like a fan catching a ball thrown up by a baseball player. "Have eyes at The Verge. But stay off our asses. We have business to conduct for Senior, and the last thing you'll want is for that focus to shift onto you."

Tyler was already thinking of the next move for the MC. What was their plan? How'd they track them? Why so sloppy? Was the MC careless? Couldn't be. Had to be a decoy.

"You guys threatened me first. I needed a little bit of time if you were on your way to make do on your threats. How'd you think I was so prepared for you today?" A lie, but he had to push. "Wouldn't you guys do the same? Come on, what's Senior paying you? I bet I can double it."

The duo scoffed at the idea. They bought the lie. They rose to their feet and buttoned up their suit coats.

"This is your last warning, Junior. Fall back or start coming to peace with your maker."

Confidence exploded inside Tyler. The MC was in. "This isn't the Wild West, is it?" His voice was sultry with sarcasm. "My father isn't that stupid. But he hired you two to keep on the payroll, so."

The shorter of Bert and Ernie stopped as if he wanted to step up onto his platform and have a go. Pummel his face until it is unrecognizable. It wouldn't take much. Thankfully, Bert pushed Ernie out the door. Keep walking.

Tyler swiveled in his chair. Sigh of relief. Blood flowed down his pants. Power. He got up and moved to peer down from his office. Russo's guys were leaving his building. He took a perverted scan around at the women. Not as arousing after sending away the heavies. He retrieved the burner phone from his top drawer and wrote a simple message.

Meeting at Au Sushi?

The read receipt flashed immediately.

CHAPTER 23

San Francisco, CA—Au Sushi

Tyler was in the middle of an empty bar at Au Sushi. He held a sparkling water with a lime and talked into the glass. "Time. It's the only thing money can't buy you more of. Tonight's the night."

He checked his Apple Watch. When would Russo show up? Would he show up? Radio silence ever since Tyler sent the message. Formal commitment is not required. It was all a mask to look like an industry meeting. A group tank discussion on the state of Bay Area multi-family real estate. Or so the other guests would believe.

Tyler took a sip of his sparkling water. Sucking the liquid in through tight lips. Enough to coat his tongue, and the bubbles kept his stomach from getting upset. The last thing he needed was to puke onto a $300 sashimi platter.

Au Sushi was his gold standard for a midweek flex. Tucked off Chestnut Street in the Cow Hollow district, Au Sushi dripped with luxury. He and God were the only ones who knew what the monthly rent was.

It didn't matter if a party reserved the secluded room in advance. When Tyler decided he needed the room, the Au team cleared the calendar. Far easier for them to piss off one customer who only makes a casual appearance. Owning the building and giving a sweetheart deal on the lease afforded him that privilege.

The entrance had dark-stained polished maple wood, red velvet curtains, and thousand-dollar bottles of cold sake lined the wall behind the bar. Gold-leaf accents and gold trim everywhere. On the other side was a collection of dimly lit tables that led to the secluded room.

He kept sipping his sparkling water at the bar. Standing up and sitting back down frequently. Li, the head server, was first through the door. He took a bigger drink and let out a sigh of relief. Without her, his plan was going to be much more difficult.

"Where am I setting up?" Li said. She carried a stack of tablets with her. Each was in a protective black case.

He resisted the urge to hug her and said nothing. Leaving his glass on the bar top, he led her to the private room. Its crimson red walls and red velvet seats made the room haunting. The continued gold trim said elegance. Statement made.

Silence filled the space between him and Li. Muffled sounds of the chefs preparing the meal came from the kitchen. Li placed the tablets around the table at each of the place settings.

The temperature in the room shifted. Li's eyes flashed at the door.

Alerted, he spun. No threat.

Holly, another server, was on time to place hot teapots and sake. Tyler hadn't seen her since the night of the Giants game. Did she notice him leave his apartment that night with Russo?

Later. Tonight's business comes first.

They strategically scattered several bottles of Dassai "Beyond" Junmai Daiginjo sake around. Not to be out of reach from any chair in either direction.

An optimally temperature-controlled cooler, tucked into the corner of the room, held the backups. Only the most attractive servers were assigned to work this dinner. He hoped the sake and the dim lights would set the tone. Each server would leave the night with over one thousand dollars in tips. Along with many offers for favorable jobs, to travel the world and earn larger sums of money.

The girls knew better. The promise of jobs, travel, and money would disappear when the girls refused a blowjob, or the wives found out. Tyler paid each of the girls another thousand to string his guests' interest along as long as possible. Then he'd be sure to end the dinner and push his guests out of the restaurant before they could sleaze their way into making the servers any more uncomfortable. The women appreciated him. Top-level confidential service was all he required in return.

"Your guests should arrive soon, correct, Mr. Truman?" Li asked. She was tall and had eyes that looked as if they had been hand drawn.

Tyler admired her aesthetic. Don't get distracted. "Yes. I believe the first one is less than five minutes out."

Li smiled, then said, "Are we missing anything?"

He admired the table. "Only our guests."

Li exited, leaving him to pace the room on his own.

He checked the place settings.

Perfect.

He selected his seat to face the entrance. A visual of the scene. His guests. Russo, across from him. Chess, not checkers.

He embraced the rare moment of stillness in the middle of the sixth-largest economy in the United States.

Poof. Gone. His guests had arrived.

Four Dassai "Beyond" sake bottles were already empty and lining the ledge behind the table. Ninety-six pieces of high-grade sashimi were nearly gone before he brought up the business of the night. He was good. So good, he didn't have to bring it up at all.

He'd been grooming them for years. We are talking about the same group. This is the same restaurant. The same open tab. The same beautiful servers. Asking nothing of his guests. Agree and deliver on the favors they asked of him. Now it was time for him to hand in his receipts.

"Gentlemen, take a break from enjoying the freshest and most exquisitely prepared sushi in San Francisco. And by all means, don't slow down on the drinks." Tyler raised his glass of sake. The men followed suit to toast from across the table before throwing back the silky, chilled liquid.

Li led the women of Au Sushi. They began refilling sake and cocktail glasses around the table. Powerful men's eyes wandered with the overload of beauty swimming around the room. Smiles and subtle touches from the servers made the expensive sake heat the men even more.

Li stayed with Tyler. His glass was only to be filled by her. Nobody else. Which included himself. Her job was of high importance - to keep him sober. But make it look like he's drinking just as much as his guests. The white dolphin. She wouldn't poison him. Would she? He paid her well enough.

Stop being paranoid.

This group of businessmen enjoyed their vices. They didn't want to be drunk during an offer meeting, while he sat back and sipped water. It would put them on edge. The theatrics of Li's sleight of hand protected him.

He held up his glass of silky liquid. The rest of the table followed. Moment of truth. "Salud." In unison, the men tapped the shot glasses on the table and sucked them back. He was still breathing. No sudden collapse of his lungs and windpipe. Eve protected him. For now.

"Gentlemen. We have scrubbed the tablets before you and tailored them for each user. No two are alike." The men opened the tablets, and he smiled at their expressions. "I know you are too smart to think I'm providing seven-hundred-dollar sake and thousands worth of sushi while you drool over the lovely women, just because we like each other."

A collective laugh from his audience.

He continued while murmurs around the table tried to derail him. A few repositioned their chairs. Tyler had details that would change their lives. Russo's eyes never left his.

The dimly lit red room glowed with the hue of blue faces reflecting the tablet screens.

"You'll be required to place your palm flat against the screen. This will give me your digital identity. It's as good as signing a contract with a dozen lawyers looking over every word. You will all do so, and there will be no discussion."

Although no one objected verbally, people expected hesitation. One by one, the tablets beeped approval of a good palm scan. Russo's red, bulbous nose matched the room's aesthetic. The final holdout placed his hand on the screen.

"Excellent. The first image you'll see is our disastrous property down in the Inland Empire."

A voice from the table interjected. "The Verge."

He swallowed his irritation like a hot wad of wasabi.

"My father's Hail Mary has been anything but lucrative. It's come under the microscope of local law enforcement."

The same voice interrupted. "What's that to do with us?"

He paused this time. Locked eyes with Russo. He carried on. "If you'll let me finish. You will learn things. The resident was David Johnson. Son of the local mayor and an associate Senior had been working for me. Helping him diversify his money through cryptos."

They refilled the sake. Faces glowed.

"Well, much like The Verge's status, Senior's crypto funds were depleting faster than 309 Eddy Street." A reference to the property they all went in on when there were talks of the SOMA project moving above Market Street. Gentrification got shot down, and the street people shot up.

A unified grumble filled the room.

The screens simultaneously transitioned to his next talking point.

He sat back and read the room. Glossed-over looks as the digital material presented itself. Some, quicker than others, were eager to start. Russo dragged. He expected Russo would. The delay made him feel even better about his decision. Russo needed to turn on Senior.

"You're free to eat and drink as much as you like. I'll be at the bar to collect your tablets as you leave. Questions need to be handled in private. One on one. This protects you, me, and our mission."

He stood. Filled his own glass from the nearest sake bottle. Li took half a step out from the corner, but quickly retreated. He raised the expensive rice wine to his newest independent contractors and took his shot. He left the men to their own devices, and Li followed him out.

CHAPTER 24

San Bernardino Mountains, CA

"You drive this every day?" Sarge asked Zane.

Zane looked over the edge of Highway 18 from the passenger window of his old Ford Ranger. He hadn't seen it from this side of the car. A ball of anxiety swelled in his stomach.

"Keeps me focused," he said. "Can't stare off into highway hypnosis. Otherwise." He whistled and animated a splat with his hands. "Good thing those archaic hands of yours have built-in grip."

Sarge looked down at the stiff joints and knuckles as they gripped the wheel. "I know what you're saying. I didn't even remember driving in on most days."

There was no reception on the radio within these twists and turns. The hum of the engine and the transmission shifting up and down gears made up their soundtrack.

Zane rubbed his palms on the tops of his pants and squeezed the fabric. Pain sparked from his shoulder, and he did his best to find a more natural position. "How'd you end up in my hospital room?"

Sarge stroked his long, gray goatee. "I'm still listed as your emergency contact."

Zane sighed and said, "That'll change."

"C'mon. Who you gonna list? Mom? Your LT?"

"You don't get to bring Mom into this. You left her. Us. The department."

"Here we go. You don't know nothing about nothing." Sarge's arthritic hands twisted on the steering wheel.

"I don't? Let's work backwards. Did you walk away from your life in law enforcement to become an outlaw? Yes. I followed *your* footsteps into *this* job, and you turned your back on that. Then there's Mom." He shook his head and went from staring out over the cliff to his old man's face. "There's no excuse for leaving her."

The vibrating hum of the tires rattling along the pavement engulfed the truck's cabin. Zane hadn't had an actual conversation with his father in years. Why would it change now? He rubbed his aching shoulder and shifted in his seat. Back to watching the cliff's edge.

Sarge shot a quick glance over. "Close your eyes, son. I'll have you home soon."

Zane wanted to, but he couldn't. "Did enough of that in the hospital." A lesser man would rely on the bottle. "Is this why you drink? Numb the pain. Drown your problems?"

The expectation was another unanswered question. A rapid response was not.

"Your mother and I are still together," Sarge said.

The pain in Zane's shoulder switched off, and another rage burned within. He took a controlled breath. A bleak attempt to weather the storm inside.

"Maybe she believes there's still a good man in there. Distraught that your midlife crisis wasn't just a convertible Corvette and spur of the moment runs to Laughlin. You already had the stache. Instead, this." He waved his hand up and down toward Sarge.

After passing the Strawberry Peak fire lookout post and another dozen rock slide signs, Sarge backed the truck into Zane's driveway.

The pitch locked the seatbelts into place. Zane groaned in pain.

"I'm going to take a quick shower," he said.

Sarge took up occupancy on Zane's large L-shaped couch.

"Big couch just for you?" Sarge said.

Zane looked at his old man and kept on walking. "Gives me options. Never know which spot I'm gonna like best. I won't be long."

His old man made some comment about a worn-in cushion. Zane ignored it. He needed a shower. Hot. Not the cold ones he'd grown fond of. Those would not take the hospital grime off.

Cleaned and smelling of pine tar, he found his old man staring blankly at the flat-screen TV. There was nothing on.

"Just checking out your reflection?" he asked. The expression on his father's face gave him pause for concern. The fading summer blew through the open back door.

Sarge groaned as he got off the couch and moved across the living room to the bar, where there were empty bottles. "Bit of a problem, son?"

Zane sighed and walked over to his old man. Now was the time. "I pour them out once I get them. My little ritual. Constant reminders of what strained our relationship."

"Expensive habit," Sarge said. He stood still, looking over the empty bottles. "You want to know the truth? You're going to wish these were full for what I'm about to tell you."

Zane couldn't decide whether to sit or stand. He sat. No. Stood.

"I'd sit," Sarge said. His voice was low, almost dull.

Zane settled onto the couch, feeling uneasy and awkward. He reached for the pain in his ribs with his free hand. Even if now were a good time to drink, he didn't keep any in the house. "Uncle Ricky."

"That's right." Sarge looked at his arthritic hands as they trembled. "Not a day goes by that I don't think about him. Losing a partner isn't a state of sadness. Its rage. Its fuel and a fire you can't extinguish. A feeling you're experiencing now. Revenge is on your mind, just like it's been on my mind every day for the last two decades."

Uncle Ricky wasn't an uncle by blood. Ricky was an uncle by bond. A man who entered the Bruce family orbit as Sarge's partner, taking bad guys off the streets. Dues paid without even knowing it. Loyalty, joy, tears, laughter, love, and dependability. Family vacations, holidays, backyard pool parties, and birthdays were all staples for the Bruce family.

The similarities between Sarge's bond with Ricky and Zane's own with Duncan weren't hard to see. "Wasn't he ambushed by some random gang bangers?" Zane said.

"Yes, and no."

"What do you mean?"

"Ambushed, yes. Random? Not so much."

Zane straightened up. For a moment, he couldn't feel the pain in his ribs. Rage soaked inside his brain, leaked down his neck, and into his chest. He felt the connection to the not-so-random attack that took the life of his partner, Paul Duncan.

"After Ricky's funeral, I begged my captain to let me run it off-book. I was told to stand down. Think about my family. Uncle Ricky was family. So, I went dark."

"Understatement."

"Mom fell victim to an attack then. Another *random* robbery gone wrong."

Zane's face twisted into a scattered puzzle. "Mom?"

"She lived, but the message landed harder than a corpse. She made me promise to keep it from you. We all know how you'd react. After that, I stopped asking permission."

Zane popped off the couch. He paced the room like a lost puppy. The pain in his ribs was a distant nuisance. "Why weren't you allowed to pursue it?"

"I was told it was a random attack by gang bangers trying to make a name for themselves. A story seen in this line of work a million times."

"Makes sense."

"We checked the box. Let's all move on."

Zane shook his head. His father's words sank into his soul.

Sarge spun an empty liquor bottle in his hand. "I used everything the badge taught me. And everything it wasn't supposed to."

"Was it hard to track them down?"

"Not really. I followed the money. No warrants. No reports. No backup. I found the men who ordered the intimidation of Mom. These weren't kids. They were contractors. Middlemen. Who knew how to make violence look accidental."

"Could have just arrested them?"

Sarge nodded. "Armchair quarterback always with the smarter play."

"You pound them into submission?"

"Something like that," Sarge said. His eyes were on Zane, but the light behind them appeared to be in a distant place. "Beat the first one so bad, he never walked right again. Dragged another into a wash, and he gave up number three."

"And what happened to number three?" Zane held up three fingers.

"He tried to run. Didn't make it. It wasn't a shootout. Wasn't self-defense. It was rage with a memory of your mom, and a badge still warm in my pocket. When it was over, I knew exactly what I'd done. Crossed the blue line so hard there was no stepping back. Not legally. Not morally."

"Did you report it?"

Sarge's silence told him everything.

"Where did getting patched up come from?" Zane motioned to his old man's leather vest.

Sarge stroked his long, gray goatee. "I didn't wear the colors for a long time. But I found refuge in a place built for men who understand violence."

"And your life as a cop didn't matter?"

"Word travels when a man handles himself the way I did. I rode with'em. I bled with'em. Ran security. Enforced debts."

Zane stood there, shaking his head. His old man was the reason he went blue and donned the shield. "When did you stop pretending you were still a cop?"

Sarge's face went stiff. His eyes searched for a memory long buried in the shadows of his soul. "The club gave me structure the department no longer could. Loyalty without paperwork. Justice without appeals. Consequences delivered immediately."

"What about your family?"

"If I had stayed, I would have poisoned you." Sarge turned to the display of empty bottles. "None of these have liquor?"

"No," Zane said. "I've had so much hatred in me for so long. I still don't understand."

"Good. Hate me. Hate is safer than understanding. Understanding makes you curious. Curiosity will get you killed."

"You didn't just leave me and Mom. You murdered people."

"I know."

Zane swallowed a large lump of anger. His heart thumped like a war drum. There was a fraction of him that understood. He wanted to exact retribution on Duncan's killers. Without paperwork. Free from the never-ending court of appeals.

"I recognize that look," Sarge said. "If you follow me there, it won't be for love. It'll be because you think violence fixes things. It's a temporary band-aid. Eventually, it just makes a life you can't come home to."

The pounding of boots clambering up the front steps caught Zane off guard. No threat. He knew who was showing up. Without a single knock, the door opened, and Carmen came in as if she owned the place.

"Only you get that kind of treatment, huh?" Sarge said. Tension still tight in the air. "Pretty sure he makes me knock. Then waits as long as possible to torture me before allowing me in."

"Oh, was I supposed to knock?" Carmen said. "Not really my style. Plus, he's damaged goods at the moment."

Zane looked around the room as if he had no clue where he was. Carmen's arrival couldn't have been at a better time. "My gun's around here somewhere for such an intruder." There were two concealed in his living room and another in the kitchen. That covered the upstairs.

"You still carrying that ugly-ass Glock?" Sarge said.

"Didn't you use to say, *I'd rather be standing with an ugly Glock in my hand than be dead with a pretty Sig.*"

"I never said that."

"Oh, well, it sure sounds like something you'd say."

"You just here to check on the boy?" Sarge asked.

"Something like that," Carmen said. She moved over to Zane and placed a caring hand on his shoulder.

His father's story about turning outlaw was still fresh. But he wanted to move on for the night. Press pause on the past.

He stroked Carmen's hair with his good arm and then looked back at his old man. "Take my truck. Leave it at the department. Have one of your biker buddies pick you up."

Sarge agreed and bowed out.

As the door closed, Carmen took a half-step back from Zane. Her brown eyes twinkled with curiosity. "What was that about?"

"Family trauma."

"Anything you care to discuss?"

"Let's just say, when I look into my future, it's me arresting my own father."

CHAPTER 25

"Where do we start?" Zane said. With his old man's exit, his adrenaline spike had faded into the background. He plopped onto his couch and groaned in pain. His ribs and shoulder ached like mini daggers stabbing him from the inside.

He scratched his chin. His mind went back to the crash. The sound of the footsteps as he hung helplessly in the truck played in his head. The silenced gunshots. His own pending death that never came. Saved by an external, split-second decision.

Carmen joined him on the couch and placed her gentle hands on him. "I want to tell you to get rest. Your body needs to recover. But I know that would be a waste of breath."

"You're right." He looked at Carmen. The empathy in her eyes glowed, revealing her soul to him. The pain his body was in vanished for that moment. He didn't want to take any painkillers. Just another poison in the body. Carmen was his source of healing. "We got the thumb drive from Vernon. He ended up full of bullet holes. That led us to the black SUV, which took Duncan. They must have been after the thumb drive."

He caught the lump in his throat and looked out the window. Carmen moved closer to him and placed a hand on his thigh. He stared out the window with glossy eyes.

Breathe. Breathe.

He wanted to scream, but didn't. Carmen came into focus. He squeezed her hand and held it on his thigh. "Thank you for being here," he said. "As long as I have the thumb drive, I'll be next."

"I'll stay with you," Carmen said. "If they're willing to take out the mayor's son. Take out a cop. Then nothing and no one is off-limits."

"That'll be up to me," he said, looking around the room. "Where are my things from the hospital?"

"You had little. I brought you a change of clothes. The ones you wore that night were trash."

Zane remained silent. His mind was where the crash had taken place. The rain. The pursuit. The thumb—

"That's it. I tossed the thumb drive Vernon gave me into the glove box."

Carmen sat back and said, "Please tell me you used an evidence bag."

"Do I look like a boot?" he said. "What about Mr. Pink?" Carmen shot him a confused look. "Duncan and I were sitting on him when the two heavies arrived. Whatever they said to him scared him shitless. He went white as a ghost. They drove off and left him in a code brown."

"Nasty."

"The muscle has to be the link between Johnson, Mr. Pink, and Duncan. Has to." His desperation made him pace. Agony, pain, and rage all rolled into a ten-foot circle in his living room.

Carmen cut in. "We should have all the requested files on Johnson sent over from The Verge. Wouldn't be surprised if it is less substance and more formality."

A bolt of theory cracked Zane's skull. "Vernon. He said Mr. Pink was a suspect. *Pervy*. I believe, to be more specific."

"Can we back up to Mr. Pink?"

"Sorry, head dick in charge at TruCapital. When Duncan and I first saw him, he was decked out in all pink."

"Interesting. Lots of dots to connect while you have busted body parts."

"Body is already healing. The hard drive…" he smacked the side of his head with an open palm. "This thing is like a steel trap."

Carmen smiled at him. Her eyes twinkled. She turned and kissed his cheek. The pain in his ribs and shoulder subsided. She grabbed his hand and led him down to the bedroom. "Let's see if we can't get you a good night's sleep."

"What did you have in mind?" He gave her hand a squeeze at the top of the stairs. "I'm not ready to lose you."

"You won't."

"I lost Duncan."

"We both lost him."

He closed his eyes. His chin sank into his chest. Her hands gripped each of his biceps. His muscles trembled as mini fireworks of electrical current exploded underneath his skin. Carmen lifted his chin and kissed him.

"You're a good man. Come on. Let's go to bed."

"Bed doesn't have to mean sleep." He took the lead, and she followed him into the bedroom.

CHAPTER 26

San Francisco, CA—TruProperties

Truman Senior slammed the handset of his office phone down so hard that it bounced back out of the cradle and spun atop his polished mahogany desk. He ignored his secretary squawking through the receiver. Senior peered through the glass doors to his office. His body heat rose out of his collared shirt and warmed his ever-expanding jowls. Maybe he was getting too old for this business.

He'd made millions, and not just one or two. He made enough in the 1990s and early 2000s to have retired then. A true juggernaut and pioneer of the multi-family residential real estate market in San Francisco. There were always rent-controlled tenants looking for a payout to move. Senior would purchase the building, he'd start sending offer letters, long-term tenants would accept, they'd get paid, and TruProperties would flip the newly gained unit at market value and make hand over fist what he paid out. Easy money.

It's after the initial wave of flipped units that things become more hands-on. Savvy tenants would hold out for a bigger offer, fine. But the ones that got ornery about it became a nuisance - pests that needed to be exterminated from the building of his empire. The ones who lawyered up were fun to deal with, and Senior knew better than to approach them himself. Enter Al Russo.

Russo lived for that kind of stuff. Especially in that era. He had pull with law enforcement. Senior loved that. Russo also had a connection to the biggest sports star, Barry Bonds. Who was launching baseballs into the bay at record pace, and the department guys loved it. Russo could grant them access. A signed baseball here, a picture for their son there, a night out at AT&T Park in a luxury box with views of the Bay Bridge and the bright lights of the city skyline. The Giants may not have been the best team in baseball during that time, but the games were popular. Watching an elite athlete, enhanced by drugs, allegedly, blast baseballs into the night sky was exciting and the place to be for athletic entertainment.

Russo would report back to Senior. The dirty tricks used to force tenants out. Piles of trash backed up the garbage chutes, so they'd have to take the stairs to discard their *Hefty* sacks. Pay the mail carrier to withhold the mail. Then, after calls and complaints, he'd dump a month's worth of mail on their doorstep in the middle of the night. With the Internet, being connected to us at all times, he and Senior wouldn't be able to get away with the childish bullying behavior as they did in different times.

Senior pined for those days.

Things were more extreme now with the wellness checks done at the Dogpatch warehouse. Once the blood was on Russo's hands, he could never wash them completely. Forever under Senior's control. Now, the blood was also on Junior's.

***

Russo needed to be focused. His new mission has been at the forefront ever since he left Au Sushi and said goodbye to Junior for the night. This was his chance to have a clear conscience. Decades of service to Senior and the hundreds of people he forced out into harder living conditions, check or no check in hand. Somehow, exterminating a resident manager was less burdensome than forcing someone out of their rent-controlled apartment of forty years.

Al Russo had reached a crossroads in his life. The angrier he saw Senior become with his failure of The Verge property, the closer he got to rambling up the highway. Enough was enough. Was Junior any better? Not by much. Junior at least wanted to run the business and return it to glory, while for Senior, it was all about money and power. A heavy, weighted boot pressed down on Russo's neck. The only relief came when he bowed to Senior's every demand.

Russo entered Senior's office and found his usual spot on a tobacco-brown leather chair. "Forty years of service and old Mrs. Teller is still barking on that phone like it's day one on the job," he said. "She hasn't figured out the intercom switch, or, heaven forbid, getting her ass up and walking the fifteen feet to your office?"

"She tried that back in ninety-seven, and she was met with an Italian loafer thrown at her head," Senior said. "Hasn't tried that since. Never got the loafer back. Part of me wants to bronze the other one and give it to her as a retirement gift."

"You still have it?"

"It's a damn fine loafer. Custom-made on my first trip to Italy. Unparalleled craftsmanship. Still hoping she'll return the other one and I can wear them again."

Russo stood and walked back to the door of Senior's office. "Mrs. Teller, for the love of God, please stop with the phone. He hasn't picked the damn thing off his desk, let alone respond to whatever the hell it is you're blabbering about."

"But, it's-" Mrs. Teller tried getting her message to Russo, but he cut her off.

"Write it down and give it to me on my way out. I'll relay it to Senior when he's ready." Russo cut her off a second time. "Write it down and hand it to me on my way out."

Russo closed the large glass double doors behind him, and he returned to his seat on the couch.

"No movement on The Verge?" Russo asked his longtime boss.

The pause Senior took told Russo everything.

"Nothing. Couldn't fill it with people I'm paying, let alone anyone willing to cough up rent. Fucking Inland Empire. What a fucking shithole. Who put that property on our balance sheet?"

"You did."

"No shit, I did. It was rhetorical, Al. Somebody's head needs to roll for this, and I can't take my own. The tribe will never pay up at this point. They're going to steal that property from me."

"The irony."

"Don't give me that bullshit. The boys are meeting with the tribe today, so we should expect their report soon."

"You're trusting those two as your proxy? Please tell me Junior will at least be there?"

Senior stared with dark eyes. He didn't say a word.

Russo continued. "For fuck's sakes, pull up a Zoom call with the Chief and handle your own business. Show them some respect. Your muscles can't negotiate."

Senior scoffed. "Out of their mouths? No, out of their hands and weapons? Speaking of which, how did Junior handle the Dogpatch wellness check?"

Russo returned the silence, contemplating his words. "He added to the cleanup when he threw up," he said. "Nothing a little extra bleach and the Dogpatch boiler couldn't handle."

"Good. Monitor him. Not sold, he does not have the stomach for this business. It'd be a real shame if he couldn't keep his head."

What was Senior saying? The aging real estate mogul was losing it. The leather chair absorbed Russo's weight as he shifted around. "He's a good kid. A loyal one. You're fortunate to have him."

Senior blew by that comment like it was a parking cone. "Get the crew lined up on The Verge and the Kizh. I want the deal done yesterday. By any means."

Senior had decided. An insane thought: bully the Kizh tribe into overpaying for a property they don't need. Starting a war with Native Americans, like it's the 1800s all over again. The hubris knew no bounds.

Russo's mind bounced to his own granddaughter. Somewhere. All the years lost. He didn't have many left. Did he really want to spend them chasing after Senior's ego?

"Al," Senior slammed his palms on his desk. "Where the hell did you just go? I'm laying out my plan, and you're off in la-la land. I know distraction when I see it. Pull your fucking head out of your ass and help me solve my problem. You've been doing it for more than half your life. Over fifty years in that seat. Now's not the time to fade away. I need you here. Focused. Locked in."

"It's my granddaughter's birthday this weekend, and I thought about surprising her with a visit."

"Grandkids," Senior sat in the thought's weight. "Junior is too limp a dick to bring me some of those."

Russo white-knuckled the armrest of the leather chair. His toes curled into his shoes.

"If you could tell me where she lives, you can go." Senior had him by the short and curlies. "I need you down south for the next several days to help with Dom and Sonny's shit with the tribe. Your expertise at The Verge needs to keep Gina out of the loop, too. She knows we're selling, but she doesn't know how or who, just yet. Junior better not fuck that up either."

Senior reached into the bottom drawer of his desk and, with a tiny silver key, popped open a drawer safe. He threw a bound-up stack of hundred-dollar bills at Russo, which he caught perfectly in his lap.

"I know the internal battle you're having about your granddaughter." Senior's eyes were almost soft and colorful. "Ten grand should clear your conscience. A midyear bonus. I need you at your best."

Russo nodded his head in appreciation and an understanding of what was being asked of him. He tucked the stack of cash inside his coat and walked out.

Mrs. Teller held out her note that Russo requested, but it went ignored. He was fighting a battle he couldn't win. Mrs. Teller's urgent message would go unanswered.

CHAPTER 27

San Bernardino, CA—Kizh Casino

"I have a meeting at the casino."

Those were the last words Tyler spoke to Snake, the biker he met through a PBR and Fernet haze at the Wooden Nickel. Snake never confirmed with him, so Tyler had to rely on hope.

Hope was a terrible strategy, but hope was all he had.

He sent Snake a text from a burner phone with the date and time. Tyler would be there, but would Snake be there to do his part? He hoped. The extraction of Senior's heavies needed to begin. He hoped.

He rescheduled his afternoon flight back from SFO to the first Boeing off the tarmac. Sitting around the city made him edgy. Stomping around Cow Hollow and the Marina would not do him any good. He wasn't in his right mind to be company for the regular cocktail waitresses he'd plucked from the scene throughout the years. Another reason he needed to end this power struggle with Senior. Get back to the city, back to the swing of things.

He pulled up to the valet stand in front of the Kizh Casino Resort. The recent influx of Vegas money had the exterior under full renovation. A co-branded partnership. Another few dozen billboards along the two-hundred-some-odd miles that separated the two casinos.

More glitz. More glam. More busloads full of retirees pumping Social Security checks into the machines.

The blackjack pit overflowed with people. The staff squeezed several tables together to plop as many asses in seats as possible. Fire marshals weren't really a concern on the reservation. Young men and women in their late teens and early twenties. College kids? Probably. Eighteen was the legal gambling age, and they all had drinks. Fake IDs? Definitely.

Probably recent graduates from the private high school down the street. Tyler weaved amongst the bodies, looking for Snake. Having only met the young biker once, he wasn't sure of his ability to pick him out of a lineup.

His anxiety vanished like an old campfire when pain shot through his foot. The weight of a heavy boot was trying to anchor his foot to the colorful casino carpet. The pressure relieved, and Snake looked up at him with a devilish smile.

He shook his foot out. "A message would have been easier and a lot less painful."

"No doubt. But where's the fun in that?" Snake spoke behind tinted sunglasses, a bucket hat, and a long cigarette holder clenched between his teeth. "Surprising crowd for the middle of the week."

Tyler nodded in agreement and waved the cigarette smoke out of his face. "Lots of people. Loud slot machines. Perfect for the plan."

Snake motioned toward an excited group by the blackjack tables. "I'll take it from here. Where will you be?"

"Senior's heavies should arrive any minute with the tribal elders. They'll be looking for me, but that's when you'll draw them out. I'll be in the lounge where I can see you work your magic."

Tyler sat in the lounge off the casino floor. Low leather chairs around circular tables. No chance any of the rolling oxygen tanks in here ever sat in them. Slot machines lined as far as the eye could see, all with their own light patterns and sounds to attract retirees to drop some of that hard-earned savings. Wheel of Fortune-themed games, Big Mouth Bass-themed games, you name it, a slot machine features it.

Another time, he'd head for the table games. People were drawn to the interaction with those at the table as much as they were to the opportunity to win by "outsmarting" the house. Which isn't a thing unless card counting is involved, but then a permanent expulsion from whatever casino catches you is certain to follow.

For most at these tables, a few hundred dollars spent in an air-conditioned sensory hell made sense. Tyler needed Snake to use it for mayhem.

Snake ordered a drink from the center bar. Its electric blue hue and obnoxious lemon garnish made it stand out from any distance. Snake never removed his sunglasses as he staggered away from the bar with his procured cocktail. Pretend sips and dance moves to Bruno Mars that played throughout the gaming floor followed. Pai Gow tables were too quiet with what appeared to be a group of three ladies learning how to play. Snake moved on.

Another sip. Another spin move. Bruno Mars played.

He knocked into a drunk girl swaying in the back of the pack. Snake didn't apologize. He forged ahead and sloshed his drink onto a few elbows. His head was down. Eyes shielded by the sunglasses he held onto with his free hand.

"Hey, bitch! Watch it," the drunk girl yelled out.

Snake picked up his act and stumbled into the back of the players at the table. The unsuspecting guy flared back in shock and pushed Snake back toward the group. He spilled more blue elixir, his aim hidden by his actions.

The drunk girl spun Snake around, pushing the lemon off at another bystander. Direct hit.

"What the fuck is your problem?" the drunk girl slurred.

Snake didn't answer. He smiled and sent the drunken hot mess in front of him into a rage.

She pushed Snake back toward the table. Snake threw the rest of his drink overhead. Glass and all. A direct hit on the center of the table. Whatever was left of his cocktail exploded all over the dealer, players, and chips across the table.

The crowd rushed at Snake; he covered his head and ducked down to avoid the top-heavy contact. Like dominoes, the mayhem fell from one blackjack table to the next. Pit bosses and security rushed to protect the chips and the money. Their fighting wasn't a concern. The skirmish grew from a few to dozens.

Drinks spilled. People cussed. Hair pulled. Punches thrown.

Snake avoided it all.

Tyler couldn't believe it.

Snake ditched his sunglasses and swapped a hat from the floor. He casually walked away, looking more like an innocent, sober bystander caught in the crossfire than the drunken instigator he pretended to be. He smiled back at Tyler and gave him a nonchalant wave.

Tyler was on his feet and had to fight the urge to break out in applause.

The dozens of tribal security members secured chips and cash, then they moved on to the swelling mob of chaos. Drunk and out of shape, most had resorted to shouting and throwing things from afar. It resembled a summer camp water balloon fight more than gang warfare. Small pockets of flare-ups dotted the scene, but they were short-lived.

Tyler stood his ground. Snake waited next to a colorfully obnoxious slot machine.

The automatic doors slid open in smooth fashion, and hot outside air pushed its way into the casino. The tribal chief didn't come without protection. His guards were suited and cowboy-booted, but walked with the purpose and attitude of being left alone. The four-team security detail entered first, followed by the chief. The doors hung open. Senior's henchmen brought up the caboose. Far enough back from the tribal leaders, but close enough to be recognized as part of the group.

A chill ran down Tyler's spine. He pictured them in their rubber coveralls, forcing him to shove Josue's remains into the Dogpatch boiler.

Tyler wanted Snake to take the smaller one right then and there. Maybe he had a small, hooked knife, holstered just inside his waistband. One poke to the carotid artery, and it wouldn't be over two minutes before he bled out on the floor. Tyler would play concerned, and Snake could disappear amongst the screams from bystanders stunned by the blood-soaked carpets.

Camera surveillance at a casino was top-notch. Couldn't happen. He was certain security was already scrubbing the footage. Before AI technology recognized the casual man in the ball cap, Snake needed to be gone.

If not here, then where?

Tyler greeted Senior's guys. Over their shoulder, Snake strolled out of the casino.

CHAPTER 28

San Bernardino, CA

Funerals for fallen officers are no small ceremony. Freeway overpasses crowded with citizens waving American flags. A sign of appreciation for the sacrifices made, as the caravan of police cars, family members, and the inevitable Hurst passed by underneath.

Zane hated them.

Law enforcement from all over the country would travel if their schedules allowed. Pay their respects and remind themselves of what's at stake every day they put on the shield.

On the other side of the freeway overpass would be the *defund the police* protesters. They'd hold up posters demanding justice and freedom for a loved one. Occasionally, they'd even make sense. A long sentence for selling weed was one example. But wanting freedom for a career criminal with a rap sheet of violent offenses, trafficking, etc., garnered little sympathy. The protest just became noise on the corner.

Another nuisance to get through an already emotional day. Zane's mortality was his and his alone. He didn't need the reminder that outside forces would work against him. Duncan writing him in as a pallbearer meant he had no way out. He'd break out the pristine white gloves, the formal uniform, and he'd help carry the casket into and out of the service. Maybe this was another reason his father sought refuge in the bottle. Another reason to keep a clear head.

Zane sat in his Ford Ranger and refused to leave his truck until the last minute. *Motley Crue* played through the speakers, and a tight grip on the idle steering wheel when a knock hit his passenger window. It was Carmen.

"Open the door," she said.

He could barely hear her muffled voice through the window and the sounds of the 1980s Sunset Strip. He acted as if he couldn't hear her.

"Don't fuck around, Zane. I'm still your CO." Her playful threat did the trick, and he leaned over to pop open the door. "You ever going to update this beater?"

"Come on? The ninety-nine Ranger is classic. No Bluetooth, no automatic doors, no automatic windows. As a matter of fact, the only thing automatic is the transmission. An absolute workhorse. Machine and man together as one. You can't tell me you feel connected to that PT Cruiser you're pushing around these days?"

"Give me some credit for my car, at least. The 4Runner is reliable. Looks pretty badass, too. My go-rig for when shit really hits the fan, and I need to head overland for the foreseeable future."

"Hard to look past all the gadgets and tracking devices on that thing. Simple man. Simple pleasures." He caressed the dashboard.

"You don't have to make yourself miserable to enjoy life. Duncan wasn't miserable."

The day was already rough, and any mention of Duncan's name grabbed Zane by the throat. She didn't stop speaking, but he was half in, half out.

"That guy enjoyed the hell out of life. Sure, fluorescent is making a comeback. But to him, it never left. Sly, Arnold, Chuck, Segal, hair metal bands. That guy lived hard and had a fun ass time doing it. That's a lesson we can all learn from. Be who you are and don't change because those around you want you to be something different."

He was back in. "You do make speeches. And proved my point. Don't change when somebody is telling you to. Copy that, Lieutenant."

"You're such a pain in the ass. You have your speech prepared?"

"I fucking hate these things. But yeah, it's all up on the hard drive." He tapped two fingers on his temple.

"No bullet points on a buck slip? Just trusting that a chilly morning shower will electrify that brain of yours to come through? Gutsy move, detective. It's impressive you don't rely on the sauce. One of the many things I like about you. Plus, saves me from having to give you a ride in the plush confines of Celine."

"Celine?"

"My 4Runner."

"You even gave it a name? Jesus Christ, that just made it all the worse for me. I'm not riding in a fucking car with a name. Would definitely have to be drunk for that, so you're in the clear."

"Celine for the win. Now, come on. Let's go shake hands and kiss babies. There's a great turnout to say goodbye to our friend."

CHAPTER 29

Zane had found solace under the shade of a cypress tree. He stood flat-footed as the memorial attendees hugged and began making their way back to their cars. For most, life will roll forward, and the only reminder of the day will be when they pass the dedicated freeway sign to the fallen. For some, an annual golf tournament or dinner to remember their friend.

But for Zane, there would be an all-encompassing reminder of his brother. Nightmares of the crash. The crunching glass under the steps preceded the shots. He feared he was next. The survivor's guilt.

Carmen spotted him and approached. "You did way better than anybody expected," she said. "You honored Duncan. Made him a hero. The action star he always thought he was. He would have been proud. Probably would have given you shit for choking up, but he'd understand."

Zane brushed the grass with his polished boots. "I'm done with this entire scene." He removed the pristine white gloves from his hands and placed them in his back pocket. "If you all think I'm scooping one ounce of dirt on the casket, you're insane. Being on the rail to carry him was an honor. Being able to speak about my friend was an honor. There's no way in fucking hell I'm laying him to rest by shoveling. I'll visit him afterwards. When the skies are moody and I can sit against his headstone. That's how I'll say goodbye."

Carmen wrapped a warm hand around his forearm. "So, what's the play?"

He wanted to talk his mind out of it, but his heart told him the answer. "Vengeance. Retribution. Justice. However you want to phrase it. I need to fill this giant Duncan-sized hole. Maybe head to The Verge. That's how I'll honor him. Find out what that place has to do with him being in a box, headed six feet under."

"Want me to go with you?"

"I'll keep you on speed dial. Do me a favor; tell my old man I went for a drive. If I need him, he'll be my second call." He squeezed her hand and walked away.

No one else got a goodbye wave from him. He didn't break stride. He couldn't let anyone else he cared about find the same fate as Duncan. Certainly not Carmen. A large refrigerator of a man approached him as he reached his truck.

The man's voice was somber. "Zane. That was a helluva speech."

The cadence and familiarity cut Zane to the bone. His skin tightened, and goosebumps sprang from his tense forearms. He stood tall and firm. Sucking the anchor in his throat, he extended his hand. The man's paw was a mitt, and it belonged to Paul Duncan's dad.

"Hey, Mike." The two embraced, and Zane stepped back to take in Mike Duncan's appearance. Mike's barrel chest and extended stomach were pushing his untucked black linen button-down to its capacity. "He was on his way to looking just like you."

"Nah, I look like a guy on his third divorce who just got done with an all-night slow-pitch tournament. He was better than that. Better than me." Mike forced a smile beneath a pair of his son's fluorescent wrap-around shades.

"Slow pitch? You mean softball? I don't have the words to express my condolences to you. And the rest of your family. He was like a brother to me." Zane's stomach tensed, and he forced his tongue to the roof of his mouth. Suppress the emotion.

"You represented my son, the department, and most importantly yourself well with what you said back there," Mike's voice broke. He cleared it and paused as a couple he didn't recognize walked by on the way to their car. "My son meant the world to me. As I'm sure you can imagine, you mean the world to your own father. Paul spoke about you like you were the messiah. His very own action hero. He may carry himself like an eighties movie star, but to him, you were the real thing. God, he loved working with you and bringing bad people to the end of their criminal careers. The stories he'd share, I'm sure, were cherry-picked from the ones he couldn't, but I could see why he was so fond of you."

Zane's face twitched. Electrodes of emotion fired off under his skin. "It was an honor to serve with him. We had the best time together and played to each other's strengths. Nobody I'd rather have done that with. I will bring those responsible to the proper end they deserve. I'll see to it." He removed his sunglasses and allowed Mike to look into his eyes.

Mike extended his paw once again. The moment Zane took it, Mike pulled him in. A hushed breath whispered in his ear. To anyone walking by, it was a friend and father embracing in a shared loss. For Zane, it was an agreement with Duncan's father.

CHAPTER 30

San Bernardino, CA—TruCapital

WHERE ARE YOU???

Tyler saw the read receipt the moment he sent the message. He needed Snake. Don't fail now. The intentional chaos cut his intended meeting short at the casino. He was back in his glass-enclosed office with Senior's duo, Ren and Stimpy. They were a lot less intimidating when they weren't standing over a bloodied man hanging over a bathtub.

Tyler installed hidden security measures after he purchased the building and began renovations. These weren't cameras and alarms, but something more permanent. Silent.

Beacons run on a simple Bluetooth connection to a smartphone. Small enough to go just about anywhere and ping a device within a 100-foot distance. Part of TruCapital's security included such a strategic plan. The main purpose of the beacon was to communicate with clients coming and going from the building, track employees, etc. Another beacon was tucked inside the walls through a discreet access panel. With an eight-year battery life, he had forgotten it was there.

He checked his Apple Watch. "How much longer you guys going to be down?"

Ren looked at Stimpy and then back at him. "Senior wants to make sure negotiations run smoothly with the tribe."

He rolled his eyes. "That's what I'm for."

"Senior doesn't think so. And actually, even if Senior did, he's paying us to be his eyes and ears. We've seen you in action."

"And?"

"We're not impressed."

Tyler wanted to hear from Eve, not these two knuckle-draggers. "Can we get you set up at The Verge while you're down? Plenty of openings."

Ren scoffed. "Last time you put somebody up there, they ended up dead. We cherish life a little more than that. The res offered to put us up."

"Least they could do after today's scuffle," Tyler said. Bullshit is what he really wanted to say. "Don't let me keep you. I'm sure a bison ribeye at The Pine's Steakhouse will do wonders in healing your troubles."

Ren and Stimpy gathered at the door before leaving. "You're lucky you're Senior's kid," Ren said. "That lip of yours should be busted up by now."

"By offering you a dinner recommendation? Seems harsh."

"It's not what you said. It's how you said it."

Tyler smiled. "Seriously? Senior's muscle is offended by tone?" He felt confident in his face-off with the duo for the first time. He'd be even more so if he knew Eve was around. "It's a good steak. Tell them I sent you and enjoy the compliments of the chef."

He controlled his breathing. Watching Ren and Stimpy lumber through the building on the security monitors. Where's Snake? His phone was still blank. Ren and Stimpy exited, and the moment his monitor flipped to the parking lot camera, his phone buzzed. Snake.

WATCH.

One word followed by a pair of eyes emoji. He sat in his leather chair. Grabbed the edges of his monitor with both hands as if trying to pull himself into the screen to see the action unfold.

Although the footage was decent, it wasn't close enough to capture personal details. The hood of the car separated Ren and Stimpy when a dark truck pulled up in front. The driver exited the cab like a freight train and exploded into Stimpy as he crossed over the front of the hood.

The force of the impact from the driver's shoulder tackle sent Stimpy flying over the engine block and into the windshield. Stimpy lay limp as the glass caved in and cocooned his body like a hammock.

Before Stimpy came to rest, the driver was on top of Ren like a lion in the Sahara. The man rained down fists in a blur of strikes. Ren's body went limp before he hit the ground. The man stood over him, heaving. He picked up Ren and threw him headfirst into the driver's door window. Ren's torso disappeared while his legs flailed into the parking lot.

Tyler stood up. Hand over his mouth as if he were trying to keep a secret from escaping. He pushed his face closer. Clicked the image to zoom, but he couldn't go any further. The man was all in black, with a hood over his head. Sunglasses concealed his face. A wildcard who showed up, annihilated the threat, and vanished as quickly as he arrived.

He sent Snake another text.

Tyler fought the urge to run outside. He flipped through other parking lot cameras. No sign of Snake. No sign of anyone.

He hesitated to call for help. He should. It wouldn't be hard. Someone assaulted two men in the parking lot. Well, then there would be questions. Tyler didn't want questions. The long arm of the law would look into the two guys. After that, it was him. Then Senior. Then…

In a flash on the screen, the car with Ren and Stimpy's bodies thrown about erupted into a ball of flames. Flames engulfed the entire car in seconds. No visible image of the two.

Tyler gasped. He threw himself into his chair. Eyes unblinking as he watched the flames eat and destroy. Black smoke billowed.

His desk phone rang.

He hit the intercom. "Yes," he said.

"There's a car on fire," Tyler's receptionist said. "We have already called it in, and fire is on its way."

"Great job. Thank you." He picked up the receiver and placed it back into the cradle to end the call.

Still nothing from Snake.

He had a few minutes to prepare himself for the emergency responders. Answer the questions and direct inquiries to his liking. Then it was on to Senior. To Russo.

Tyler was free from Senior's threat. Now, he needed to press forward with Russo and push Senior out for good.

CHAPTER 31

Before Tyler could head north, he allowed the relief to wash over him. The next step was to dispose of his burner phone.

A small janitorial closet located outside his private bathroom would do the trick. He kept his own supplies, but did none of the cleaning. Another facade that would make sense to most people, but Russo taught him a thing or two about common household items that have applications not directed on the label. Using a tightly wrapped rag soaked in bleach, Tyler easily destroyed the cheap burner phones he preferred for his communication with Snake. Sure, he could have used a hammer like a former politician, but he wasn't one for tedious cleanup.

He recalled a simple line Russo gave him, "These things don't need to be complicated."

He remembered how casual Russo was about it all. He suppressed his emotions and focused on the next phase of his plan. Russo and Senior. The day had worn him thin. Now, he had to use his means and expertise to pay Snake his final sum.

He scheduled the wire transfers from USD currency into multiple cryptocurrencies - some pegged by the almighty dollar, but many not. Then he'd buy up Non-Fungible Tokens, NFTs, through various shell accounts. From there, he'd send to various other real people (likely, but not guaranteed), and as that money merged in his MetaMask wallet, he'd use Web 3.0 apps to send the total sum owed to Snake in the adjoining cryptos used for those platforms.

He loved flipping NFTs to launder money and pay off his debts of gratitude. Sometimes, depending on market conditions, he'd even make a profit on the NFT sell-offs.

Dumb kids buying JPEGs.

This process was tedious and not quick, by any means, but it beat placing stacks of cash in Manila envelopes and hoping on confidential drop zones. The increased use of digital banking and electronic monitoring had long compromised those. The PATRIOT ACT, enacted shortly after 9/11, eroded privacy for Americans and increased the private reach of the US government's surveillance.

Circumstances forced him to move to the dark side of the web, yet he never had to dive into the actual dark web. He had his own version of the Silk Road that was only known to those he let in. It wasn't a free enterprise of illegal activity made famous by American Kingpin, Ross Ulbricht, aka the Dread Pirate Roberts, from the early years of Bitcoin.

Tyler was relaxed for the first time in what felt like forever. Another surf trip down to Costa Rica was sounding better and better. He stood from his trusted desk chair and walked to the floor-to-ceiling windows that looked down on the workers below. He knew it was only a matter of time before some of his favorites noticed him looking down.

He wasn't wrong.

"Oh, how I've neglected you." The words to himself fogged up the glass. He peered at the first woman to walk underneath him with a loose-fitting teal blouse. He carried similar thoughts for each of the women that paraded below over the next several minutes until an alarm from his computer interrupted him.

Russo wanted to meet.

CHAPTER 32

Zane pulled up to the bustling scene in the strip mall parking lot, where he and Duncan first laid eyes on Mr. Pink, Tyler Truman Jr. The burning smell of destruction permeated his truck before all four tires were on the property.

His throat clenched as if a hand had come out of the steering wheel and squeezed the breath out of him. The attention garnered by the emergency personnel on site told him one thing. He wouldn't be avenging the murder of his fellow officer.

Somebody had beaten him to it. Who? Mr. Pink? No chance he had the stones to do it himself.

He swallowed his rage as if he were eating raw testicles and approached with caution. Still in his dress uniform from Duncan's funeral didn't help him fit in any better. His eyes searched, hoping to connect with a friendly face. Or, the face of the killer. He had no room in the middle. He got neither.

A sea of the same blurry faces connected to bodies that seemed to move in slow motion. The air molecules wafted off the parking lot asphalt from the summer heat, and he felt a momentary pity for the firefighters. He found the EMS Incident Command Officer and got caught up on their findings.

He called Carmen, but she didn't answer. Her voice cut through the scene's chatter as he went to call again.

"I'm not answering just to be five feet behind you," Carmen said. "Break it down for me so far."

He exchanged a smile with her. Then wiped it straight.

Carmen continued, "Some elderly lady said a truck pulled up, a man in black jumped out, and then the fire started. Hence, firefighters."

Carmen's attitude didn't match the scene, but he knew she was trying to cheer him up. Duncan had been buried in the earth only a couple of hours ago, with six feet of dirt on top.

"Any bodies?" Zane said.

"Medics and fire extracted the bodies and are prepping for transport."

"You get a positive ID?"

"Negative."

The crowd of bystanders wasn't anything impressive. The heat kept people away, but civilians naturally gravitate toward an emergency at any time. For better or worse.

"See any familiar faces?" Carmen asked.

"None so far. I'm not sure whether that's good or bad."

"Copy that."

Zane spotted the ICO, and Zane introduced Carmen.

"Sorry for the loss of your officer," Fire Chief Solorzano said. "I ran a scene a few years ago with Duncan. Heck of a police officer. Quirky, but damn good at his job. He hit a ball that I'm certain is still orbiting Earth in the last fire versus police softball game."

Zane chuckled and collected himself. "Thank you. He could hit a softball a mile. You should see his dad. And quirky is a delicate way to describe him. We use more colorful words, but we appreciate your sentiment. And yes, he was a heck of a police officer on top of it all."

He squirmed in his shoes during the conversation about his dead friend. Even if it were paying compliments. Just didn't feel like the right setting for it. He wondered if he'd ever find the right setting for talking about Duncan.

"Any idea who these guys are?" Carmen broke in.

"Haven't come across any direct IDs yet," Chief Solorzano said. "You guys want to run the car and see what you find?"

"That'll work for us," Carmen said.

"We're sweeping the vehicle now for chemical detection. Once that's done, and we can ensure the scene is one hundred percent secured, it's all yours." The chief ducked into a small sliver of shade and looked Zane and Carmen over. "You two are thick as thieves. The ambulance chasers run for the hills at any mention of a possible chemical agent. I suppose that's why they're them, and you're you."

"If you're here. I'm here," Zane said.

"Fair enough," Solorzano said. "It shouldn't be much longer. That vehicle is no eighteen-wheeler that jackknifed on the 210 overpass. You guys remember that? With the winds howling and swirling that day. Had to close the freeway in all directions for five miles. Really screwed up some commutes with that one."

Zane tapped Carmen on the shoulder and pulled her aside from the fire chief. "These are the guys who killed Duncan and wanted to add me to today's funeral service."

Carmen looked back at the charred SUV. "Are you sure?"

"Positive. I've been seeing that vehicle everywhere I go. Playing back on the drive on the freeway. Sitting in the hospital. Sitting at home. Sitting in my truck."

"You do a lot of sitting. You should really be more active."

He rolled his eyes.

"I'm not bullshitting. It's definitely them. We need to ID them and find out who they're working for. Well, worked for."

"Roger that," Carmen said. "Let's run the VIN and see what comes up. I'll be back."

"I'm going to keep looking through the crowd."

He walked around until he found shade from one ambulance. He still had a good view of the scene and personnel on site. The crowd kept their distance, which made familiar faces all the blurrier. Heat waves rose off the pavement, distorting everything on the other side. A young firefighter walked fire badge stickers over to the kids in the crowd. Zane shook his head.

What do firefighters and cops have in common? They both want to be firefighters. He laughed at the joke his dad always told him as a kid.

"If you want to be loved by the public, go into fire," his dad warned. "If you want to be covered by the grime and shit of life, become a cop."

Zane was reluctant to do so and dragged out the decision as long as possible. To the department, his dad was The Sarge. A larger-than-life cop who came up in a time when brute force was more often the solution to any problem. To Zane, he was his dad, the man that he never knew if it would be the last time he saw him whenever he left for his sworn-in duty to protect and serve.

Then came the drinking. The absence. The unreliability.

If it hadn't been for his love for his father, there's no chance in hell he would have become a cop. Redo the wrongs. Rebuild the Bruce family name.

As it was, he wouldn't change his decision for the world. The grief he felt at losing Duncan. The ass-chewing he'd taken from superior officers. Sleep disorders. Post-traumatic stress. Lonely nights. Solitude living. Those last two were changing. At least he'd avoided the bottle. More nights next to Carmen weren't a bad thing.

Carmen's voice broke through his thoughts. "Got a hit. Vehicle is registered to some property management firm up in San Francisco."

He blinked himself back to the present. "San Francisco? What are they doing down here?" He had a hunch that would send them back to The Verge. The dead body that set this whole thing in motion.

"Not sure yet, but I have Corinne pulling the firm's records to find out. She said whatever she finds, it'll be ready by the time we make it back to the station. You find anything here?"

"Only how nice it must be to be a firefighter."

Carmen nodded in agreement. Then smirked. Her eyes softened. The late afternoon sun was turning her brown eyes into butterscotch.

"I can't believe I missed. I won't be the one to avenge Duncan." He wanted to be anywhere else in the world. Just the two of them. Soon enough. He had one more thing to do. "I'll meet you back at the station. I need to talk to the coroner for a minute."

"Make smart choices."

"I always do."

CHAPTER 33

Tiburon, CA

Tyler sipped a peach bellini on the sunny patio of a trendy Tiburon restaurant. North of the San Francisco Bay, a short ferry ride across the frigid waters gave him a view of Alcatraz. Though now a family-friendly tourist attraction, it once housed America's most notorious criminals. If the prison were still operational, would the Truman family belong within its walls? Behind its bars?

He carried the burden of Josue's fate. How many more went up in smoke through the Dogpatch boiler? He sucked down the rest of his drink and waved to the waiter for another peach bellini.

He set in motion the take-down and demise of his own father. His flesh and blood. The man he idolized his whole life, and still does.

For the better part of three decades, Senior was the man in San Francisco. He had connections that opened doors to anyone and anything. However, Senior failed to realize that the game had changed. He wasn't about to let the world tell him what to do. Every time Tyler tried to influence his dad, the changes went on and were totally overlooked.

"You're barely out of diapers, kid," Senior would balk. "What do you know about this business? I had bought my first twenty buildings while you were still suckling at your mother's tit. You don't know shit about how the real world works."

Tyler winced during those conversations.

Gone were the days of what Junior called "childish" tactics. Senior preferred "guerrilla" tactics. It was an enormous benefit to San Francisco's property owners. The demand for occupancy was always there. With a limited supply comes high demand and higher costs, economics 101.

Tyler looked out at the water and back at the city from his position at the restaurant. He could see Karl the Fog lurking a couple of miles out in the Pacific Ocean. The clock was ticking before the fog would envelop the western part of the city to Divisadero. Over in Tiburon, it was a picture-perfect day for the bay.

He checked his Apple Watch and eyed people coming through the entrance to the patio. His lunch guest was due to arrive at any moment. For a split second, he wished it were a date showing up. Gina? No, those days were long gone, but maybe that would be the next phase of his life. For now, he focused on taking over the business and taking down the man who built it. He ordered another drink. His eyes darted between his watch and the entrance to the patio.

Tardiness was not something he tolerated. He finished the next drink, and then another. He asked for the check while the chair across from him remained empty. A different server delivered the tan leather bi-fold with the restaurant's embossed logo on the table than the one who had been attending to him. He didn't notice until he opened the bifold to look at the check. There was no check, but in its place was a note.

Not here. Meet me back at BV. Your tab has been paid. Take the next ferry back.

He looked back and saw the server, but she disappeared in a sea of other servers. No chance of telling who dropped the note. He thought about going over to interrogate them, but what was the point? The note came from Russo. Now, he had to find out why Russo had stood him up, and a change of venue was required. He had about an hour ferry ride to rack his brain for the solution.

The sunny shores of Tiburon gave way to dense gloom. Karl the Fog had arrived. The warmth of the sun on his face and the sweet palate of peaches were all but a distant memory. The cold summer air snapped through his thin linen shirt, and he longed for one of the tourist SF fleeces. That's the irony. He stepped out of his Uber Black ride, which he had taken from the Ferry Building to the Buena Vista Cafe.

At the end of Fisherman's Wharf, on the corner of Beach and Hyde Street, The Buena Vista opened in 1916. However, it didn't become world-renowned for the Irish Coffee until the 1950s. The owner at the time challenged a travel writer to recreate the drink he had at Shannon Airport in Ireland. Seventy years removed, The Buena Vista pours up to 2,000 of its famous libations a day.

It was clamorous inside once Tyler finally ducked in from the chill outside. Coffee filled the cafe. Tourists lined up at the bar despite the bartender's efficiency. Their white hair and the bartenders' coats proved they'd been perfecting the cream for ages, like something from a fancy old movie.

Tyler didn't immediately recognize anybody, so he pushed himself through the crowd to the far end of the bar and ordered what put The Buena Vista on the map. Once his drink arrived, it wasn't rocket science to see why they poured so many in a day. You'll be refilling that glass in no time. He held up his second one, simplistic beauty.

Russo finally arrived. "They are elegant, aren't they?" he said. He saddled up to the bar next to Tyler and motioned to the bartender for the same drink. Russo's bulbous nose glowed red the closer he got to the alcohol. "Been coming here for as long as I can remember. Which is pretty damn long. Not much has changed. Same drinks. Same bartenders. Pretty fucking amazing, actually."

Tyler wanted to questioned Russo's tardiness, but he was still in the, *I love you, man* phase of drinking. "In all those years, you ever eaten here?"

"Never."

They shared a laugh and watched the bartender line up twenty glasses to begin a fresh batch of orders. Russo's included.

The process was flawless, producing whiskey, coffee, and perfectly frothed cream that floated atop like a sweet cloud.

"Never gets old watching them work," Tyler said. "Not a splash on the sleeve of his coat either. Fucking impressive."

The bartender handed an Irish Coffee right to Russo. "Here you go, Al," the bartender said. "Been a while."

"Yes, it has," Russo said. He took a sip that left a white foam mustache on his upper lip. "Thanks Dan. Good to see you still have the touch."

"First name basis with what was it? Dan?" Tyler said. "This was your old stomping ground, wasn't it?"

"I've had my time around this city. I got Dan his first place at 2600 Van Ness. He ran it for a little while. Until your dad put that tart up there, which he was putting through nursing school. I kept his rent as low as I could for as long as I could, but eventually your old man wanted him gone."

"Why'd he even care?"

"Because I cared."

The pettiness rattled Tyler's insides. He finished his drink and motioned for another.

"It was all about controlling me. He didn't give a shit about Dan's rent, but it made me jump through hoops. Senior got off on watching me do the damn dance for him. Not so different from why he kept pushing you off from working for the company. Make you sweat. Make you think he held some higher power over you and everybody he let in."

Russo saw him. Russo cared about him.

"You were probably ready the moment you could drive from North Beach to SoMa. Your old man would not allow you to waltz right in and start working for him. You had to be below him. By a large margin. You could have filed building papers or swept the floors to earn it, but even that put you too close. He knew you'd learn too much too soon. This meeting we're having now. The Dogpatch. What you set up at Au Sushi would have taken place ten years ago if he had done that. Gotta cut Senior some credit. He knew this day would come, eventually."

"You think he knows now?"

"No. He won't see it coming until it's too late. Stubborn son of a bitch still won't recognize it. Trust me, he'll spin the shit out of it to make it seem like it was his intent all along. Never will that old man show signs of defeat. Or wrongdoing. Haven't seen it in fifty years. No way, we're watching it now. Would have been an ideal politician. Could have been Governor."

Not in San Francisco. Even with his connections.

"His hubris will be our greatest strength in this."

Russo finished his drink and held up two fingers to the bartender. "Yeah. But let me ask you a question. Dogpatch was too much?"

"This didn't happen overnight," Tyler finished the last of his coffee. "In a strange way, I'm proud of what I did that night. It's more than that. It's been years in the making. Every step has been a calculated one. For once, the stars aligned, and the moment was right. I'd push him off into the sunset where he belongs. He's too stubborn to ride off on his own. His ego too massive. His empire in this city is crumbling, all because he didn't notice the world changing. The Truman name once meant something. It stood for the growth and development in San Francisco. Was it clean, no?"

Russo shook his head and mouthed the word, "No."

"But it was more about the why than the way. He got away with so much shit for so many years because he was cleaning up. Making the city better. Bring glory back to San Francisco, but once every other Tom, Dick, and Harry started filling the voids and swinging their dicks around town on bigger properties. More capital. Larger investors. Senior couldn't suck it up to ask for help. Wanted it all to be done on his own."

"He always thinks he knows best."

"The problem is, he overbid himself by forty percent on buildings simply because he feared more money would come in. Snatch up the deal at the eleventh hour. You see him with the tribe? I brought them in to help with The Verge, and he refuses to participate. It's his out on that dumpster fire, and he can't play ball. Swallow his pride."

Russo laughed. "Never going to happen, kid."

"He's gonna shove a bunch of beat-up cars in the parking lot to make it appear as if people live there? How dumb does he think the tribal leaders are? It's fucking insulting to them and a goddamn embarrassment to us. The tribe doesn't fuck around. He thinks his Dan and Stan muscle can out-muscle the reservation. He's lost his fucking mind."

"I told him the same thing. Well, not in those exact words. I still have to report directly to the man. It's good work you've done by bringing in the tribe. Cutting our losses on The Verge and moving on with anything other than a BK would be brilliant work."

"It makes sense for the tribe to move on that property. They can bulldoze it for all I care. Build whatever they want. It's the land that's valuable. Right outside their boundaries would be perfect for their mid-level clientele. The ones coming out for concerts. The ones that drink a little too much. Spend too much. And the ones they want to monitor without making them feel uneasy about staying on the reservation. Too many folklore stories floating around of people who stayed on the res and never came back."

"Or came back as different versions of themselves. I've heard the tales."

"They'll get it at the absolute floor price, too. They'll have to pay twice as much if it gets reverted to land from another buyer. We need Senior to play ball. Show up to the meetings for fuck's sakes and at least pretend to care about the deal."

"He's running out of options." Russo's phone must have vibrated in his coat pocket, and he reached inside. "Bat phone, so I need to take this." He stood up.

Tyler waved him off and watched Russo walk out of the crowded bar, and could see him through the windows as he paced back and forth with a look of concern painted upon his face. Russo's pacing stopped, and he looked back at him through the windowpanes of the Buena Vista.

A rush of energy surged through Tyler's veins as he waited for Russo to cut back through the crowd. His fingers tingled around the warm glass of a fresh Irish coffee. The look on Russo's face was about to shift the mood of their afternoon. The loud, playful atmosphere of Buena Vista became an annoyance as he strained to hear what Russo was trying to tell him.

"They're dead," Russo fought to keep his voice low enough not to be overheard, but also loud enough to break through the noise of people several Irish Coffee deep.

"What? Who?" Tyler feigned shock. His stomach knotted. His tongue sweated.

Russo dropped a hundred-dollar bill on the bar top and pointed at Dan to cover the tab and keep the rest. They walked toward North Beach before cutting into Chinatown and felt more at ease with their conversation.

"That was Senior on the phone," Russo finally spoke. "His crew is dead."

"Beavis and Butthead?" Tyler joked. "Senior thinking the tribe had something to do with it?" He played it off. The urge to vomit faded.

"Yeah, of course he does. Wants to pull the plug on any sort of negotiation and start a fucking war with them."

"Well, that's dumb. How'd he find out about Bartles and James?"

"He wouldn't say, but I made a call to verify his information. I'm not doubting the fact that they're dead, but who is behind it is another matter. They made some enemies of the police down there in quick fashion. No doubt they were on their radar. If it wasn't from their end, I'm sure there's a trail somewhere that doesn't lead back to the tribe. Senior is fishing and hoping it'll fit his narrative."

"What can I do to help?" Tyler said.

They walked through the crowded streets, and the smell of savory gyoza and dumplings filled their nostrils, making them both hungry.

"I'll need the security footage of your parking lot."

"Of course." The video wasn't the best, but it didn't show him doing anything wrong.

"And one other thing. You're not gonna like what I'm going to suggest," Russo said.

"What?" Tyler knew the answer as soon as he asked. "Oh, come on! She fucking hates me."

"Maybe, but whose fault is that? Sure as shit isn't mine. You need to find out what she knows. Nobody has had to deal with them more recently than Gina. Call her and start making amends for your past. It's the only way forward. And hell, you want to make something of your father's legacy and this company? You pull the rabbit out of the hat with The Verge, and you'll be well on your way. Come on, let's eat, and you're buying."

Russo tucked into the House of Nanking and left Tyler outside to contemplate his next move. He pulled out his phone and pulled up his contacts for Gina Kramer. He admired her caller ID picture before putting his phone back in his pocket and following Russo inside.

CHAPTER 34

San Bernardino, CA—Kizh Casino Resort

"What the hell, Truman?" Gina said.

Tyler expected a more cordial greeting. Well, not really. Nobody invited him. Gina adjusted into a defensive position, and he knew he had to land softly.

"I sent you a thanks for the ticket," Gina said. "But that sure as fuck wasn't an invitation for you to ruin my night."

He put his hands up in defeat. A green Heineken bottle in one hand, and an open palm in the other. "Relax, okay. I'm not here to sit through a fucking EDM concert. I knew you'd be here, and we need to talk. This isn't about us; this is about The Verge."

Gina's eyes remained suspicious. She softened her posture by a degree. "The property you banished me to, because your little dick couldn't handle me running properties in the city? That property? The one I've busted my ass in this hellhole of the suburbs, so you wouldn't have to deal with me and how you treated me? That property? The one your dad is too chickenshit to visit himself, because his ego is too great to acknowledge the mistake he made and lost a sizable chunk of his worth. How did he screw up the company? You? Me? All the employees who rely on this? Yeah, this sure doesn't sound like it's a talk about us."

"Well, not us-us." He took a pull from his Heineken. The casino lights gleamed off the green bottle like a kaleidoscope as he tilted it back to his lips. "Let's not forget, I got sent down here as well. Senior fucked up by outbidding himself on The Verge, yes. He hasn't been down to see with his own eyes how bad it is, yes. He's completely mishandling the sale of the property, yes. The rumor mill at the office has Market Street chirping with concern, yes. Will they lay off staff? Yes. But not if we can turn this around."

"We?"

"Yes, we. You're vital to this whole thing, Gina."

Her position shifted from defensive to soft to intriguing. She looked like a model sitting in front of an art class. "Well, tell that to Senior's goons he sent down to scare the shit out of me. I've been around too long and seen too much both to believe them and not give a shit about what they're telling me or threatening me with."

"I would if I could, but I can't, so I won't."

"What do you mean?"

"They're dead." His eyes locked with hers. This was critical.

Gina froze. "Dead?" She sat back before swirling the onions in her Gibson martini. "They were literally just at The Verge, stomping around my poolside office the other day. What happened? Did they finally go too far with their double-pegging sessions?"

He needed to lie. She wouldn't go along if she knew the truth about him. About his ties to an assassin. He'd be just as bad as Senior.

"I'm still unclear on the details. I was up north with Russo when he got the call." He couldn't told if she could see through it or not. "I'm gonna go check it out tomorrow when it's light out. I'm pulling the video tomorrow. Dead though. Definitely dead."

She looked around the Overlook Bar. With the gold lounge chairs, the purple accents, she could have been anywhere in the world, but she wasn't. She sat, legs crossed at the ankles, a martini in her hand. He remembered why they had dated. She had a natural elegance. It sucked him in.

"I can't say I'm upset," she said. "Those two were up my ass the other day with their typical bullshit. Wannabe gangsters. Is that why you're here, to tell me that? Come on, Tru, this isn't your style."

"No. I need more. People. Faces. Names. What's been going on at The Verge with the sale to these people?" He held his palms out wide and spun to showcase the casino resort behind him. "Look at this place. They have the money."

"Just cops roaming around asking questions about David Johnson." The sound of hundreds of slot machines whirred away. Gina finished the last of her martini and popped a gin-soaked onion in her mouth. The crunch must have given her a rush as goosebumps filled her legs.

He wanted to reach over and rub them away, but knew better. This was a rare moral decision. "I have a meeting coming up with Lynn Sanmaura," he said. "I assume you know her."

She hesitated to answered. "I'm sure I've met her at a chamber event or two."

He couldn't tell whether or not she was being cautious.

"You'd know it if you did. She's the chairwoman of the reservation. I thought her name would be Running Water or some shit. I need to pull the strings of this deal along, because Senior is fucking it up."

Her face twisted in disgust. "Running Water? Really. You are a pile of shit up in your San Francisco-raised ivory tower."

He waved the comment away. "Not now. If this deal is dead in the water. So are we. You can give me your sensitivity training once the deal is closed and we survive this. Otherwise, stay in your lane and get out of mine."

"There's the Junior I know. You're such a little dick. Are you done ruining my night?"

"Careful, Kramer. One text and your tickets for a DJ in a space helmet are as good as toilet paper."

"And there's that vindictive charm we all know and love. So, what do you need from me? I'd like to enjoy the rest of my night. Whatever semblance of fun is left."

"Soon as I schedule the meeting with Lynn, I want you there."

"You said you already had the meeting. So which is it?"

"I already have a meeting, but she doesn't know it yet."

Gina rolled her eyes, and he continued.

"Senior had Billy Bob and Tweeter down here to meet with the tribal council, but those two nut bags didn't have a clue what they were doing. Now they're gone." He fluttered his eyelids and crooked his neck, and tilted his head sideways. "So, asking them what the old man's original request was is out of the question. Senior stood the council up time and time again. They're pissed he couldn't be bothered to meet them."

"How hard is it to join a Zoom call?"

"They were okay with him not coming down. They didn't love it, but will meet online. Once he no-showed, they got pissed and are out for his scalp now."

Gina rolled her eyes again.

"Lynn is our connection to stopping that and maybe getting this deal done without losing the entire company. You know The Verge better than anyone. All the challenges you've faced since it opened. What it needs to succeed, and how it can turn it around. You can read people without fear of objective opinion."

"You need a woman," Gina said. "Lynn has been dealing with the boys' club her whole life, and you and Senior are just another pair of dick swingers trying to push her around. You're done before you even enter the room with her. Wow. The almighty Truman Junior needs a woman to do the job he can't."

His eyes narrowed in displeasure, but it didn't change the truth.

Gina's eyes widened. "Oh my. You need me to set the meeting as well. I must say, this is going to be fun. The only way this will work once we're in the room is if you completely stay in the background. You apologize for Senior's lack of attendance, acknowledge all of his faults, and then open the floor to me. Lynn will need to know you have full confidence in me. In women. To make this happen on our own without another man interjecting their opinion on business."

His shoulders slumped in defeat. "You're right, Gina. I can play the game. That's why I'm here." He stood up and threw a couple of hundred-dollar bills on the lounge table next to his empty Heineken bottle. "This will cover the rest of your night. Text me in the morning or afternoon, whenever you recover from flashing lights and electronic beeps. Pretty sure I still haven't recovered mentally from the concert you dragged me to eight years ago."

"Damn, you've gotten soft with age." Gina grabbed the blue C-notes and tucked them into her clutch. "Now, if you'll excuse me, I have time for a couple more martinis before I go to my seat. Talk soon."

He waved goodbye and shouldered his way into the swelling casino. A salmon against the stream. He was returning to San Francisco. Again. This time, for a face-to-face with his father.

CHAPTER 35

San Francisco, CA—House of Prime Rib

"Please, join me and sit down, son," Senior offered Tyler a seat in the booth.

The aura of the House of Prime Rib with Senior in it was always different. Two staples of San Francisco's history, but for two very different reasons. Tyler pushed his tongue to the roof of his mouth and fought off his father's intimidating presence. Accepting Senior's invitation, he slid into the red leather booth.

He didn't want to. This was his chance to assert himself with Senior. Show his old man he's ready. Been ready.

San Francisco's finest packed the dining room. There was a two-hour wait for those naïve enough to think they could merely walk in. They'd have much better luck walking a block over and enjoying oysters at Swan's Oyster Depot. If you didn't have the right connections or win a charity raffle, you would not see a table on the weekend.

A wine sommelier appeared as Tyler worked himself into a comfortable position. Feet firmly on the carpet. His back was straight and tall. Good posture. Shoulders back.

The waiter presented Senior with a 2019 Kosta Browne Sta. Rita Hills Pinot Noir. "One glass," Senior said. "The boy can order on his own."

The boy. Asshole.

Tyler wiped his palms on his pant legs. "I'll have a Godfather."

Senior swirled wine in his mouth before swallowing. "Godfather? You think you're running this family?"

"It's a classic drink for this classic restaurant. Having a sit-down dinner with my father. Are they bringing us menus?"

"What's there to look over? I already ordered for us. Prime rib. Creamed spinach. Table-side salad."

Chefs in tall white hats manned stainless steel Zeppelin carving stations on wheels. Rolling from table to table to provide fresh cuts of beef, hot au jus, and a choice of horseradish.

Tyler inhaled the aroma that had seeped into the walls for decades. "This is how I know that veganism was not for us. My mouth never watered smelling a salad."

"One of the smartest things you've ever said." Senior raised his wineglass to toast.

The old man's gesture caught him off guard. He hesitated, but gave in. His father's love was rare, even if there was an alternative motive. "Why isn't there more of this? Always something with you. Can't just shoot things straight with me. Gotta send me to work the pier or run your investments from the other end of the state."

"Stop being so dramatic. Look at a map; we're practically neighbors."

"Well, now that pleasantries are finished. What do I owe this dinner to? One of your side pieces canceled?"

Senior checked his cufflink and twisted it as he delayed his response. He admired Senior's timepiece, the Rolex GMT Master II white gold Pepsi bezel. Despite the technological advantages, his Apple Watch suddenly felt inferior. He tucked his watch into his sleeve and gave mental praise to the tailor who had left his sport coat sleeves a quarter inch too long.

Senior finished his glass of wine and snapped his fingers toward the waiter to refill it. "Let's just say two of my assets have gone missing, and I don't think I'll ever get them back."

Tyler shifted uneasily in his seat. His toes anchor down in his secondhand Italian loafers. His stomach knotted. He was on the ropes early. With the tableside salad, the waiter arrived in time. The delay gave him a chance to think.

A stainless-steel bowl was spun by the waiter on a bed of ice. Tossing the lettuce mix of romaine, spinach, and iceberg inner mixed with beets, sourdough croutons, tomatoes, and hard-boiled egg. The dressing cascaded like a waterfall onto the spinning bowl of greens.

Tyler held his defense until the waiter was at the next table. "What do I have to do with something you've lost?"

"You're too smart to play naïve with me. A gift inherited from me. Sadly, your gratitude seems to be something that is missing. Maybe start a morning journal to help you sort through it. But I'm not here to press you on that. We can save that for Thanksgiving dinner."

"Then please explain to me why I am here."

"The Verge."

"The Verge?" Senior's sudden interest surprised him. "I thought you'd lost something? Maybe your mind is going." The jab at his father's memory would sting, but to his surprise, the old man remained calm on the outside.

"Yes, they're involved, but what's gone is gone and no longer my concern. More important is my portfolio. I sent you down to diversify. We're clearly having issues moving it and selling to the Indians."

He blinked at the word but remained unmoved. His brain was working overtime to decipher pulling himself back into the game. He had an edge. Senior needed him and was finally about to admit it.

"Having problems with the tribe? Gina is at the property. Rest assured, it's in great shape."

"Let's just say a little of both. The property is substantial. The location, well, that really only serves one purpose. That city has fucked its residents over consistently with how little it cares. A gorgeous property like that can't get any attention." Senior clicked his tongue. "Nobody wants luxury apartment living there. The tribe asked about converting it to extended-stay business suites for their high-roller travelers. The Orientals, Chinese, and Japanese are coming in spades and aren't big on staying on the reservation. Their boundaries are just outside of The Verge. They can shuttle them back and forth to the casino. Give them the peace of mind that a vision quest into the surrounding desert won't come into play."

They polished off their salad plates, which were quickly swept away to the kitchen. The waiter was back with a small silver tray and a matching scraper to clean the white linen. Prime rib would be inbound soon. Tyler's mouth watered. For once, it wasn't to lube his throat for vomit.

"I'm aware of their interest in the property," Tyler said. "The tribe is extremely active in the community. Your continued disrespect toward my knowledge is part of your hubris in this whole thing. You think just because you sit up here in the big city that the tribe should bow at your feet and take whatever garbage deal you put together. They will not let another white man push them around and fail to hold up his end of the bargain. Just be a man of your word. Show up when you say you will. Be impeccable with your word. It's a code of honor. The tribe operates more from honor and their perception of it than by your white teeth, money, properties to sell, or the muscle you send."

Senior's gray eyebrows raised.

Tyler didn't think he had the stones to bring it up. Confidence pinging. Senior held position.

"My muscle?" Senior repeated. He sat up and folded his arms on the table in front of him. "What do you know about my muscle?"

The corners of Tyler's mouth curled upward as he reveled in his newfound confidence. "You sent them to the casino to push the tribal leaders into accepting your sale price. Babysit me. You once again misread the situation. Didn't get the results you were hoping for."

"Oh, it would have worked. A brawl broke out inside the casino. Distractions caused the delay. You know, it wasn't long after that incident that my muscle, let's say, atrophied and could not make the return trip home."

He would not take the bait. "It's a shame to hear about your muscle. Maybe eat more steak. Surely the big city hasn't outlawed that yet. Unless Russo overtook your spot here. He seems better connected to the older parts of this city."

Senior scoffed. "Russo is lucky he has toilet paper to wipe his ass. He'd be licking pine tar off baseball bats if it weren't for me."

The zeppelin cart rolled up, and the chef in the tall hat locked the wheels. The chef sharpened his knife and carved. He plated the prime rib cuts.

In front of Senior, he placed the King Henry VIII cut. Finish that, and he has the option of a complimentary second cut of beef.

In front of Junior, the chef placed the children's portion.

His eyes were daggers, looking at his dad. "Really?"

Senior sliced a portion off his King cut and spoke with a mouthful. "Must have been a while since you've eaten here. I told them I was with my son, and the usual would do. Oops."

Tyler grabbed the edge of the zeppelin. "I'm not a child. King cut. Please and thank you."

The chef nodded and swapped out his plate. Tyler shook his head and picked up the conversation.

"Maybe that's your problem. Always doing as you please. Not considering how your actions impact others. It's only a matter of time before the bigger bear has all its paws on your back and pushes you out the door. Retirement can't be that far off for you. What are you hanging on for? Step aside. This is a young man's game now. It's changed. Evolved. I'm afraid that you haven't, though. Still the same tired tactics you used in the nineties. You're washed up. Face it and let the rest of us handle the actual business."

He was hoping Senior's insides shook like a rusty carnival ride at the county fair. Senior ate as if he were alone. The spicy scent of straight horseradish Senior smeared over the top of his King cut punched Tyler in the nose. He fought to keep his eyes from watering. Don't give the old man an ounce of satisfaction. He smeared his own layer of straight horse over his cut. A root vegetable pissing contest.

A thought hit him as hard as the horseradish. "Why don't you just sell it to me?"

Senior paused his gluttony. Finished another glass of wine and snapped for a refill. Tyler was as invisible as the profits on The Verge. Press on.

"You launched TruCap for the original loan," Tyler said. "Which you outbid yourself on. I've been running the numbers on that property ever since, and know how much you've lost up to this point?"

No answer.

"The tribe will never go for your asking price; nobody will. Every buyer will pick you apart once you have to open the books for due diligence. Nobody would miss it. You're stuck with me as your out. Overpaying for a dying property. Who would do that?"

No answer.

"You don't have to answer. You're a man of extreme pride. We both know your bank account fuels what's inside you. It's part of what makes you a valued contributor to the San Francisco skyline. I admire what you bring to the table. TruProperties wouldn't be a fraction of the company it is without your knowledge and business intellect. I'll put this to bed for you easily. An NFT smart contract could be your best bet. Weave in a detail that you can make a small - and I emphasize a small percentage on any future sales."

The expression on Senior's face morphed and twisted from disdain to one of deep thinking. Did Tyler finally capture his attention? NFT? Smart contract? What was he talking about? The dead air gave him a chance to enjoy his own King cut.

Senior sat with an empty plate. "You're not speaking my language. Percentages of future sales has my attention. I don't know what the other things are."

Tyler conceded he couldn't handle the horseradish and scraped it off. "I had a feeling. Arrangements with the tribe are made. Gina will be there. The tribal leader is a woman, and it'll do us a ton of good to have her spearheading this conversation. It'll make up for your absence."

Senior's face contorted back to the stoned anger he held for much of this conversation. "You already contacted the tribe and are bringing in Gina? The woman you screwed over and had sent packing down south in the first place?"

Tyler's turn. No answer.

"You think you can just go around me on my property." Senior's heat index increased more rapidly. The bottle of Kosta Browne must be empty. "You don't go to anyone unless you go to me first. That's how it's always been. Always will be. I'd ask where you got the nerve, but I know the answer is seated across from you."

"First, calm down. You don't want to have a heart attack in this place. CPR will be tough with that much horseradish. Secondly, why waste the time of going to you first? You'd spin in circles for weeks before realizing what we already know. Third, Lynn Sanmaura is not just a female face for the tribe; she's incredibly business savvy and has positioned them incredibly well. You'd know that if you ever joined the Zoom calls."

Senior checked the bottle for more wine.

"I know what you're thinking," Tyler cut off Senior's train of thought. "I'm not conspiring against you." A lie he hoped his father couldn't see. "We're saving time. The tribe is tired of waiting for you to show up and get this moving. They're interested, but it comes at a price for them; you only have one way out of it. Long term."

"How long?"

"You won't see the return in your lifetime. Your legacy will be in setting precedent for future property contracts in perpetuity. Generations of property owners, from me to the high prince on his third island in the Mediterranean, will know what you established."

Tyler couldn't believe where he was. An out-of-body experience, hovering over himself, watching his own struggle, an unknown way to extend Senior's legacy. Battling on could leave Senior with nothing. He recalled every property Senior had overpaid for.

1080 Sutter St. 660 Clipper St. 2240 Golden Gate. 1440 Washington St. 1225 Jackson St. 2600 Van Ness. 1245 California, and the list went on. Washing away money satisfied their insatiable appetite to dominate San Francisco real estate as a multi-family property owner.

Senior pushed himself up. His elbow joints cracked and stood for a moment as his body calibrated to being fully upright. He checked the time on his Rolex.

"To quote John Updike, suspect each moment, for it is a thief, tiptoeing away with more than it brings," Senior said. "I'll be in touch, son. I can't say this has been my favorite father-son dinner. Should have stuck with the child's plate. You and Gina need to hold your positions until I make my decision. It's still my name that's signed on the bottom of the normal contract. Legally binding me to all matters of sale."

Tyler ordered another Godfather and only finished about half of his plate. He didn't want to harsh his buzz. Senior had a running tab, so wasting food wasn't his concern. He slid his sleeve up and checked the time. Gina should have a head full of electronic music by now. It made him smile. Thankful for the short flight. He'll be back in the morning for their meeting at Kizh.

CHAPTER 36

San Bernardino—Police Headquarters

Zane's phone vibrated away on the cloth passenger seat of his Ford Ranger.

Ignore it.

He had spotted Mr. Pink in the crowd of onlookers at the scene in the parking lot outside TruCapital. Doubt was clouding his judgment.

The coincidence piqued his interest. It could have been just that: a coincidence, two dead guys and a charred vehicle in the same parking lot as TruCapital. Or, it could be the reason they were dead. No chance Mr. Pink did it himself. Did he have the means to call it in and orchestrate it? Possibly. Humans are all capable of doing the worst when pushed to shove.

While he ignored his phone, he couldn't ignore the crackle of the department radio shoved into the cup holder of the center console.

"Lieutenant Cruz to Detective Bruce."

Her formal address made him sweat.

"Copy, this is Bruce."

"Come back to the station; we have to talk."

"Roger that, LT. Was just heading back."

"Copy. Oh, and answer your damn phone once in a while. See you soon."

He holstered his radio back in the cupholder and smirked. Carmen knew how to flirt professionally.

Mr. Pink was on his mind, though. Was there a connection between Duncan, the two dead heavies, and Johnson at The Verge? All too close to one another not to be connected. Regret boiled in his veins, a thirst for vengeance. His emotions cycled. Sad, angry, and relieved. The relief only made him angrier. Somebody needed to pay, and he needed to see it through. Somebody else doing his work, his mission, was not an option. He was ready for a fight. He needed that fight.

The black Ford Ranger made a smooth transition over the entry speed bumps at the police department parking lot. Away from the other trucks, which likely spent their off days pulling speedboats to the Colorado River, he slowly drove to his usual parking spot. He would rather fish in solitude than chase adrenaline on the water at high speeds.

The air inside the department felt lighter to him after he buzzed himself in through the back security door. The weight of burying a fellow officer weighed down all those who proudly served in the shield's honor. No matter how hardened they'd become by years of service and working the streets, every man and woman in the department was aware that the end could be every time they said goodbye to their loved ones.

It didn't matter if they loved or hated or never really knew their fellow officer; the date of the memorial service draped like a wet blanket over every department that had to put one together. Once they were over, anxiety fell, and those who cared the most finally got a sense of honor, and the survivors' guilt began to lift and lighten. It never truly went away, but away enough to laugh again. To smile at knowing such a human who would sacrifice themselves for something greater than the image that stared them back in the mirror every day. Paul Duncan was the type of man Zane's father spoke about as he pushed his son into law enforcement and down his path.

The shiny linoleum floors had an extra squeak to them as he moved down the hall. The weightlifting room had more people inside who were getting after it. Probably more for mental clarity and stress relief than to compete at the next bodybuilding competition. He wanted to join in. Throw something heavy around, but later he needed to change and meet up with Carmen.

He found her in her office. Her presence comforted him. A reassurance that someone was on his side.

"You definitely give off a Riggs vibe," Carmen teased.

"I take that as a compliment. One Duncan would have loved," he said. "I hate breaking out the formals. They're crisp and restrictive. Pretty sure I'll have a rash after today."

"That's a lot of complaining for a few hours of wearing them to honor our friend. Now that you're here, I'm going to call Alyssa and have her come over to discuss the findings. She's been digging ever since I got off the radio with you and we had our initial findings on the vehicle. If she finds what I'm hoping she'll find, we'll finally have our first concrete lead."

He interlocked his fingers and put them behind his head as if he were on vacation. "Can't wait. You really need to order some new chairs here. These make me feel like I'm sitting at an old diner that serves bad chili."

"That's the point, Riggs."

He rolled his eyes. Carmen continued.

"You think I want people sitting there for an extended period and making themselves at home in my office? Oh, hell no. Next thing you'd know, I'd have street-clothed cops in here telling me I need new chairs. Can't have that."

He laughed. A bond shared during stressful situations. A way of diffusing the moment, but not the overall aim. They got through the academy using the same method. Carmen was another of his people. A blossoming relationship beyond the department walls.

Alyssa Williams walked into Carmen's office, and the air shifted. She walked with a confidence that made her appear to float as she entered. It wasn't to intimidate, yet her presence ensured you paid attention. She was a top mind in all things digital forensics. It was only a matter of time before she moved on to bigger and badder cases with agencies that go by initials and whose reach had no boundaries. Until then, Zane would squeeze every bit of knowledge from her to help him solve this case.

Alyssa sat down across from Carmen. "First and foremost, The Verge is a ghost town," Alyssa said. Her voice was soft and authoritative. "Which isn't a bad thing in my line of work. Reviewing hours of tape when the bodies are zipping all over the place is much more tedious and requires top-dollar facial recognition software, which, frankly, this department will not spend the money on. And two don't need it. Anyway, David Johnson was a hermit for much of his time at The Verge. Mainly popped in and out at regular hours. Maintenance staff were the only visitors, and they always gave at least twenty-four hours' notice before entering. Whoever was behind pushing him toward his end sure wasn't about to come visit for tea."

"Any familiar faces, or changes in behavior?" he asked.

Alyssa slid her head to the side. "Never. Like I said, a hermit. A loner. His hours of behavior changed, though. He started carrying items out of his apartment every couple of days. Then he picked up the frequency. Seemed to leave his place with something in his hands every time."

"How'd he move the big stuff?" Zane asked. He got animated as if he were picking up a couch on his own. "Couch, bed, tables, that sort of stuff? His place was pretty empty when I went by with the building manager."

Alyssa casually leaned back in the chair. "I saw no large items. Coming or going. Duffle bags were about as big as they got. I'll put together all the clips of him."

"Thank you for your patience with the video and with us," Carmen said. "Let us know when you're ready to premiere your film, and we'll be on the red carpet."

"Will do. I'm looking forward to doing the work and helping however I can. We'll get this sorted out. That I promise you." Alyssa left as powerfully as she had entered.

Zane stared at the office door. "Anyone else impressed?"

"I'm right with you," Carmen said. Her line of sight matched his. "Impressed, and she didn't really give us anything impressive. Is that the most impressive part?"

"Right? No visuals, just her telling us what we kind of already knew. I'm blown away. Add in the video next time, and wham." He held up his hand and received a high-five. "We'll be able to put Duncan's case to rest."

CHAPTER 37

San Bernardino, CA—The Verge Property

Four hundred and thirty miles later, Tyler was back in Southern California. He was pulling into The Verge parking lot and had Gina Kramer on the phone.

"You don't sound as hungover as I expected," he said.

Gina's peppy voice powered through the speakers of his BMW M-Series. "I'm a professional. Why do you sound worse than I do?"

He looked in the rearview mirror as if his appearance matched his sound. "Had a turnaround dinner with Senior."

"How'd that go?"

"I'm here, aren't I? See you soon."

His phone chimed with a message. It was from Al Russo.

RUSSO: The old man is ripped shit pissed.
TYLER: Guessing he's a little hot from our meeting?
RUSSO: Bingo.
TYLER: Well, does he have any idea you're working with me?
RUSSO: Not that I can tell. He's too angry with you to be looking at me.
TYLER: Let's keep it that way. I'm meeting with Gina. Heading to the res. All goes well, I'll be back up to the city in no time, and we'll be done with this fuckstain of a property.
RUSSO: And Gina?
TYLER: Don't worry. I'll handle her.

He put his phone back in his pocket, checked himself in the rear-view mirror again, and stepped out of the car. His manicured hair immediately became disheveled as the Santa Ana winds whipped through the parking lot and pulled the BMW's door out of his grasp. His Prada sunglasses stuck to his face like ski goggles.

The wind blew hard against him as he made his way toward the automated glass door entrance. The immaculate landscaping impressed him. Maybe the landscaper was ready for a change of scenery. Bring him up to work the high-end Pacific Heights, San Francisco properties once the deal for The Verge is done. He noticed the police car in the lobby's reflective doors as they parted ways for his arrival.

He attended the Chamber of Commerce's ribbon-cutting ceremony, which was the last time he was here. He forgot how much he loved the design. The marble flooring throughout the lobby was higher-end than the surrounding area deserved. Floor-to-ceiling windows opened up to the resort-level pool scene, which was something to behold. There was no scene to view, but that was the point. Scottsdale would have been a perfect fit for the property.

Gina's voice broke through his thoughts. "You're actually on time. I hardly expected you for at least another twenty minutes."

He shook his head. "I'm early for the tribal meeting, not for you. Let's not get the two confused."

Gina laughed. "I'm not confused. I know exactly who you are." She stood strong in front and unfazed by his attempt to rule over her. "You need this deal to get done with Lynn Sanmaura. You're not dealing with the tribe as much as you're dealing with her. I want this deal to be over. But not like you and Senior do. I've run into Lynn at some parties and events over the past couple of years. She commands a lot of respect. You need to acknowledge her."

His eyes drift and wander to what was going on behind Gina. A voice. He moved past her and walked up to a kiosk with a bright display screen. "That's your kiosk assistant."

"Becca. The assistant who doesn't age. Wasn't that how you sold it to Senior?"

Tyler's great and powerful idea. "Hey," he said. "Just because you suffer from progeria doesn't mean others do."

"Wow, look at you with the big words. Here I am thinking mayonnaise was your greatest achievement in modern lexicon. Silly me," Gina held up a tablet. "It's loaded with all the relevant data and information you requested. The rest is clean."

"Can never doubt you for being prepared. It's why I kept you around. Lose value in one area. Always deliver in another." He held up his arms like scales balancing each other.

"You are insufferable. Please check that at the reservation gate."

"Knowing how the world works shouldn't be an insult. I follow patterns and then execute what I've learned. It's a formula that's worked well in life and one that I'll continue to use."

"Is being an asshole a pattern?"

"Enough of this. Get your head in the game, Kramer. Debrief me on the drive over. We should arrive there a little early to show our commitment."

Gina didn't respond and began walking toward the automated glass lobby doors. Her head was up, and she dodged the man entering just as she exited. Tyler wasn't so lucky. The cadence of Gina's high heels striking and lifting off the marble floor distracted him. The man clipped Tyler's shoulder with such force that it spun him three hundred sixty degrees.

"Look alive there, Mr. Patterns," Gina said over her shoulder. "You never know who you'll run into."

He looked back just as the sun crept over his back and filled the entrance of The Verge. The man's image faded into a silhouette.

CHAPTER 38

Zane was strategic with his walk into The Verge. He stalked the entrance for an hour before he saw Mr. Pink pull up. He wasn't expecting to be rewarded so quickly, but his gut instincts kicked into gear when he saw the BMW M3 pull into the parking lot. California vanity plate. 2BEATLA.

His 1999 Ford Ranger blended in seamlessly with the other twenty-plus-year-old cars. The man who got out of the BMW dressed in a way that didn't fit the usual customers of The Verge. Gina Kramer was the only person who suited the fashion of The Verge's well-manicured landscapes and high-end interior design.

He thought of the simple advice his father had given: "Show up and pay attention." Words given to him throughout his teenage years, into his academy days, and throughout his years in the department.

He sidestepped Gina with ease. Her head was up, and she saw him coming. When he saw the well-dressed man distracted, his mind shifted to that first flirtatious interaction at The Verge.

This was a perfect opportunity for Zane to break out his *Terry Tate Office Linebacker* impression. He leaned hard on this man's shoulder with extra force. Like he was trying to disrupt a pass over the middle. A courtesy check from an old friend taken too soon. This unknown visitor wasn't his target this morning, at least not yet. With Gina on her way out, his plans would have to wait.

The sunbeams blared through the lobby entrance, and shadowy figures formed across the floor as if they were searching for something. There was nobody to impress with his balance. His feet anchored to the marble floor. His body remained symmetrical as he pressed on, walking into the vacant lobby. The kiosk screen came to life. He ignored the introductory message it displayed. Through the windows, he found the deserted pool scene. The sunlight warmed the still pool, promising a bath-like experience instead of refreshment. A far cry from his icy cold showers. Hard pass.

He took a lap around. The furniture seemed uncomfortable, and probably leased from a high-end boutique agency. He marked the time on his Panerai and didn't plan on sticking around much longer. He still needed to visit Duncan's burial site, refusing to call it a grave, even in his own mind. Pay his respects. Say goodbye to his friend and partner. Not today. Not until he finished what they started. He was overdue for the tow yard. Retrieve the USB drive from the glove box, if it was still there.

CHAPTER 39

San Bernardino, CA—Kizh Reservation

The low-profile tires of Tyler's BMW M3 screamed as he raced up the side streets toward the Kizh reservation's nondescript security gate. Nestled in a suburban neighborhood, the location offered an exclusive feel for those with substantial reservation wealth.

Gina white-knuckled the grab bar above the passenger window. "I should have driven separately. You drive just like you interact with people."

He smiled. "Calm, charming, and well designed?"

"Like an asshole," Gina rebuked.

He brake-checked her for no other reason than to prove her point and possibly spill the iced coffee she was holding.

"You're such a predictable little dick."

"If I remember correctly, you were quite fond of my predictable dick."

"You're repulsive. Don't forget the *little* part. I could use a puke purge of breakfast. I fancy doing it myself rather than from your heinous narcissism."

He sarcastically drove ten and two, the gears whirring as he slowed down. "I can't risk that this morning. I need you to be on point with Sanmaura. Hell, *you* need *you* to be on point with Sanmaura."

She eased back into the leather seat and eased her grip on the handle. "Like I've said many times, stay out of my way in there. More importantly, stay out of your own way. This is the last place you want to strut around peacocking. I've worked with the tribe on many events throughout my time down here, and it's always been a great experience. They're smart and hardworking. Extremely loyal to their own and those who have helped them build better lives and wealth. Something TruProperties has lost sight of over the years."

He ignored the critique of TruProperties. "Wealth? Their wealth has more to do with federally assisted government checks getting deposited into the slot machines. While a diabetic on a rolling stool smokes off-brand cigarettes and sucks down a sixty-four ounce diet Shasta."

"The American dream. The tribe has donated millions and millions of dollars to some influential organizations around the Inland Empire. They're the high-dollar sponsors. Lynn's savvy. She shows up and puts out, and who does the same. We've connected at these events. You need to recognize their contribution to the area. Be prepared to answer why TruProperties isn't on more donor plaques and sponsorship titles. They will ask."

They spent the remaining minutes in silence. He wasn't driving to the main entrance of the casino. He drove through the residential area to reach the back entrance. Lawns were mostly green unless people had already transformed them into drought-tolerant plants. Every fourth house looked the same. Cars and trucks that lined the streets and filled the driveways weren't much different from any of the others. The occasional bro truck stood out until the next one. The only difference was Truck Nutz. A sophomoric novelty item that dangled prosthetic testicles from the truck's rear trailer hitch. A novelty that had long overstayed its welcome.

The entrance gate was nondescript. Reserved for residents and their guests. The latest GPS update for Waze would not pull it up. Visitors from this gate needed private instructions. He had Gina.

He eased the BMW up to the guard structure. A large member of the tribe stepped out with a tablet to greet them. He couldn't remember the last time a security guard had intimidated him. This was one of those moments. He rolled his limo-tinted window down and gave his best smile.

"Good morning. We have a meeting with Ms. Sanmaura."

The security guard didn't bother to bend down. Tyler remained staring at the large man's belt buckle. Its appearance suggested considerable value, with its silver rectangular frame and the highly polished turquoise stones embedded within. The muscles in his jaw tensed up. The silent guard scanned his tablet for the visitors. Discomfort hung in the air of the German sedan. The air was thick like mud in a broom closet.

Gina came to the rescue. "Hey Robert," she said. "You'll find us under my name, Gina Kramer."

Tyler's head pivoted as if he took offense. His attention quickly shifted back to the security guard, who had spun on his heels and lumbered around the front end of the trademark kidney grille.

Robert's head was still not visible through the windshield.

Gina rolled her window down with a cheeky smile on her face. Robert bent down for a better look. Tyler saw her reflection in Robert's mirrored aviator sunglasses straight out of the security guard costume box.

Robert's face wore a serious look with deep lines that told the story of long hours in the intense Southern California sun. Tyler seemed to shrink the longer Robert surveyed the two. It was Robert's gate in every sense.

"Gina Kramer," Robert said. His voice was rich. His reflective sunglasses shifted between his tablet and Gina's smiling face. "Damn good to see you again. Ms. Kramer." The intensity on his face broke into a pleasant, warm smile. "I thought I recognized the name, but I can never be too sure of that at my age. Seen lots of names over the years. Your face, though. And that smile. Finally popped the light." He lightly tapped the side of his colossal head.

"It has been some time," she said. "You know, that whole pandemic thing. It's good to see you again."

"You too. I'll let Sanmaura know you're here and on your way up. Enjoy your time on the reservation. Let's please not go another three years and four months since your last trip through my gate."

Tyler chimed in from across the driver's seat. "That's oddly specific."

Robert spun his tablet around to show him and Gina the display. A picture of Gina smiling from inside her Audi A8 greeted them. Her profile followed on the screen: address, phone number, date of birth, height, weight, eye color, and then the dates of every one of her visits.

"We keep a well-detailed list of who gets to drive through my gate as visitors."

"Impressive," Tyler said. "I hope you don't need my ID. Lost it in San Francisco right before coming down here."

"Oh no, your vehicle provided it for me already," Robert said in a heavier tone than he used with Gina. He swiped on the tablet screen and flipped it around to confirm with him it was all there. A picture from when he first rolled his window down and stuck his head out. "We're a bit more sophisticated than a lost ID."

Gina gave Tyler a look that told him he was skating on thin ice. Underestimating the tribe was not something they tolerated. He acknowledged that he understood. Shifting into a more passive body position behind the tan leather steering wheel, she was ready for instructions from Robert.

"Once this swing gate opens, you're free to proceed up to the main office," Robert said. "Do not stray from the path. From this point on, your position is being tracked. Diverting from your course will cause immediate removal from our land."

The large infotainment display screen in the middle of the dashboard quickly flashed to an updated GPS map and directions.

Robert continued with a well-rehearsed speech. "The directions are now on your dashboard. There won't be any confusion in direction, distance, or the time it should take you to reach your destination. Questions?"

Tyler diverted to Gina.

"No, Robert," Gina said. "You've been so generous with your time and set us up for a successful route to our meeting. It was really nice to see you again." She gave a flirtatious smile.

"You too, Ms. Kramer. I'll be here to check you out when you're finished." Robert motioned with his arms for them to proceed and stepped back into his guard station like a bear protecting its den.

"Keep your pants on," Tyler said. "I'm shocked you didn't slide right off your seat. You owe me a detailed clean."

"Grow up. You understand the rules of this game. Don't get distracted by the supercars in every other driveway, and we won't have to be escorted off the land the moment we arrive. At least survive the meeting before we leave on our own."

The size of the houses was impressive. The shiny sports supercars, more so. Lamborghini, Ferrari, Bugatti, and McLaren were as commonplace in these driveways as Tesla and Rivian were in Silicon Valley.

He was driving a car more fitting for the Bishop County Fair Demolition Derby than a luxury sports car. "I think we're even with them now. For fuck's sake, it's not even just one Lambo. It's multiples. They park them outside like horses to show their neighbors who wears the biggest feather."

"Dear lord. Feeling little dick syndrome kicking in?" Gina kept her eyes on the street. "Get it all out now. Once we step foot out of this dilapidated automobile, you're gonna need to be Marlon goddamn Brando regarding your respect and humility to them. They will own your ass if you do not. You're struggling to realize the magnitude of the situation. They are out on The Verge. Fuck it up, and you might as well file a BK and tuck your tail back to daddy."

The vein on his temple pulsed. His jaw clenched, and he resisted the urge to chew on his thumbnail and beg to keep the vomit from rising. He remained quiet for the rest of the drive through the gorgeous neighborhood and toward the base of the San Bernardino Mountains.

The residential views gave way to the sprawling and breathtaking spread of the tribal council's headquarters. Five stories of complex craftsmanship deserve a cover feature in *Architectural Digest*. Outdoor facilities to handle everything from ceremonies to art to workshops to sports. It was state-of-the-art. A true hidden wonder compared to the condition of the city just on the other side of the reservation's boundaries.

He backed the BMW into a stall that was away from the other cars parked there.

"A little intimidated, are we?" Gina said.

"Not too far away to make it noticeable. Just enough so I don't have to rub mirrors with a million-dollar McLaren F1. It's Jay Leno's garage around here."

"That's the self-deprecating humor that doesn't appear as a bigoted asshole. You pay them a compliment to one of the most famous car collectors, and you recognize your inability to keep up in your BMW mom mobile. That's what the 'M' series implies, right? Mom mobile?"

"You're dumb." He buttoned his blue windowpane sport coat. Checked his reflection in his tinted window and looked back at Gina. "How do I look?"

"Professional. Now, let's keep it that way."

"You look-" he began before Gina cut him off.

"I didn't ask you. I know how I look. Confident. Tits and ass will not work here. They want class. Respect. Humble. Remember that while we're here. Check your ego with Robert until we leave. Got it?"

He nodded in reluctant agreement. They took in the glass facade of the tribe's headquarters.

"If you ever wondered where the design elements for The Verge came from," he said. "You are looking at it."

"Well done."

The pair walked in lockstep toward the entrance, taking in the valley below.

"Can hardly tell what a dumpster fire it is from up here," he said.

"The air is cleaner just a few hundred feet higher," she said. "Especially with the Santa Anas blowing through. Can almost see Catalina Island. On a still day, the smog will remind you of the vapid life below."

A loud female voice broke their amusement at the view and admiration of the architecture.

Lynn Sanmaura approached them. "So great to have you back up here again, Gina." Her tone was sincere and diplomatic. "I hope it wasn't too much trouble finding your way and getting through the gate. I know Robert takes his job rather seriously. Which makes him the best at what he does."

Lynn extended her hand to greet Gina, and the two shook hands. She then turned to Tyler, and they exchanged pleasantries. "You didn't have to park so far away. The BMW M-series is a magnificent car. Do not let the others intimidate you. If they really knew what they were doing, they would race them around Laguna Seca. Not obeying residential speed limits around here."

He appreciated the words and thanked Lynn for putting him at ease. The trio walked into the sprawling headquarters, and suited-up tribal security guards followed the echoing sound of their footsteps.

There was a notable silence to their footsteps as they walked through the open lobby and into the hallway. The gymnasium was being set up with large banquet tables and plenty of folding chairs. The workers buzzed about like an ant colony. Each with their own separate jobs, they work as a cohesive unit. He tapped Gina on the elbow and pointed through the open double doors.

"What event are you hosting?" Gina asked Lynn. "The crew is getting down in the gym."

Lynn spun on her heels and walked backward as she spoke. "This weekend is our annual community resource fair. There will be everything from sobriety experts to employment staffing centers to credit unions explaining personal finances. That's one of the most popular programs. So much so, we had to invite more than one institution. For every mansion with supercars in the driveway, there are another dozen rundown houses with families struggling to make it through their day-to-day. The drive you took through the neighborhood to get here is misleading as an overall look at our community. People are struggling. We need to fix it with the help and resources they need."

"Truly inspiring stuff," Gina said. "Taking care of your people and offering them something like this is incredible. If there's anything we can do to help, please never hesitate to reach out."

"Well, depending on how this goes today, that might be the only help we'll need." Lynn spun back around to walk forward and led them to a courtyard on the back side of the building.

The landscape comprised red rocks, drought-tolerant plants, and ponds that flowed from one to the next. It was both rugged and tranquil. With the clear skies, it felt more like they were at a retreat, focused on inner peace, rather than preparing for the last season's planting.

Lynn stood at the edge of the outdoor seating, arranged in a rectangular pattern, and faced inward toward a glass rock fire pit. She directed her guests to sit down and motioned to an underling to bring refreshments. An underling delivered water and hot tea to all three. She took her seat directly across from Tyler. The steam rising from Lynn's porcelain teacup fixated her momentarily.

Lynn swirled her tea with a miniature teaspoon. "Jasmine and lavender. A lovely combination. I like to stir the tea and release more of the notes. Jasmine is good for your brain, teeth, and maybe even your heart, plus other stuff. Lavender reduces inflammation, boosts the body's natural immunity, and aids respiratory health. Breathing is a key element of life. It aids and nurtures us in ways that are vastly overlooked and underappreciated in today's culture. By controlling your breath and slowing down, you can resolve much."

He absorbed Lynn's words and followed her lead. He stirred the tea, and then he brought the cup to his nose. Taking in a slow inhale of the bouquet being released. The lavender reached his lungs first before the warm hug of the jasmine wrapped his head and mind like a merino beanie on a cold winter morning.

He wanted to be unimpressed. Instead of judging, he understood his role was to show care for the tribal people and a genuine interest in their lifestyle. He was here for the deal, and there was no mistaking that part.

"I appreciate you trying," Lynn said. "You have made up your mind about visiting me today, which isn't necessarily a bad thing. I prefer not to go through the motions of making a deal."

"So we are going to make a deal," he said. "You plan on us driving off and having a deal done. Right?"

Lynn sat back, and the sun kissed her cheeks as if it were the most natural thing in the world. "I'm certainly not here to sift through the bullshit and nitpick every detail. That's what the lawyers are for." Her face glowed, and her rich black hair shone as if it were wet. She had the clientele to fix TruProperties' woes instantly. Unlock the potential of The Verge. Lynn's eyes were like a hawk. "I'm intrigued by the NFT smart contract, but that seems to benefit you the most. We have no plans of selling and flipping the property. I had my people look it over. It doesn't seem to make much sense for you either. A shiny coin at the bottom of the wishing well. Something more fitting for your big city properties in San Francisco. Assuming at least a few of those would be next to hit the overpriced market."

"The old man is stingy," Tyler admitted. "I needed the smart contract to get to this table. We needed a hook. I can do without it. It's a financial pyramid for future purchases to throw a kickback to the prior owners. Maybe that drops the initial sales price by a percentage. The money lost up front will swing back on the next sale and the next one after that, and so on."

A man who was approaching neatly tied his raven-black hair back into a ponytail. Pearl snaps on the front of his button-down shirt sparkled like diamonds. The man's walk had a perfect cadence. Boots that were no doubt the man's cherished possession. This was a man who would rather travel on foot than by sports car. Pride beamed from his broad shoulders and booming chest. Tyler shivered. The man made everyone uneasy.

Standing like a well-trained soldier, the man stopped behind Lynn. A man of security. A man of principle. Do not mess with this man or his people. After a quick scan of Gina, the man darted his eyes and fixed them on Tyler. The man pulled an envelope from his back pocket to present to Lynn. His movements were natural and smooth.

Tyler wished he had brought his own security with him. They never would have made it past Robert at the security gate. The man retreated into the shade. Somehow more menacing from there than he was standing close by. A warrior in a garden.

Lynn opened the envelope and read the contents. Tyler looked on with eager anticipation. His heart thumped. New tension hung in the air like a thick cloud of smoke. Breathing labored. The tips of his ears burned with fear. He resisted the urge to reach for Gina. Something was uneasy. Unsettling. Paralyzed in the moment.

The man in the shadows lit a cigarette and began singing and chanting in his native tongue. He held his hands high as they danced through the exhaled smoke.

Thunder and lightning cracked and sparkled overhead, but the day was clear as ever. Lynn's figure broke in waves and floated like August heat waves above asphalt, but she was of flesh and bone. The unfamiliar chanting provided the soundtrack to Tyler's new reality. A dimension and portal into another plane of existence. The morphed, wavy figure of Lynn floated over his teacup. Like a curious puppy, his head tilted, and his jaw hung like a chandelier.

Lynn's voice broke through like a great wizard from Oz. "You're going to be okay. Relax and resist the urge to fight these feelings. Embrace the inner peace you're so close to experiencing. This will help us reach the decisions we're here to make."

He blinked hard through his brain's fog and distorted vision. He wanted to be back to normal. If normal was even a possibility anymore. Maybe there is no reality. This is reality. Does he even exist in the chair? Or is the chair just a particle, as he is? As we all are?

He white-knuckled his Armani slacks and curled his toes under his Nordstrom Rack loafers. His skin needed to rip and split through every seam of his clothing. His insides needed to be out. He saw his dad; he was younger, and Al Russo.

Was Tyler crossing his father for the right reasons? Or was Tyler being selfish? Maybe both? Has to happen. Needs to happen. For Tyler? Why the third person? Is any of this real?

Lynn's voice was back. "This is real. Your inner dialogue is very much verbal. I knew this was about your father. You wouldn't admit to such tactics without opening up your conscience. That's all this tea did. Now, we'll have you both sip another tea that will bring you back to your regular state of being. Unless, of course, you would like to ride it out for the remaining five minutes? See what else bubbles to the surface? Gina seems to enjoy the ride."

He twisted his neck to where Gina had been sitting, but she was no longer there. Her blurry figure stood up on what he knew was a large red boulder. She spread her arms wide, like an eagle ready for flight. The colors of the sky and landscape seemed to blur and washout like an oversaturated watercolor painting. His jaw numbed as if it were on Novocain. His fingertips searched for every minor bump of razor burn and every new facial hair protruding from his face. The sun. The bright sun. So full and intrusive. This wasn't San Francisco.

Gina twirled around like a flower child of the 1960s Haight Ashbury counterculture - carefree, spreading happiness, joy, and love. She looked at peace. A look he hadn't seen on her since she began running The Verge for TruProperties. Maybe this needed to be her new life. An eternal search for the present. What would it take without the tea?

Lynn poured from two new pots of tea and topped each hot cup with a paper-thin slice of yellow lemon. Two staff members assisted him and Gina back to their seats. He ignored the pain of the steaming liquid sloshing through his mouth and down his esophagus. He longed to return to his asshole circadian rhythm. The bouquet of citrus pulled him from his hypersensitive sense of self and freedom. The steam he blew off the top of the cup vanished into the blue sky.

A beautiful siren song slowly played through the speakers, easing his transition back to reality. The music was peaceful and made for a softer landing. Business still needed to be done.

Ceremonial tea was a peace offering. His inner turmoil became apparent. The things that stirred and rattled his soul.

"Don't rush it," Lynn said. "Fear is not the way out. You must focus on your breathing and stay in the moment. It's not about staying in the tea. Allow your mind and body to clear on their own terms. Quiet your mind and breathe."

Gina reached over and placed her hand on his forearm, and he relaxed. A few minutes later, he tapped her hand and sat up with eyes open and a clear mind.

"Thank you," he said. "I think I'm ready to do it again."

They all had a light laugh.

"Another time, for sure," Lynn confirmed. "For now, we need to finish this deal, and this is where we part ways. I'm thankful for you, Gina, in bringing this together, but now I ask that you go back to your offices. My team will assemble the documents and deliver them to TruCapital. The lack of surprise on your face, Mr. Truman, tells me everything I really need to know. We may have removed our poker room with our latest remodel, but that doesn't mean we've lost the ability to read people. We've merely trimmed the areas that don't make us any money."

He sat in disbelief, but ultimately nodded as he focused his attention on the two teacups in front of him and Gina. Lynn had an outside glimpse into his soul while he took it from within. He fought for a rebuttal. But facts were facts. The deal was done. The Verge would have new owners. He and his father were relieved of the sinking ownership. His ego was crushed, and he felt a weight lifted off his chest in another way. No longer a burden. Except for one more piece, removing his father. His flesh and blood. The man he had looked up to his entire life. Senior was destined for the sunset road. Tyler, the road to succession.

CHAPTER 40

San Bernardino, CA—Police Headquarters

Zane's energy was building during his recovery. Rest wasn't his strong suit. Pushing his body to move. Forcing blood into his shoulder, followed by ice baths, was his preference. He felt back where he had been physically before the accident. He eased past the threshold of Carmen's office.

"What are you working on?" He asked.

Carmen looked up from her computer. "Johnson. For the son of a local mayor, he sure was an enigma."

"How so?"

"Other than Dad. No family. No relatives. No friends. No leads to his life. No social media."

"That's a tell."

"Not even a suicide note."

He paced in Carmen's office. Only one personal photograph was visible. It was he, Carmen, and Duncan posing in front of the SWAT truck as if they were dropping the latest hip-hop album. A stark contrast to the captain's office.

"What are we missing?" He asked.

Carmen invited him to look at her computer screen. He crouched down by her ear, fighting the urge to kiss her neck. *Not here. Never here. Back home or at her place. Never here.*

"Duncan hated this system," he said. "Manila file folders. Paper-clipped mugshots. Handwritten details. That was his method."

Carmen paused her digital scroll and halfway leaned into him. *Maybe here.* "Duncan was a work of art." Her temple nudged his, but she snapped back upright when a few pairs of boots walked by her office. *Never here.*

He caught his breath. "There was an art to the files. Now we have to run through these databases built by some Silicon Valley tech nerd with no law enforcement background. Least they could do was ask for some input from the ones actually using the system."

Carmen nodded. "Use it or lose future funding. Pretty sure whoever bought this software is sitting on the shores of Big Bear Lake fishing for trout."

"Doesn't sound too bad." He left the blinking cursor on Carmen's computer. Took a lap around her office. Stared at the certificates on the wall. The ceiling. Then she went back to looking at her monitor. Brain fog. What happened? His memory, wiped clean like a chalkboard at the start of the school year. Duncan lay in a mangled heap. The rain diluted the thick maroon blood. *Think dammit.*

Carmen broke his negativity. "Let us walk through the steps, following the captain's brief."

"We all met at your office."

"Really gunning for the finer details."

He shrugged. Duncan's death loomed like a storm cloud from hell's pale rider. "Duncan would know. He studied his ass off. Loved the job. For every Rambo reference, there was a man who sought justice. Gave his life for it." His throat seized.

Carmen stroked his forearm. "You all right?"

He swallowed and nodded. "He was the type of cop my dad always told stories about."

"So will we. So will we."

He circled and plopped down into one of Carmen's desk chairs. "Fuck. I thought you were getting better chairs. Did my past critique mean nothing? I will have to write another strongly worded letter."

"Can you think of any suggestions you've made in this building that resulted in change?"

They both laughed.

"We met with you, and then we were sent for doughnuts," he said. "The guy was sketchy and had the confidence of a meerkat."

"Vernon. Victim number one."

"Number two." He held up two fingers. "Utah, get me two." The pain in his shoulder spiked. He grimaced and pulled his arm down. Maybe he wasn't at full strength like he thought.

Carmen's eyes confirmed it for him. "Two? You think Johnson is one?"

"I do. Then Duncan. That's three. Then our dynamic duo. Makes four and five."

The morgue was getting busy.

"What did the custodian give you guys? Names? Information? Can you remember anything?"

He cleared the lump in his throat. He shook his head like a wet dog. "Yes, he did."

Carmen straightened up.

"A USB drive."

"A USB drive? Of what?"

His mouth fell open. "Damn. We never saw it. The crash was right after." He lightly slapped the side of his head. "You know, likely CTE and all."

Carmen shook her head. "I don't find concussions hilarious. Especially when it's someone I care about."

"We need the truck. Fuck, we need to see the truck. Where is it?" He shot up like a bottle rocket and left with Carmen on his heels.

"Impound evidence," Carmen said.

Fifteen minutes later, he pulled the department F-150 onto the impound lot. Other than dispatch messages they ignored, he and Carmen rode in silence.

"I sure hope this is worth it," he said.

"Hope? That's not like you."

"I know. Hope isn't a strategy. But it's all we've got."

"Maybe. We need to find out. Impound is notoriously slow. I swear they go even slower when there is an officer involved."

"Another politician's handshake deal with these people. This one needs to break in our favor."

A faded sign hung on the side of the square office building. It looked like someone had made it of corrugated metal and a handful of rivets.

A+ TOWING AND GARAGE

He looked around. "*Garage* is an overstatement."

Carmen followed him to the front door. "It's amazing we still do business with these people. Shall we head inside?"

He didn't answered. He pressed himself close to the reinforced door.

Camen tapped him on the shoulder and pointed up at the CCT camera. He smiled at it and turned back to the door. He pressed the buzzer and followed that up with a status quo police officer knock. Dogs barked in the distance. The dogs sounded big. That was enough for his skin to tighten. Shooting a junkyard dog was the last thing he wanted. His sleepless nights didn't need any help.

Slow shuffling sounds came from the other side of the reinforced door, and the heavy bolt locks slid open. Dust popped off the hinges as the door groaned open. Santa Ana winds ensured dust and dirt were bound to find their way and settle. The oldest man Zane had ever seen looked at him with deep-set eyes that had witnessed life twenty times over.

The old man pulled a cigarette from behind his ear and began waving it between two fingers. "Is it necessary to hit my door with the damn police SWAT breacher? I can see you on the cameras, and I sleep ten feet away. A simple, polite back-knuckle would have done the trick." He rapped his knuckles on the door.

Carmen cut in over Zane's shoulder. "Thank you for opening up. We will make a note of our tactics." Always diplomatic.

The man took half a step out of the door. "I'm Cliff Scott. I'm the proprietor of this place."

"Who gave you the grade?" Zane pointed up at the faded sign with the lot's name.

"That's a holdover from the phone book days. Most people would only look at the first couple of businesses in a category. Had to be at the top alphabet. Would you like to come in? I do not enjoy the Dust Bowl."

Zane and Carmen accepted the invitation and followed Cliff inside.

Tattoos, likely telling an intriguing story, covered Cliff's arms. The ink matched his rich mocha skin, making the story difficult to read. Deep ravines that outlined his facial features softened him to look like a bloodhound. The office and what was apparently also part of the living room reminded Zane of Duncan's work habits: unorganized chaos only layered in nicotine and tobacco. It was strangely comforting. Newspapers, invoices, and receipts were stacked high. A locked cabinet of keys adorned the wall behind the desk. A computer monitor sat on the desk, appearing unused. The monitor probably hadn't been plugged in. More likely to be used as a self-defense aerial weapon than for record-keeping.

One thing on the wall that caught Zane's eye was a framed newspaper. The date would have put him somewhere around his tenth birthday. The top headline was about Magic Johnson's retirement from the NBA after contracting HIV. Seemed like an odd choice given the lack of clues around that suggested Cliff was a die-hard Lakers or Magic fan. Cliff was a fan of paper and doing things the long way. Below the fold was another article with no photo and less pop: "Police officer and owner defend tow yard amid gang violence."

"I take it you're here for the truck?" Cliff said. He placed the unlit cigarette back behind his ear. "Pardon the mess. Been a little busy lately. Lost my last driver, so it's back into the field to hook up the unregistered and the stolen. Probably been a decade plus since I last had to do that more than once or twice a year. Nobody wants to work anymore. Especially in this line of work. It ain't for the faint of heart, and I'm getting too old for this shit."

Carmen stood wide of the door and kept surveying the room. "How long have you been working with the department?" she asked.

"Oh, early nineties. You'd have to check that paper on the wall that this young man was eyeballing a minute ago." Cliff pointed at the framed newspaper with the unlit cigarette between his index and middle fingers. "You look an awful lot like him."

"Him who? Magic?" Zane laughed. So did Cliff.

"Sergeant Bruce," Cliff answered. "Seeing your name across your chest had me thinking you're somehow related."

"That's my father, sir."

"Good man. Helped me keep those thugs from looting and destroying this business. He was a raw son of a bitch that spoke fear into young men."

Still does.

"Didn't quite have the security as I do now. No dogs. No cameras. No connection to law enforcement. I was an easy target for the gangs that liked to bust through my fence and steal whatever they could. Car stereos were a hot item. They'd take hubcaps, hood ornaments, windshield wipers. Crazier times. Tow yards aren't as hot an item from a vehicle standpoint. Less hassle for the thieves to steal catalytic converters from home driveways than it is to deal with my yard. They'd more than likely try to hold me up at gunpoint and rob me for the cash."

Carmen jumped at the opening. "Sir, we're looking for a particular truck. It came a couple of months ago from an officer-involved incident. Sound familiar?"

"I know the truck," Cliff said. "There's nothing in it. But if you'd like to take a look for yourself." He pointed at the back door with the unlit cigarette.

"That would be great," Zane said. "We're looking for something tiny. There's a chance you missed it or it slid into a crevice somewhere." He took a deep breath as he contemplated coming face-to-face with the vehicle he last saw Duncan alive in. He looked over at Carmen for support. A look was all he needed from her. The time for her gentle touch would come later.

"I can go check," Carmen said. "You don't need to see it."

"No, I do need to." He held firm. "Sir, please show us the truck."

"It's in bad shape. Guessing you were involved."

"Your hunches are strong," Zane said. "I was the passenger with my partner driving. He didn't make it." His voice broke a touch, but he quickly suppressed his emotions. There was a job that needed to be done. "Sir, lead the way and we'll follow you."

The trio exited a back door of the office, which was just as sturdy as the front. They weaved through a mismatch of deserted Honda Civics from the mid-nineties to unregistered beat-up camper vans with the encyclopedia of parking tickets still plastered to the windshield.

The front passenger wheel, which had caved in under the weight of the rolling truck, caught Zane like a stiff jab to the chin. The blown-out windows and streaked scratches that covered the once shiny black pearl paint a body blow. His shoulder ached. The sight of the mangled truck took the wind out of him. Carmen was right, and he shouldn't be there. What was he trying to prove, anyway? He stepped back and then up to the passenger window, where he went dark and woke up in a hospital bed.

"You got a pry bar?" he asked. Cliff answered by handing him one.

Zane scrubbed any broken window shards away from the door and leaned in. The dust from the exploded airbags still hung in the air. The white bags lay lifeless. With one foot on the side running board, he used the pry bar to gain leverage to lift the passenger airbag. The glove compartment popped open.

"Can't quite reach all the way in," he admitted. "May need to pry the door open. Not sure how that impacts our internal investigation. LT, any suggestions?"

"You try the door handle?" Carmen answered.

The door opened with a smooth pull on the handle just as the day it was driven off the showroom floor.

"You men are always looking for the most destructive answer to simple problems," she added.

Cliff lit his cigarette. "Impressive," he said.

Zane slid into the passenger seat and felt ill. Duncan's ghost loomed. His skin prickled with goosebumps. He felt a strange comfort in the scent of Cliff's cigarette smoke mixed with the dust and damage of the truck. That comfort evaded him quickly. The rusty smell of dried blood penetrated his ego. He rummaged through the glove compartment without success.

Carmen's constant peppering of questions about whether he had found anything only escalated his irritation. He white-knuckled the pry bar and slammed it down onto the dash with such force it sent a shock wave to his lieutenant and the ancient tow yard proprietor. He sat back with his eyes closed, wishing he were anywhere else in the world. Back on the lake with a fishing rod in hand and his old man next to him, telling him stories of the good old days. Hell, even the beach, and he hated the beach.

Cliff's voice broke through the tension. "Son, I can't imagine the emotions you're experiencing at this moment. Take a breath. I get it. I also think you're not done yet. There's more of that energy built up inside of you. Windows are busted, airbags flat, and it's dented all to shit. Have at it, young man. We'll be waiting for you in my office."

Cliff motioned to Carmen, and they left him to his own devices. He burst through the back door like an eighties soft-drink commercial shortly after they returned to the office.

"You're a smart man," he shouted. "One good boot to that fucking box and she sprang loose." The heavy back door closed with a thud, and he displayed his hand. An almost mint-condition USB thumb drive. "Damn thing looks like it's fresh out of the box. Cliff, you're a gem of a man. Anything we, the department, or I can do for you, just give us a holler."

Cliff nodded graciously. "I'll keep that in mind. Break-ins aren't as common these days. Like I said, more likely a stick-up for the cash I don't have, or some deadbeat trying to get his car back. Been handling them for most of my life."

They shook hands before Zane came in for a bear hug.

"Don't squeeze me," Cliff said. "I'm too old for a fucking squeeze."

"Wouldn't dream of hurting you in a hundred years," he said, and the two shared a smile. "Thanks again."

The wind and sun swallowed him and Carmen up as they exited the small tow yard office and made their way toward their vehicle.

"Where to now?" Carmen asked.

"Our trusted digital forensics department, aka Alyssa Williams."

CHAPTER 41

Zane marched back into department headquarters as if he were carrying the Olympic torch. Carmen was hot on his heels. He knew where to take the USB drive and who would help. He wasn't halfway into Alyssa Williams' office before she greeted them.

Alyssa stood up. "Lieutenant Cruz and Detective Bruce. What do I owe the pleasure?" She appeared to be lost in an endless list of department what-tos, how-tos, and to-dos. "I was just about to put on my Scotland's Best playlist and drift away to the Highlands."

He made room for Carmen to join him in the cramped office. "It should be more lively than procedural bore."

"One checked box after another," Alyssa said.

He checked the halls and then closed the door to Alyssa's office. The air stiffened between them.

"We have something, but it needs to stay between us," Zane said. A mole in the department wasn't off the table.

Alyssa confirmed with Carmen that they were on the same page, like two boats navigating the same waters.

"This might be nothing," he said. "It might be something much bigger than we've dealt with."

"What is it?" Alyssa sat tall in her chair.

"This," he said, opening his hand to display the nondescript USB thumb drive.

"Can't you do that yourself?" Alyssa said.

"It came from a source," Carmen said. "A source who is now dead. And one of our own followed suit." She pointed to the black stripe that was across her badge.

Alyssa rolled back in her chair. "Paul Duncan?"

"Yes," Zane said.

"So, then wouldn't that make us next?" Alyssa said. Discernment painted her face like a mask.

"This is going to be the evidence to confirm Mr. Pink is behind all of this," he said.

He gave Alyssa the rundown of their encounter with meerkat Vernon. The ensuing crash took Duncan's life. Then, retrieving the USB earlier in the day. She nodded and dug through the cluttered top drawer of wires and cords.

"Got it." Alyssa pulled out a USB that looked an awful lot like the one he possessed.

"A-nother, USB drive?" He questioned.

"Yes, but special," Alyssa answered. He hung on her every word. "This one goes into the computer's USB drive. Then, your USB goes into it. That way, if there's anything virus-related, it'll get captured within the buffer USB and won't infect our system."

"That's pretty smart," Cruz admired.

"There are two small lights on the top of this one. Red flash means bad. I'm sure you can guess, green flash is good."

"Any chance it'll fail, and the virus could still infect the computer?" He asked.

"Yes, but the odds are minimal. Like less than less than possible. That would be for the world's super hackers and encryption code writers."

"Plug her in." Carmen's authority was more than enough. "Let's see what we've got."

He paced the back of the well-lit office. The cooler temperature setting to keep the computers running at optimal limits was right up his alley.

"Can I move my desk? You can hang meat in here." He took a breath. What could be so vital that it got at least two people killed? Four, once he lumped in Duncan's killers, who showed up dead in the TruCapital parking lot. The raw sensation of fear and anger penetrated his ego. Somebody needed to pay for Duncan's death, but those two already met their maker, so who now? Anticipation balled up in him like a cement fist.

"What's taking so long?" he asked. Anticipation had him bouncing up and done on the balls of his feet. "Shouldn't we know green or red by now?"

"On a shitty one, yes," Alyssa replied. "Those have leaks, and mid-level viruses can seep through. I don't mess around. This will take a couple minutes. You're free to pace in the halls if that'll make you feel better."

"We'll get it," Carmen said. "I'm just as eager as you are. Payback, yes. I also have a case file I'd like to close and solve. Remember that."

He nodded and took an impatient seat on the most uncomfortable office chair imaginable. It made Carmen's chairs feel like heaven.

"We're green." Alyssa held a thumbs-up. Her eyes locked on the screen for the next phase of the process. "Now, we need to figure out what level of encryption the files will be under. That will determine if it's going to be a few minutes, hours, or days."

"You're fucking with me, right?" He launched back up onto his feet. "We are on the goal line, and I'm not sure I can handle a few days."

The first file folder contained a multitude of extra files. Initially, their labels looked like gibberish. Yet, the longer they examined the ordinary file names, the clearer a pattern became.

"Do we just start opening them and see what's inside?" he asked. Nobody answered. They remained locked on the screen. The time passed in silence.

Alyssa pushed back from her desk. "No. But this will take some time. I'll know more in a few hours."

Carmen shot him a look that told him to calm down and find any semblance of patience. Patience wasn't his strong suit. She was right, though. Forcing something when he's knocking on the door rarely leads to the best of results. At best, he mangles it, and he wastes more time repairing the damage. He needed the files that would tell them why David Johnson ended up in a bathtub and triggered a wave of death that included his partner. He plopped back into the awful office chair, and an unwelcome glance met him once again. This time from Alyssa.

"Sorry," he said.

Alyssa offered a peaceful smile. "No offense. I can't fully focus with you or anybody else in the room. I need it all to myself. The lights will be off, the music will play, and my mind will work. I'll call you once I'm ready and we have some answers."

Carmen pulled him out of the chair. "Thank you, Alyssa," she said. "Holler when you're ready."

CHAPTER 42

San Bernardino, CA—TruCapital

Tyler nervously twirled his fine-point Pilot fountain pen between his fingers and checked the time on his Apple Watch. His stomach knotted with unease following his meeting with Lynn. His attempts at stoicism were a losing battle. He wanted to run - fight or flight. He had never won a fight. Not physical. The Dogpatch warehouse wasn't a fight. It was a lamb led to the slaughter.

He pushed to be a mental champion. Decades of outsmarting and out-thinking his opponents. He worked over Senior by going straight to the tribe. They were very ready to play their part. His play against his father made him proud, though he hadn't considered the other side of it.

He did not despise his father. He turned a small crack of animosity between father and son into a savior for the family legacy. The prodigal son. The only other person tired of Senior slipping was Russo. Where was Russo now? He called Russo again, but once more, right to voicemail.

Russo's long-resigned office assistant did the voicemail recording. A once sexy voice was now the bane of Tyler's existence. There was no need for him to send a follow-up text message. That would be just as unfruitful. The thought of standing back at his glass perch and gazing down at the women on the first floor didn't even appeal to him. He had a larger matter at hand. He grabbed his key fob from the top drawer of his desk and headed for the door.

Heading north on Interstate-5 in his BMW M-series, he called again. "Russo, it's me," he said. "We need to speed up our end. The tribe is way savvier than expected. Call. Me. Back."

He ended the call from the beautifully lit tablet screen on the dashboard. He paid no attention to the fine details of the German craftsmanship that went into making the luxury automobile. Senior, Russo, Gina, Lynn. Fuck, he didn't know which way to turn. He would have been shocked if he hadn't blinked once all the way through the Grapevine and up into Modesto. He had little time before he was back in the city; less than three hours remained on his drive, but that time would come and go in a blur. Sooner rather than later, he would face Senior. He'd better have answers.

CHAPTER 43

San Francisco, CA

After eight hours of panicked, white-knuckled driving up Interstate-5, Tyler pulled up to his burner apartment building on the border of the Cow Hollow and Marina Districts back in San Francisco. He kept this apartment as a spare. Something he paid for under the table as a getaway from Senior's reach. A place to collect his thoughts.

One of the tallest buildings in the area, his north-facing apartment offered 180-degree views of the Bay. The view encompassed the Berkeley skyline, extending past Treasure Island to the chilly Pacific Ocean that passes beneath the Golden Gate Bridge. He especially enjoyed hosting a small party, composed mainly of women, during the vibrant and noisy San Francisco Fleet Week. His speakeasy-like apartment offered one of the more unique views of the Blue Angels screaming through the skies. On the best of those days, he'd lead the group up to the rooftop to sip expensive champagne while the jets raced overhead and around the city's iconic skyline. Coit Tower, the Transamerica Building, Palace of Fine Arts, to name a few.

Fond memories, which he longed to be in the middle of once again. Instead, he had Russo and his father to deal with. He knew Senior was stewing and eager to light him up like a Christmas tree. That his phone had yet to ring with his dad on the other end was intimidating. A flex play by his Senior, but that didn't make the uneasiness go away.

Senior hadn't built up his wealth and assets because he was timid and could not play the game. Senior exercised that from when Tyler was a young teen, trying to break into the family business. This was something else, though. Senior was vulnerable. Tyler pulled the strings from the top like a marionette, working with the dexterity of a wily veteran of the arts.

Senior should respect that play. However, the part of the deal that Senior would not respect, the part of the deal that had Tyler holed up in his paid-for-in-cash apartment, was the tribe taking the last bit of power in the situation away from him.

Subsequent generations of the Truman family could no longer reap long-term residuals. Herbal tea sent Tyler into the truth-telling land of his subconscious. A legacy of an awful deal that left behind Josue, David Johnson, a dead cop, and two of Senior's trusted servants.

He called Russo. "I'm dropping you my pin. Meet me here." He hung up the phone and walked over to his mirrored bar. The fine crystal glass of C.E. Taylor bourbon took purchase in his shaky hand, and he embraced the sultry burn as it filled his throat and imagination. His hand slowly settled.

It wasn't long before Russo arrived. He handed Russo a freshly poured bourbon and refilled his own glass. The warm flavor of the initial drink still hugged his insides like a long-lost friend.

Russo joined him as the two overlooked the blue waters of the bay toward Tiburon. "Were you in the area?" Tyler asked. "Thought I'd be a couple more drinks in by the time you got through the city from SOMA."

Russo raised his glass and brought the caramel-colored liquor to his lips. "Yeah. Palace of Fine Arts. I still don't understand that damn building. But it's my little sanctuary to walk around and think. My daughter used to love it. Helps me clear my head. She was smart to leave the big-city life and take my granddaughter away from it all. This is no place to raise a family. Especially on your own."

"She's made of iron."

"I don't give a damn how built you are. This city has changed. It's dirtier and more dangerous than ever."

"It's always been dirty," Tyler said.

"Yeah, but it was more politically dirty. Simple bribes and favors from one industry to the next. People got greedy. Corruption always finds a way. There is a fine line between the two, and human nature can't resist the urge to become greedy."

"One of the seven deadly sins for a reason. Greed is a tractor beam for the undisciplined."

"Once the train runs down that track, there's no stopping it." Russo's bear-like paw smashed into his fist. "The only thing that matters is the will of those on it. How much greed can you handle? How much corruption are you willing to live with? Once you answer those questions, you'll sip three fingers with the son of the man who got you on that train. Just trying to figure out if there will be any life worth saving once you jump off. Or if there will only be the need to pull the plug and let it flatline."

Tyler looked into his glass for liquid answers. "Any ideas on where your train began? Guessing it was once you got hooked up with Senior."

"Started way before I met Senior and started working for him. Few people jump on and then find dirt under their nails. Our greed attracted us to each other. We went about it in different ways. Greed masked as ambition. I wanted a better job. More money. Nicer place to live. I believed that compromising myself was the trade-off to achieve those goals. It was hardly the case. The secret is, though, I could have improved all those things if I had chosen the harder path. Not to say that working side by side with Senior was a simple path. Once we filled the void of the other's weakness, the money started coming, and fast."

"What's changed now? All these years of loyalty to him. Now you will help me take him down."

Russo sat on the armrest of a leather chair. "As the old cliché goes, I'm too old for this shit. At a certain point, the old warhorse needs to retire. I'm certain Senior doesn't have that plan. It's either a polished mahogany box six feet under or steel cuffs around his wrists. I'm damn certain that wouldn't even stop him. He's too ornery for that."

"No shit. Probably just piss him off even more and refocus his crosshairs."

The two remained locked in conversation without looking at one another. They embraced the view that spanned out across the blue waters. Tyler wondered if he'd be having this open discussion if it weren't for the tribal tea. He'd feared this conversation with Russo beforehand, or would he? Was his mind deceiving him? Whatever it was, he had inner peace.

"Plus, if Senior goes in cuffs," Russo said. "I'm not far behind." His eyes widened around his red, bulbous nose. "Then, one way or another, you'll be next. Your hands might be cleaner than ours, but there's plenty of shit on them."

The threat was the truth.

Tyler turned to face Russo. "Senior's coming for me already," he said. "He's not dumb enough to do it through law enforcement. My guess is he's going to reach out to you, if he hasn't already."

With those words, the air in the room flattened like day-old soda. A rush of cold came on like an arctic front.

His face flushed with pale sweat. "He already got to you?"

"Loyalty," Russo's voice was deeper and intense. Russo set down his glass and retrieved his Beretta sidearm. A relic from his Gulf War days. "You're a good man. Always have been. This is the hardest job I have ever been tasked with. And I've been neck-high in the shit for decades. Take a seat."

Russo motioned with the end of his Beretta, and Tyler obeyed without taking his eyes off Russo's trigger finger. The tan leather of the chair held a matching cold that swept through his apartment. Russo being so close was no longer a coincidence, because it wasn't. If Russo knew, then so did Senior.

Russo checked his smartwatch and made a couple of taps on it with his off-pistol hand.

Tyler already knew the answer, but he asked anyway. "He's coming, isn't he?"

"Yes, I'm afraid." Russo's tone softened. He walked over to the seating area where Tyler was stationed and joined him in a matching chair across a glass coffee table. "I will not hold my Beretta on you. You know the threat. I'm not putting it away either. I've known you since birth. Let's try to keep this civil."

"Fuck, Russo." Tyler squeezed the leather of the armrests. "Seriously, what the fuck? Senior has gone mad. He's holding up his only son in his apartment, and he's using you as his proxy to do it. How does this make any sense in your head?"

"Question and answer time has been completed. Senior will take over once he's here. I advise you to remain with a clear head. Sip your bourbon. It was mighty tasty, if I say so. Try to relax. He should be here any minute."

They sat in silence for an eternity. Tyler spun the crystal glass in his hand, but didn't take a drink.

Russo huffed as he stood up from the leather chair. "Ah, the moment has arrived. Do you want to answer the door, or shall I?"

Silence.

Russo motioned with the end of his gun. "Why don't you lead the way? After all, this is your place, and it would be weird if I answered your door. Don't let fear take hold of you. I'll be right behind you."

CHAPTER 44

"My boy. My boy. My boy." Senior took his first few steps inside Tyler's stowaway apartment in Cow Hollow. "Did you really believe you could live anywhere in the city and I wouldn't know about it? Hmm?"

Tyler received a few rough slaps on the side of his face from Senior's open palm.

He didn't answer. His disbelieving eyes remained fixed on his father as he stalked around the room. The bay view, a blur in the distance. The end-to-end windows were more like a zoo exhibit than a high-market-value amenity. He was the prey.

"It wouldn't matter how much you slid under the table at this place. Word always gets around." Senior continued to circle. "I've been doing this longer than you've been alive. Sure, it's cliché, but it's just the facts. My connections run deeper in this city than you'll ever know. That goes for both of you."

Senior momentarily threw a dark look at Russo before turning back to Tyler.

"Let's not focus solely on this apartment. Decent view at least. I know all the broads you've had up here. Your parties. How you prefer this place over Russian Hill when you've had your little midweek Au Sushi meetings? I've been greasing palms for decades just in case an event like this would ever transpire. With the better part of four decades' worth of cash handouts, and here we are."

Senior walked over to Tyler's bar and looked at the bottles of whiskey that would impress many.

Russo pulled a long black cylinder from the inside breast pocket of his overcoat and screwed it onto the tip of his Beretta. No explanation was necessary.

Senior moved from the whiskey collection to Russo's shoulder. "And let me not forget Al Russo. You really thought you'd flip my longtime confidant against me? With what? More money? You could never top, hell, or even match what I've already paid this man. Prison for me meant prison for him, and prison for you. Poor strategy. What, were you going to off me? With who? You didn't have the stones to handle our Southern California problem. His granddaughter?" Senior laughed. "Please. If he wanted to have a relationship with her, he would—"

Senior wouldn't finish his rant. The suppressed 9mm bullet ended his life before his old, vengeful body hit the parquet wood flooring in Tyler's not-so-private apartment. His brain matter and warm blood sprayed across his whiskey collection like an abstract scene from the San Francisco Museum of Modern Art.

Tyler's face contorted through all the stages. First, the shock at seeing his father's life end before his eyes in graphic detail. Then, the denial that the life he was in was actually real. The anger twisted him up for not doing it himself. For not saying what he wanted to say. For not winning and for besting his dad on his own. He bargained for a few seconds, that he had actually won. Neutralized and no longer a threat, Senior was gone. Tyler's shoulders sank. He had lost his father. The man he both despised and envied. Russo accepted his decision. It was an outcome they had previously discussed, but hadn't officially settled on.

Russo dropped the firearm to his side and slowly approached him. "It's alright, Junior. I'll handle the cleanup. Been doing this a long time."

Tyler's eyes swelled with tears, and the dams of his eyelids were about to burst. The grapefruit in his throat was suffocating. He placed his head in the empathetic embrace of the man who had just shot his father.

"It's alright, Junior," Russo repeated over and over in a calm tone. "Let it out. It's alright. Now, you're going to do exactly as I say."

Tyler quietly sobbed. The shoulder of Russo's overcoat got more saturated with his tears. He took a deep breath and raised his head. He looked at Russo. A man who'd been like a second father to him. The soft landing when Senior wasn't there. Through his fear, there was also trust.

"What is the plan?" He forced out through shallow sobs.

Russo motioned for him to pull out his phone. "You're going to call the police. Tell them exactly what took place." Russo nodded to confirm it would be okay. To trust. "Go on. There is a video on my phone explaining my actions. Don't worry, you'll come out clean."

Tyler pressed 9-1-1 and began explained his location and the events of his father's demise. "Yes, the man with the gun is still here."

"Good," Russo gave him confirmation. "Now, tell them you've been shot too."

Tyler's eyes narrowed in confusion before his eyelids peeled back in a wide display of reality. Russo aimed the end of his Beretta at him. He hit the floor before a tear slipped down the edge of Russo's red, bulbous nose and down his cheek.

The wind left his body, but he was alive. Breathing was a struggle as if a rhino were standing on his chest. Getting the words out to tell the dispatcher he'd been shot was even harder. He felt the warmth of the wet, thick blood oozing out of his back.

Russo reached over and ended the emergency call. His sad eyes met the shock and terror in Tyler's. Russo helped place Tyler's hand over the wound to slow the bleeding.

"You've done good, kid," Russo spoke softly and low. "I'm proud of you, and the soul of your old man was so as well. He didn't show it, but he was. Don't move. Wait for the medics. You'll survive this. Maybe a day or two in the hospital. My aim has never faltered. You were a good son."

Russo showed the video he'd recorded to Tyler. It was the ultimate act as Tyler watched Russo's boots walk out of his apartment.

Tyler heard the distant sirens getting closer, and then he faded to black.

CHAPTER 45

San Bernardino, CA—Police Headquarters

Zane breached the threshold of Alyssa's office with pace, eager to find out what she had learned. He wanted to ensure he was first, a well-timed separation from Carmen. Avoid suspicion of their outside relationship.

"I was just about to text you," Alyssa said.

She appeared more frazzled than the last time they were together. Staring at a blue-light monitor while recognizing patterns and solving problems has that effect on people.

"Crack the code?" he asked.

"Yes," she said. "It actually wasn't that complex once I saw it. I think you would have gotten it eventually. Maybe not a couple of hours, but a few weeks."

Carmen laughed as she entered the office. "She's funny. I like her."

"I'm still on the fence," he said. He winked and immediately regretted it.

"The files were scrambled according to their filenames. Which were also the numeric dates sandwiched between random numbers." Alyssa pointed to the files on the screen. "See? Just two numbers on the front and back to mask the dates in the middle. This folder starts the sequence. Eight-five, those mean nothing. Then zero, two, eleven, twenty, twenty, eight, zero."

"February eleventh, twenty-twenty?" He asked with little confidence.

"Bingo," Alyssa confirmed.

He stood tall and puffed his chest out at Carmen. He received a playful backhand to his inflated chest for the effort.

Carmen shifted her attention from him and back to Alyssa. "What happens when you put them in order by date?" Carmen's posture was curious but concerned. "Virus?"

"No, viruses here, remember?" Alyssa said. "I've sorted them already, and at first, nothing. Every file is still empty inside. Except for one. Smack-dab in the middle of the series. Like a bullseye."

"The date?" Carmen pushed.

"July twenty-fourth, twenty-twenty," Alyssa answered.

He stood under the air vent at the back of Alyssa's office. "What's the significance? Like what's in the file."

Alyssa double-clicked the folder. "We're about to find out," she said.

A list of HTML files filled the screen. The system saved all of them on the date associated with the file folder. The first couple of links opened to different blog sites. Each with the same message.

This article has been removed by owner.

The list of HTML files in this folder was fifty-odd deep. Every link clicked offered the same result. Different blog sites, from crypto reviews to entertainment gossip to political commentary.

Article removed by owner.

He stubbed the toe of his boot on the floor. "Think these articles were ever live?"

"Tough to say. The HTML seems to be coded to a dummy page. It is my best guess. Let's do a quick search on the Google machine before our good friend ChatGPT, and see what pops up."

Zane made a sucking noise through his teeth. "You mean the Wayback Machine?" he said. "Why not just start with Chat?"

Alyssa typed, and the results weren't much more than the few local articles on Dave Johnson's death. No crypto websites. No entertainment chatter. No political sentiment related to Dave Johnson. She went back to the list of HTML files.

Double-click, open, and repeat the same message.

He paced behind Carmen. Which didn't help the tension and frustration. He couldn't stop. Even the combination of subtle and not-so-subtle looks from Carmen couldn't contain his frustration. Closure for Duncan.

Carmen rubbed his forearm. Alyssa's eyes met the point of contact. "We'll get through this," Carmen said. "I'm as eager as you are for this closure. Both through the justice system and whatever has you wearing a pathway into the floor of Alyssa's office."

He didn't answered. He grunted.

Carmen looked at Alyssa for interpretation. "That means, *okay*."

Alyssa pointed at her monitors. "I'm focused here. You two do whatever you need to do. My lips are sealed." Alyssa paused. "I got one."

No response other than the continued pacing and shared looks between himself and Carmen.

Alyssa cleared her throat and let it rip. "I got one!"

The silent bickering stopped like children caught by their parents.

"Come again?" he asked. He moved around the desk to close in on the digital action.

"One finally opened to something meaningful. An icon set to mirror the HTML code, just like the other false hopes. But this one sprang open an actual file. Looks like dates. Account numbers. Financial balances. But I'm not seeing any names."

"Names of people, no. But what about names of financial institutions?" he asked.

"Negative there. We have routing numbers, which will connect us."

"Anything local or familiar?" He followed up.

Alyssa nodded. "We have several duplicates. So, the accounts are going to the same place. Could be different people receiving the money."

"Or, one person with multiple accounts," he said. "There's no indication of whether the monetary amount is coming or going. These could all be payments. Or, could all be withdrawals? Or a combination of the two."

"Lucky us," Carmen said with a flick of her eyebrows. "How hard is it to find these routing numbers?"

Alyssa gestured towards the screen, where the search results were already visible, triggered by the first routing number entered.

"Pacific Bank of the West." He read the screen. "What's their story?"

Alyssa typed them into the search engine. "A community bank hanging on by a thread. Local community banks are a dying breed in the state of California. Swallowed whole by the megas, B of A, Wells, Chase, so for these names to pop up on the routing number search results is a bit of a shock."

"I've never heard of most of these banks," he said. "Must be from a bygone era."

Carmen moved in. "I'm not recognizing them either," she said.

"Fuck around and find out," Alyssa interpreted. "Got it."

"Wait, go back." Zane about jumped over the back of Alyssa's chair. "I know that one. *We* know that one." He looked back at Carmen as he held his balance on one leg. "Mr. fucking Pink."

"Or Dave Johnson?" Carmen offered another opinion. "Either way, it looks like we have a return visit to our new friend's place of business."

"So, should I keep going through these?" Alyssa asked before he and Carmen exited the cool confines of her office.

He stopped on a dime. "Yes, compile them all. How often each one was used, ranked from most to least? Both in terms of balance coming or going and the institutions that were most popular to least."

He couldn't wait to track down Mr. Pink again.

CHAPTER 46

TruCapital—San Bernardino, CA

Beaded-up sweat covered Tyler's forehead like teenage acne. He couldn't recall the last time he had felt this bad. Maybe the flu in 2019, but this wasn't an illness. His father was dead. Executed at close range by his right-hand man, Al Russo. As for him, he had a hole just below his clavicle from Russo's pistol. A minor act of kindness before Russo walked away clean.

The emergency team at Saint Francis Memorial Hospital patched him up and placed his left arm in a sling. He couldn't eject himself out of there or San Francisco fast enough. The city that had once held his father and his adoration now churned his stomach. His eyes sparkled with excitement as he imagined the successful completion of the endeavor with Lynn Sanmaura. One more meeting with Lynn to make the pain in his body, mind, and spirit all feel like it mattered.

His eyes were dry as he stared at the security camera. Looking for the slightest bit of unusual behavior. A suspicious glance over one's shoulder. A lingering hack at the copy machine. People arriving too early or staying too late. He saw nothing. He was the only one acting out of sorts.

The pulse in his carotid artery pumped hard and thick, like a swelling river during a storm. His hands moved his mouse. The videos captivated his eyes. He swallowed hard without realizing it. He had no sensation other than his pulse. Each throb reminded him of the unraveling deal.

His inner dialogue was getting the best of him. He was restless. He knew that likely made him his greatest threat. His gut didn't lie. He hadn't betrayed himself in decades. He was right.

His intercom squeaker hissed at him. "Mr. Truman," the woman's voice said.

"Yes," he said. He didn't hear the follow-up. His mind went elsewhere. To Senior's longtime assistant. What would become of? He should send flowers. A card? No, too obvious. It was his father. She should send him those items.

"Mr. Truman? Hello?" The intercom squawked again.

He blinked clearly. "What is it?"

Before the lobby concierge could answer, he saw the trio of tribal members climbing the staircase with purpose. Lynn Sanmaura led the charge, and just like that, his tension was gone.

The deal was back at his doorstep.

No time to ponder the consequences. He made moves. The tribe came to him. The financial war was on his turf. He was big-chested and confident despite knowing he missed with Lynn on his visit with Gina. There's no other explanation for why they'd be here. Unless there was enough meat on the bone to gnaw at.

Don't sit back. He adjusted his sling into a more comfortable position and marched toward Sanmaura and her crew. For all his cowardice, he was in the game.

He greeted Lynn and her team. "What a pleasant surprise. I will not waste your time asking what I owe for the pleasure of your visit. That would be an insult."

"Nobody ever doubts your intelligence," Lynn said. She continued to his office without breaking stride. No handshakes exchanged. No one exchanged pleasantries. This was business. Her rich brown eyes focused on his supported wing. "Well, that's a fresh look than you have. I hope you'll heal up quickly and that your recovery is already underway. However, for your inner dialogue and your intentions, that's a whole other ballgame."

Lynn took a slow walk along the glass of his office. She scanned the scene below like a hawk looking for an afternoon rabbit. She encountered the motion of busywork and the uncomfortable glances from a sea of mid-level talent.

"You appear to be a much more confident man in your office. A far cry from the Bay Area boy you presented as at our tea ceremony. Even with a wounded arm." Lynn turned away from the glass and addressed him. "I like Gina. Probably should have sent her long ago. But you and your father have your egos to tend to."

He stood behind his desk as if it were a presidential podium. "Let me guess, the tea."

"Ding ding. You let it all spill. Your need to out your own father. Where's the loyalty? Strike one. The desperation to offload The Verge. Strike two. That bullshit NFT smart contract. Strike three."

"If the deal is not up to your standards, why are you here? Negotiation?"

"Come on now. No room for negotiation. We ended up on the reservation because of negotiations. This is the ultimate offer. One that is final and already signed. You just don't know it yet."

Lynn read his face. His expression told her he was searching deep in his memory bank for what was to come. He wasn't anywhere near the right place.

"Let me help you. Despite the tension over this deal, I like you."

He straightened his suit jacket with his good arm. Suddenly aware of his appearance.

"You seem like a person lost in trying to please your father. An accolade likely unachievable from what I know of both of you."

Lynn's words caught him off guard. Surprising even himself, he nodded in agreement. "So what then?" he asked.

"The Redlands Mall project. It's been vacant for two decades. How many developers have come and gone in that span? The city keeps voting down limits on building height, number of stories, parking spaces, etc. Their insistence on the homeless overtaking the place is as mind-numbing as the city council's lack of leadership."

"I've tried." He was ignored.

"The money from San Francisco has been good to you."

He took a seat in his chair and took a deep nasal inhale. "You can get me the votes?"

"Yes, but not by the people. The language in the general voting proposition is too clouded. The voter doesn't understand that if they don't pass it, the state will take over the project to appease its housing growth goals. Putting in whatever they want. The vote will never come from the public. You need the influence of the city council and other local government officials. Nobody has more pull in that arena than we do."

"And by pull, you mean money." He thumbed the rolled-up blueprints. A neglected project.

"It's the name of the game. It always has and always will. A hard lesson for many who came before us. That's the answer to just about every challenging question we face. All you have to do is find the right development team. I'm sure with your connections, you already have five lined up. So, once they've received the buy-in from city officials, the chamber of commerce, etc., it won't need a vote from the people. The city council will be more than happy to push it through on its own. Tucked away in some bureaucratic loophole that happens time and time again."

"And in return for this generous offer to sway the city officials, The Verge is yours for pennies on the dollar? Tsk tsk. That doesn't add up. Where does the tribe line up with the development deal?"

"We simply need our people to be hired first."

"Your people? Explain."

"Our workforce development team has been training our tribal members for over a year. But they could not find work. Turned away over and over. We are a proud people. Many are hurting."

He shot her a look to said he saw the lineup of supercars on his drive.

Lynn put her hands up. "Sure. Some have luxury homes on the hills lined with cars. A mere facade to the hidden realities so many face. Depression. High suicide rate. Drug and alcohol abuse. It's a grim reality. With this deal, our trained workers can help the construction crews dig trenches and lay foundations. To the retail therapist assisting some half-dead South Redlands soon-to-be divorcée part with some of her ex's money."

"Jobs. That's it, just jobs? Still doesn't add up. What's the catch?"

"If you keep interrupting, we'll never reach the good stuff."

He looked over Lynn's shoulder at her two escorts and rubbed his wounded shoulder. His gaze didn't linger long. He went back to her and repositioned in his leather high-back office chair. "My apologies. Please proceed."

"All good press gets filtered to us. We helped bring in the local workforce. The tribe is offering complimentary shuttle service to and from the resort. You name it; if it's positive, it has our name on it. And on the flip side, construction delays. Poor parking. And the like — well, that's the city. Think Lebron James. When the Lakers win, they post his face on every one of their social media channels, but when they lose, they won't show as much as LeBron's shoelace in the photo. The project wins, we win."

"This is about publicity? The public will catch on eventually."

"It won't matter by then. Nobody cares about LeBron not appearing in the loser posts. They want to see him win. Sure, he has many others who want to see him lose. It just doesn't come from the Lakers' loyal fans, and it doesn't come from the Lakers. Our determined people land skillful jobs that add value to their lives off the reservation. The community finally gets to transform a homeless dumping ground into a vibrant live, work, play space. We receive great publicity as the lightning rod for all things good. And you. Well, you ride off into the sunset on a private jet filled with cash."

He picked up a stainless-steel ballpoint pen from his desk and twirled it between his index and middle finger. "What's the other option?"

Lynn shook her head. "There is no other option."

"I cannot agree to these terms. There's always that option." He sat back with a smirk that was met by an ice-pick stare back from Lynn. Could she tell he was bluffing? He needed a bigger guarantee for himself.

"You're cute. Do not meet our terms, and this all goes away. The Verge sits on your books and drains you like a slow bleed. Your relationship with your father continues to eat at you from the inside. We ensure the mall never gets developed and your reputation takes the form of the guy who can't close the deal. Not the Truman name you want remembered. And this," Lynn held her palms upward and twisted back and forth at her shoulders. "In the end, you can say goodbye to your perverted perch for the murder of Dave Johnson."

The smirk on his face disappeared as quickly as the blood did. His father was no longer alive, and that wasn't the sucker punch that rocked him. Lynn mentioned Dave Johnson, and that rocked him. His skin went cold and clammy. His mind and vision were dizzy. He fought the urge to dry heave into his office waste bin. The acidity in his stomach was rising through him, and he could taste it on his tongue.

"By the twist in your face, I can see the bullshit seeping through your pores," Lynn said. She approached his position behind his desk and began rubbing his good shoulder. "This tension doesn't need to exist. I gave you the easiest and least resistant path. You are trying to play hardball with me. Forget about the tribe. Your mistake is aiming your hubris at me. Well, that's just a fool's errand." She leaned down and whispered in his ear. "Free your mind of trying to figure out how I know. It won't do you any good."

Lynn removed her hands from his shoulder, adjusted the strap of his sling, and switched to a peppier tone. "So, let's get this out of the way." She motioned to the two sentient men.

Tyler had forgotten they were even in his office.

A Samsung tablet with a stylus was presented to Lynn, who gently accepted it before placing it upon his desk and handing over the stylus.

"Our side has already signed," Lynn said with the bounce of a real estate agent presenting home ownership documents to a first-time buyer. "You're familiar with the rest."

Tyler went through the motions. Muscle memory digitally transferred his signature onto the electronic documents. His brain did not engage with the reality of his signature and initials.

Lynn pulled back the tablet once she finished walking him through the paces. She made a few swipes and taps with her fingertip on the screen before closing the case and handing the tablet back to her detail.

"Lovely," she said. "Your lawyers have the contract in their inbox for the formality of their review. We didn't screw you. So expect there to be no blowback for signing it before their review. It's cleaner this way. For us in this room, at least."

He absent-mindedly shook Lynn's hand before she left. Detached from the entire experience. He felt betrayed, but he didn't know by whom. It didn't matter. He was out of place and out of touch for the first time since he had moved down to run TruCapital.

As the sight of Lynn and her two-man detail faded off his security cameras, he retrieved the wastebasket from under his desk and dry-heaved until the warm, tart texture of blood cleared his system.

CHAPTER 47

The walls were more restrictive than ever for Tyler. He wanted to make a run for it, but even that thought caged him in further. His fists clenched, a seething frustration bubbling within as the thin air offered no relief.

The meeting with Lynn went in the right direction, but something unsettled him. More so than anything Senior ever accomplished in that department. Despite Senior's intent, he always knew those threats were more about intimidation than actual harm. Those threats were no longer viable. They were dead.

He read the articles in the *San Francisco Chronicle* and the *Sacramento Bee*. He was the only one who gave a damn down in the Inland Empire. Hell, even his new acquaintances from the local law enforcement department didn't care. They didn't know either. He cared. His biggest threat was also his biggest anchor. Both were gone. Occupied by a force that was a payoff, or would have been a payoff. His minute-long interaction told him that a substantial bribe to an open-palmed cop or politician wouldn't help.

The anticipation of getting Lynn Sanmaura moving on the mall project was his priority. The general vote was long behind him, which led to his blueprints rolled up like childhood posters. He needed the next city council meeting for the overriding vote. Then he'd drop a sizable goodbye deposit in his Banco Nacional de Costa Rica and ride off to the greater Pacific. Bask in the sunsets and equatorial life. The vote was something he needed to be confident about. He called Lynn, but voicemail answered before it even rang. He hated this position.

He stared at the clock as if it were a timer on a television game show. He needed this out as much as he needed oxygen. Like now. Time evaporated into the construct while he waited for the city council vote. He needed to have faith. Faith, his agreement was solid. The tribe would pull through. Finally, faith that he'd be on the western shores of Costa Rica by the time anybody knew he'd left. The last phase was in the bag. The steps to the finish line left him dry heaving into his office wastebasket, again.

He felt the clamminess of his scaly hand as it reached for the phone, which he only ever used to contact Snake. Lynn Sanmaura finally picked up.

"How fast can we move on this?" he breathed into the phone. "That Tamarindo sunset sounds really nice. I need to be gone. Like yesterday."

Lynn slowly spoke back. "My part is done, Junior. How's the shoulder?"

"It's fine." The pain was worse than ever.

"I told you the votes from the council will be there. The rest is on you. TruCapital needs to fulfill its portion. This is where you come in as the proxy. The guy who sets up the other guy. The tribe moves on to development, community affairs, and expanding our reach. Throughout the hard work of our people. Building back the community with the sweat and will of those who need it the most. You can sip your coconut lattes on the beach if you like. Your money will keep showing up in your account."

He sat still in his leather-backed desk chair and tried to calm his mind. Push the pain in his shoulder away. Visualize the Costa Rica coastline. He wanted out. To leave and only think about this place on deposit days. He needed to ensure his team at TruCapital was secure. He couldn't take off with a deal hanging in the balance. Too many of these deals had fallen through over the last two decades. So close, yet so far away. He was never closer to getting the boulder, which was this project, to the top of the hill. A nudge was all that remained, and then momentum and gravity would quickly send the boulder back to the finish.

"Tyler?" Lynn called into the static air of the phone.

He liked her calling him by his name. "Yes, I'm still here. I'll still be here to see this get off the ground. It's only right, and will allow me to board the Delta flight with a clear conscience."

"I'm happy to hear that. Though we both know your conscience will never be clear. Not by then, at least. We can help you with that as well."

"You may very well be right. But I'll pass on the help. Eighty degrees and the soothing sounds of the ocean lapping onto the shore will be all the medicine I need. That and the mailbox money."

"Yes, don't forget the important stuff. It's settled then. Our people go to the front of the hiring line. You'll be well on your way to a retirement lifestyle."

The call ended, and he found himself back in control of his emotions. He approached his office window to resume his perch above the women he employed. The control over his emotions evaporated in an instant. He looked down to meet the glaring eyes of two people.

Two police officers had a casual interaction with him regarding the death of an employee. The eyes that met his now were not casual. That warm, acidic swell of vomit once again rose inside. A man regretting his decision not to board the first Delta flight out of Ontario International Airport.

CHAPTER 48

Zane blocked the glare coming through the glass doors of TruCapital with his hand and looked over at Carmen.

"What's my role?" he said. "Something about this place really pisses me off."

Carmen placed a light hand on his shoulder. "We both know what that something is."

As he turned to face her, her hair, pulled back, revealed her round eyes and slender jawline. He gave in. "Yeah. So, what's my role?"

"Just don't throw him through a window."

"Does sound fun." He moved his shoulder around to check its mobility. "Maybe not just for the fun of it."

"Do what Duncan would do."

"Chew on a matchstick and be clueless."

"Have some fun. We both know he was never clueless. An act to put the suspect at ease."

He smiled. "He was damn good at it. I'm ready."

Tyler started speaking before he was in front of them. He approached with his working hand outstretched. "What may I assist you with?"

Carmen greeted him first. "Good afternoon. I'm Lieutenant Cruz, and this is Detective Bruce. You look a little banged up."

Zane acted as if the tall window ceilings and the open floor plan distracted him.

"Detective?" Carmen called.

Zane spun back around, acting oblivious to the whole thing. He wasn't. He played it up as an inconvenience. "Yes?"

"We're doing introductions," Carmen reminded him by throwing her head toward Mr. Pink.

"Oh yes, sorry." Zane lunged toward Mr. Pink and shook his hand with frenetic energy. "Lovely building you've got here." Mr. Pink winced and reached for his shoulder. "Oh, sorry again. I get a bit overexcited. I didn't hurt you too badly, did I? I've been going through a minor shoulder injury as well. Getting better, though." His words shot out like machine-gun fire. "These windows and high ceilings. Well. I tell you, I could just get lost daydreaming around here. I think you caught a glimpse right now, didn't you?" He laughed awkwardly and stepped back behind Carmen.

Mr. Pink's eyes darted between Zane and the windows and back.

Carmen snapped like a hypnotist reviving her patient. "We're here to talk about your former employee. David Johnson."

"David. So sad." Mr. Pink said. His tone was mellow, but his eyes followed Zane's every twitch. "But I have nothing for you."

"We have questions about his time here as an employee," she said. "Who he ate lunch with, working environment, company culture. You know, those things that aren't in a manicured HR file. Those daily things that wouldn't be handed over to authorities."

"I see," Mr. Pink muttered.

Zane stopped his erratic behavior and stood strong.

Mr. Pink continued, "Well, please speak with my receptionist and we can book a meeting on the calendar. Today is tight with city meetings. I'm finally getting my mall project pushed through."

"Congratulations," Carmen said. Sincerity was absent from her tone.

Mr. Pink nodded his thanks without skipping a beat. "And there's a lot of moving pieces to that. Have you ever tried to get a building permit in this town? Wild process. Molasses. Really have to know somebody if you want things done promptly. Lucky for me, I'm the guy to know because I know everyone. The important ones, at least."

Mr. Pink side-stepped his exit as he spoke. Zane didn't mind. He was here to read the room. Too many long-distance views from the parking lot of Mr. Pink coming and going, but never inside.

Zane and Carmen braced the high winds on the walk back to the police SUV. "Well, that was fun," he said. "I can see why Duncan loved doing this shit so much."

"He was much better at it than you," Carmen admitted. "I could feel the *fuck you* pouring out of your body. It's who you are."

"I take that as a compliment."

"I'm not sure you should."

They fastened their seatbelts in unison, then exchanged a glance.

He threw the SUV into drive, but didn't release the brake.

"What is it?" Carmen asked.

"I'm not satisfied." He slid the gear back into park and cut off the engine. "I'm heading back in. You're free to join me. Or not."

"You definitely need supervision."

CHAPTER 49

"The deal is done," Tyler said into his mobile phone. "Don't review it. Don't look for loopholes. Process it. Notarize it. Do whatever the hell it is I pay you to do and send the executed agreement back to the tribe. Notify the team that we'll have the votes of the city council, and get that contract closed on the mall project by end of day."

He ended the call and tossed his phone onto the office chair. He stared down at the busy sea of employees below his glass-tower office. His insides were a dark pit of nothingness. He had gotten what he wanted, but it hadn't filled the hole inside him. Is this how his father felt, and why he kept pushing Tyler away from the business? The thrill of the chase.

He examined a lone picture on his desk.

A photograph he took of a purple and gold sunset in Costa Rica. The surf, the sun, the women, the year-round climate. Maybe it was time for a relocation. Away from the pressure. He no longer had his old man to fall back on. The Truman name was his and his alone. There will be business ends to finish for TruProperties; the lawyers already had that underway. Senior was deep in the shit, and Tyler realized maybe that wasn't the direction he wanted to spend his earning years. Cleaning up his father's mess. Too many deals that Tyler warned him about fell on deaf ears. With each bad property, Tyler had to be the song and dance man to flip it around. Surfing sounded better.

The *San Francisco Chronicle* was the first to break the news of the Senior's murder. Real estate moguls with a history easily linked to corruption, lawsuits, bribery, extortion, and just about any other accusation to drum up public distaste. The article detailed the Truman family's four-plus-decades-long quest to be the top multi-family real estate owners in the city.

The modest start in the Outer Richmond district on the border of Little Russia. A property Senior could get a deal on, as almost every investor was fearful of the Cold War in the 1980s, and the idea of Little Russia made their bowels churn. The Outer Richmond property wasn't about flipping or generating immense wealth; no, that first property was about connections.

Senior took those early forged relationships and helped him land a handshake deal on his first Tenderloin building. Downtown, with its high crime and dirt, had some of the most inexpensive rents in San Francisco. This was the property where Senior got his education in rent control tactics and fair market value. All was quiet for the first few years, but as his small empire expanded, thirsty lawyers started tracking his property growth, and lawsuits soon followed.

Senior had to cut a few extra court-ordered checks over the decades, but they were a drop in the bucket. He attended fundraisers and city galas. Made the right political donations and supported the proper judges, but it all got swept under the rug. There's always something bigger and higher up the food chain to deal with.

With every unchecked step, TruProperties swallowed up real estate, forced long-term tenants out, and jacked up the price. Sure, there was a fair amount of value added to long-neglected buildings: stylishly renovated apartments, fresh common area carpet, vibrant exterior paint, refinished hardwood floors, etc. However, the wake of disgruntled residents and eager attorneys never ceased.

The article briefly mentioned the recent transgressions of Senior, how he outbid himself in recent years and dug himself into a financial hole. The strained relationship and heightened tension with his son, Truman Junior, who was also a victim but survived. Those things were hardly public knowledge. Like much of current journalism, the article mainly pulled from prior articles written and a simple police report on the events that led to the discovery of the bodies. Even the picture that accompanied the article wasn't current or even accurate, The Painted Ladies.

Public comments at the bottom of any online article are rife with negativity, and this one mirrored the sentiment the article sought to capture. Tyler couldn't resist the urge to read through a few of them. Against his better judgement, he began reading.

"The city is better off without them."

"Rent control stopped monsters like them."

"Deliver us from evil."

"Sued them, won, hardly saw a dime."

He didn't need to scroll through the comments section, and after reading the first few, he had seen enough. His self-loathing was a dark, solitary companion. One less problem he had to think about.

His deal with Russo wasn't supposed to end that way. Russo went off-script. At least he left the video.

A flash of bodies twisted his mind from what-if scenarios to the present. Two police officers were back inside his building. They moved at a pace. Their mannerisms made Tyler more curious than cautious. He just spoke to them. What now?

CHAPTER 50

Zane stormed into Mr. Pink's office. Carmen was hot on his heels. Playful nature be damned; Zane cooked from the inside out.

Mr. Pink white-knuckled the armrest of his chair and stood. "I didn't expect your return so soon. I don't have any party favors ready. Though I'm sure I can make a call and get you a travel mug." He slid open a few drawers in his desk to find something.

Zane smirked and suppressed his desire to walk over and break Mr. Pink's nose with the palm of his hand. "A thought popped into my head just as we were about to head out for doughnuts."

Carmen jumped in to change the mood. "We've discovered some new information," she said. "Something tells us your former employee-"

Zane cut in. He couldn't resist. This man had something to do with Duncan's death. He needed to press on the wound. "You know? The one we found in a bathtub." He flashed his teeth at Mr. Pink like a wild animal. "Son of a local politician."

Mr. Pink stood and moved around to the back of his leather chair, another barrier between himself and Zane. "Please, Detective," Mr. Pink said. His voice was weak. "We don't need to relive the details of the fallen. He was a friend."

Fallen. A word reserved for the men and women who lost their lives in the line of duty. Zane did not miss it. An adjective rightly reserved for Paul Duncan.

Mr. Pink took a slow, methodical walk around the back of his desk. He hung close to the windows overlooking the first floor, making his way to the other side of his office. He carefully sat on the black leather couch, as though it were made of papier-mâché. A trifecta of vintage travel posters hung on the wall above. Destination Costa Rica: Surf, Adventure, Pura Vida.

Zane's jaw clenched, and his fists balled as he stared at the alteration, his anger barely contained. Mr. Pink adjusted his shoulder sling.

More theatrics? Maybe. Maybe not.

"I can sense your hostility," Mr. Pink continued. "You're angry. But why is it directed at me? I experienced a gunshot. My father, murdered right in front of me. Why don't you solve that one? Oh, that's right, not your jurisdiction. Even knowing who shot me, you still couldn't track the man down. You came by. Asked questions. Which I answered." He held up a finger and smirked. "Then we all went on our way. So, now, what brings about your return? Pointing the barrel of your gun at me?"

"One question," Zane said. "All we have is one question. We'll be on our way shortly. Fair?" Mr. Pink nodded, and he continued. "What secret financial dealings led to a man's murder for finding a USB drive while emptying the trash?"

Mr. Pink chewed on a thumbnail. "Tragic, what happened to Vernon. Soft on crime policies allowing criminals to walk the streets. Free to commit violent acts against the innocent. Must make your job extremely difficult. I'm sure whoever caused the violent scene outside my building recently is already back on the streets."

Zane's veins ran cold. He popped his knuckles and silently gave Carmen a look to tell her that Mr. Pink was not wrong about their uphill battle against the lawmakers in Sacramento. "Looks like I'm staring down a two-for-one. Crack two cases that are flying around your orbit and bring you down. Let the city get back to normal."

Mr. Pink scoffed. "Normal? There's nothing normal about what's going on out there." He pointed toward the door. "The pandemic was the great shift. Mistrust of our so-called legacy institutions. Remote work. Money and benefits to stay at home. Politicians are more eager to placate anyone claiming to be a victim than the ones footing the bill."

"Is this your supervillain monologue?" Zane said. "Half-truths you spin into something believable."

"Half-truths?" Mr. Pink said. "Where's the lie? You and I both know you're not angry with me. You're angry with the system that's been established. All the hoops you jump through just to make an arrest and have that person back on the streets within days."

"Hours," Zane said. He took a half-step forward before Carmen grabbed the back of his uniform. He wanted to blow out one of the office windows and dangle Mr. Pink by one leg over the ledge of his office. Drop him like an egg in front of his staff. He'd need an adrenaline surge to push through any pain left over from the accident. That could be his test. Mr. Pink wasn't *that* big. Be an unorthodox physical therapy session, but his mental clarity would vastly improve.

Mr. Pink's head came up from his phone. "You know, I'm glad you came back into my office. There's something I want to show you." He pushed himself off the couch with his good arm and approached Zane. "You're so interested in murder. Here is one for you. Happened just the other day." He spun his phone around to display the video.

The video's timestamp coincided with the day they laid Paul Duncan to rest. The hours of that day were a blur to Zane, so it could have been during or after it. On full display was the TruCapital parking lot. Two men exited the building and headed toward their car. Their faces weren't visible. They each walked as if they carried extra weight in their shoes. Once the men arrived at their vehicle, another pulled up to a stop in front of them. The distance in the video made it difficult to see.

"Can you zoom in?" Zane said. "For as high-tech as you appear to be, this video is shit."

Before he got an answer, a slender-looking man emerged from the truck and attacked the other men. Even in a pulled-back video, the carnage was apparent. Then, as quickly as the violence began, it was over. In its wake, two bodies burned inside a vehicle. The video cut off, and Mr. Pink tucked his phone away.

Zane's legs locked at his knees. His back became rigid as if someone had inserted a rod where his spinal cord once was. There was a familiarity to what he saw, like a violent ghost from the past.

"Video was sent over to your department the day this happened," Mr. Pink said. "See. I'm as cooperative as they come. Here to assist. Now, concerning your original question. Truly tragic, what happened to Vernon. We hired a janitorial company to clean up after hours. He wasn't a direct employee. I suggest you check his background. See what other enemies he had. I'm too busy defining my legacy. Restoring my family name from being bogged down in your investigation. Detective. Now, I think you've taken up enough of my time." He pressed himself back down into the leather couch as if he were trying to push himself into the stuffing.

Carmen held one of the glass doors of Mr. Pink's office open for Zane. He stopped before exiting. "I'd call your attorney. That's not a threat. That's a prediction."

Zane stopped before he and Carmen had completely left the TruCapital building. He gave a last look up at Mr. Pink's office and found him standing. Staring through the windows of his office down at the women below. Handcuffs would not bring the satisfaction Zane needed. The closure of Duncan. Wherever Mr. Pink ended up, he was going to be there to take him down.

CHAPTER 51

Rim of the World, CA

Zane turned the knob for his headlights off and placed his phone into his back pocket. The sound of shattered glass interrupted the quietness of the thick fog. The passenger window of the 1999 Ford Ranger exploded, and bits of fragmented glass smeared the faded dashboard and came to rest in a pile of sparkling shards. Small lacerations on his hands formed as he shielded his face as best he could in a split second. He knew he was bleeding from his face, but he didn't know how bad or have time to investigate.

With one hand on his off-duty Glock 17, he rolled out of the truck and took refuge behind the engine block. He stayed low while wiping his face and examining the amount of blood on his hand. He couldn't tell the difference between what came from his face and what came from his hand. There was blood, but nothing throbbed. He was lucky, for now.

Where did the threat come from? He didn't hear a shot, so was it suppressed? Would have to be close range if so. He leaned around the tire, looking for feet. Nothing. There was only stillness through the white haze of fog.

His eyes remained on the hunt. Focused on anything that moved outside the wisps of silver fog as it slowly enveloped the rest of the mountainside. He thought something moved across the pine needles twenty yards away. A place where the road meets the front of his property. He slid around to the back of his truck and remained low to the ground.

The evening chill overcame the adrenaline that had been concentrating on the mini cuts on his face and arms. There was movement of feet again, this time paired with the sound of voices.

"Sir, are you okay?" the voice called out from within the dense fog. "I'm sorry about that. My boy threw a rock blindly into the world, and I didn't have a chance to stop him. Thought nothing was over there until the wind swept through and I could see where we were."

Zane addressed his adrenaline before addressing the man's voice. He still couldn't see the body that was attached to the familiar voice. His mind searched for the matching set. "Mike, is that you? Did you and Jax break my window?"

"Mr. Bruce?" the little voice of Jax answered. "I'm really sorry, Mr. Bruce. With the fog, I didn't realize how close we were to your house."

"It's all right," he said. He pulled himself up to his feet and dusted the pine and gravel off his pants. He intentionally concealed his firearm before showing himself to his young neighbors. "You're just keeping me on my toes. I've done plenty worse when I was your age. Probably still do to a certain extent."

The fog broke for a moment, and he could see Jax hugging tightly to his father's leg. "Thanks, Zane, for your kindness. Got a little turned around in the fog. Scared both of us quite a bit when we heard the glass shatter. Lesson learned here for young Jaxon Reid." The father and son's faces contorted at the surprising amount of blood that ran down Zane's face and onto his crossed tomahawks tee shirt.

"Oh, don't worry about me," Zane assured them. "I've cut myself worse shaving." He opened the passenger door as more broken glass fell onto his driveway, and he grabbed the duffel bag from the floor of the seat. "The fog is breaking a bit, so you guys should head straight home before you get lost in it."

"Yes, sir," Jax sprang sharply to his heels and saluted.

Zane returned the gesture and spun around to start the climb up his entry stairs. The quick footsteps behind him stopped his climb.

"Zane," Mike said in a subtle, more sober tone. "Hey, the reason we were out in the fog is that earlier. Like, not even an hour ago, we saw some strange cars and people around the neighborhood. They weren't the typical flatlanders eyeing vacation property. We were out walking when the fog started rolling in, and it moved quickly."

"Copy that, Mike. Thanks."

He stood on his porch and waved to young Jax before watching them fade around the bend of the street toward their home. He took inventory of his front door, and all checked clear for entry.

CHAPTER 52

For his chosen profession, Zane didn't set the defense of his house to model that lifestyle. The distance and mountain drive were enough of a deterrent for just about everybody he'd come across. Even the gangbangers and drug dealers stopped going hard with the serpentine drive up Highway 18. Part vertigo, part rock slide. Too many variables for the uninitiated. Anyone else coming onto his turf would be at a strict disadvantage. High-end security cameras and motion sensors were unnecessary for him. He was both. He was primitive and excelled at being tested. His simple lifestyle was his built-in motion sensor.

He kept a tray two steps inside his front door to catch his wallet and keys. Something felt off. He hesitated to release his belongings. After completing his third stride, he glanced around the room and set his keys down softly in the leather tray.

Controlling his breathing, he drew his Glock 17 from his waistband holster. Slow, methodical steps across the open living room toward his kitchen. The silver fog outside the windows provided enough light that he didn't need to retrieve his tattered Mag-Lite. He moved past the entrance mirror with its wooden frame carved out in the shape of a bear.

While making it out alive was toward the top of his to-do list, he had a fear greater than whether he'd live or die. The last thing he wanted was for a young kid to wander into the wrong house and lose his life because of it. His finger remained outside the trigger in such an instance. Trigger discipline. Could it cost him his life by delaying the action? Possibly, but will it save the life of a mistaken kid? That was the plan.

He moved with more grace than he had any right to. He stayed present. Be in the moment. Breathe. Focus. Breathe. Stay disciplined.

Approaching the kitchen, his thoughts of relaxing on his oversized couch were absent. Silence greeted him, and he saw nothing out of the ordinary. He swung into the kitchen, and all was normal. He flipped the light switch, and it illuminated the window above the sink and sent the fog into a bronze glow.

With his house built along the sloped mountainside, the entrance to the house was technically on the second floor. He wanted to check the bedroom downstairs, but thought about a Diet Coke poured over ice. Everything was normal. He holstered his weapon and pulled an Art déco rocks glass from a dated wooden cabinet.

A subtle tan ring was at the bottom of the glass from the last time he poured in his favorite elixir. He grabbed a DC can out of the fridge before heading back to the living room and the sectional couch he had neglected on the initial pass through. A brief disturbance came from downstairs. Maybe he should have cleared the downstairs before settling in. The rock breaking his window gave him pause, but that was in the moment. He had been here before.

The stairs creaked under the weight of something climbing to greet him. He could see where the top step gave way to the landing. He fixed his eyes above the top of his glass as he took a sip of his fridge cig. The light from the kitchen provided enough visibility to identify an intruder or intruders. They may have resembled bandits from old TV shows and movies, but they were not to be trifled with.

"Well, if it's not the Wet Bandits," he said. He replaced his Art déco glass with his pistol and pointed it at his uninvited guests. "How many did you bring this time?"

Three sets of eyes peered at him behind black masks. Their white and gray fur completed the outfits. The raccoons hissed in response to his line of questioning.

He wagged the Glock at the varmint. Finger still outside the trigger. "Now, don't make me use this. I don't feel like cleaning and skinning you tonight. Just get on out of here, and we won't have any trouble. I'll assume you'll let yourself out the same way you let yourself in."

The raccoons hissed again. Their fur puffed out.

"You're right, that was my mistake for not covering the door. Still doesn't mean you can come in. The dogs have been gone a long while, so there's no more food for you to steal."

The gaze of raccoons started walking toward him, but stopped the moment he stood up. He hollered and hopped and threw his hands in the air.

"Go on, get!"

Their bandit eyes locked, and they wanted a fight. He raised his Glock 17 and aimed.

"Alright, you leave me no choice. Which one is going first?"

The showdown was interrupted by a knock on the door, breaking the tension. Like torpedoes, the raccoons broke free from the standoff and shot out the kitchen dog door into the dark unknown. Their claws scratched at the wooden deck as they raced along.

He kept struggling with his firearm, unsure whether to put it away or keep it ready, as the knocking persisted. He chose protection. Two harmless close calls were telling him his luck was running out. When he looked through the peephole, his assumption was correct.

CHAPTER 53

Zane kept one eye pinned to the peephole. "Unless you have Girl Scout cookies, go away." He called through the door. "Tagalongs, too. Don't give me any bullshit about Thin Mints." He remained behind the peephole and awaited the response from his visitor.

A middle finger answered him. It was feminine, but strong. Carmen.

"Stop fucking around and let me in," Carmen said. "It's cold and foggy, and I'm not acclimated to this kind of weather."

Carmen handed him her coat as she stomped into his house. She gave extra force to it. He hung her coat on a decorative railroad tie that was anchored into the wall next to the entrance table.

"Jesus, your face," she said.

"Merely a flesh wound. Tiny nicks that'll heal by morning."

She kissed his forehead and scanned the room. "Sounded like you were under a little duress when I walked up?" She kissed him on the cheek.

"Only the Wet Bandits." He walked over to pick his drink off the coffee table.

"The Wet Bandits from Home Alone were in your house?" She didn't budge from her position just inside the door. "You gonna offer me a drink? And don't even think about handing me the one you've been drinking from."

"I hardly touched it. DC needs to be savored." He retrieved a can and poured it over ice. He kissed her cheek as he handed her the glass. "Don't mess with raccoons. You give them an inch and they'll set up camp. I saw you not too long ago. Miss me already?" A question he didn't expect an answer to. He was glad she had surprised him.

"You gave that video a look," she said.

"No, I didn't," he said. He moved to the couch and took up residence on his favorite cushion.

"You're lying to me. That's going to be a nonstarter in our relationship."

He sipped his Diet Coke, wanting the conversation to move on to something else. After he finished his beverage, he put his eyes back on Carmen. She had crossed her arms. Her raised eyebrow seemed to wait until he came clean.

"There was a familiar look to the man in the video," he said. He leaned back into his couch, hoping he'd fall through the back and into another dimension.

Carmen unfolded her arms. "That wasn't too hard. Now, can you find a lady a blanket and a warm spot on the couch?"

"Sure thing, soon as I see one."

"Don't fuck with me, Bruce."

"See? The language. A lady would never use the F-word in such a threatening manner."

He topped off their DCs and clinked their glasses. He then pulled an oversized throw blanket from the side of the couch. They plopped down side by side. Eye contact was heavy as they allowed the moment to linger. Where was their relationship heading? He didn't want to be anywhere else with anyone else. She was his person.

Carmen set her glass down first. "Who do you think was in the video?"

He pondered the question, replaying the video in his mind. The man in black was fast but stiff, like his body was going. An explosiveness without the youthful bounce of good joints. "I don't know. Wouldn't mind watching it a few more times. Put my high school football days of watching film to good use."

"I've never seen you lock up like that. And I've seen you in every position."

"Not every position." He winked, and she rolled her eyes. He broke the moment and looked out the front window. Something was off. Or was it the rock through his window and the raccoons in his house? The night had an edge to it he couldn't shake. "Anything from the CIs we work with?"

"Just the typical BS. There is an added element of bounties on police heads."

"That's nothing new. Just the ebb and flow of the periodic hatred for cops."

"Correct. Gang bangers will always have it out for us, but this part is new. Money backing it. The CI didn't know who the backer was. They mentioned only dollars per police rank. Higher the rank—"

"Higher the payout," he finished her sentence. His gaze remained fixed out the window. The fog rolled.

"That's right. We have to stop the flow of money before the next badge is black-ribboned with an End of Watch."

"I'm guessing you drove up here because you're having the same feelings about who the financier is that I'm having?"

"Who has access to funds and a new axe to grind with the department?"

"Mr. fucking Pink."

"Mr. Pink?" Carmen questioned the nickname.

"Remember? It's the name Duncan, and I gave him when we first began detailing him. The guy showed up at the office in an elaborate pink outfit with a matching wig. Knowing what I know now about this bozo, he did it to lure his female office staff into a false sense of security. Give off the vibe of how he feels about their health. Clears his conscience while he ogles them from his glass office. And they don't suspect a thing. Mr. Pink is a gold medalist perv and sleazebag."

Carmen sipped her Diet Coke. A palate cleanser. "Must not have a thing for women in uniform."

"Too authoritative. He's the kind of guy who needs to be in control. Hold all the power."

"You're quite the psychologist on this one."

"Work the streets long enough and fight in the trenches of the neighborhoods, and you learn how to spot them. Glass office that overlooks the main floor. How many guys did you notice working? One or two? Busy bodies, so it seemed, were more of them. Probably related to Mr. Pink."

"Maybe nephews or cousins of staff."

"Exactly. My guess is poor Dave Johnson was a rare outsider. A favor to someone, but an outsider. Somebody, Mr. Pink, manipulated and got to mask his financial dealings. The weight of playing in the shadows was too heavy a burden."

"Or maybe after discovering the transactions, he made a fatal mistake." Carmen sipped her drink. Her cheeks glowed. "He thought he'd found a career-changing error in the books and took it up the ladder. Only Truman -"

He gave her a look that told her to use the right name.

"Fine, Mr. Pink. Didn't want those found because they weren't errors at all. Then Tru…Mr. Pink pulled him into his web. First, by thanking him, then by offering him other reports. But they were decoys hidden with subliminal messages."

He beamed with pride. More at the use of Mr. Pink than the theory they were spinning. "Are subliminal messages still a thing?" He continued to listen while fog swept across the front.

She searched for the answer at the bottom of her glass. "We're in a digital world now, so more than ever. The bots alone can get you. Add in the algorithm once it's directed at you. If your head isn't in the right place to begin with. Doesn't matter if you're a teenage girl or a middle-aged number cruncher at an investment firm. The outcome is grim."

"Fuck, that's dark." His turn to bottom out his glass.

"Reality and darkness can closely relate."

Before she continued, beams of light broke through the fog and refracted through the front window. Like spotlights in a lighthouse. Parallel light raked across the living room. The two held still and focused their eyes toward the window. Dry pine needles crunched under the tires, and the headlights stayed on. The conversation remained paused. Senses heightened as the uneasiness set in.

Carmen slowly set her glass on the stone coffee table and reached for the Kimber 1911 she had concealed in her waistband.

He retrieved his trusty Glock 17. The only other person they'd want in this room at this moment was Paul Duncan. He was in a grave, so they had each other. They would deal with whatever came their way accordingly.

He took up post next to the open front window. "Those headlights paused too long for my comfort," he said. "Cut the lamp light next to you. Gotta reach underneath the lampshade and click it off manually."

"You know, they make smart bulbs now. You could just ask Alexa or the Google machine to do it for you." She clicked the lamp off, and the room went black. "Closest neighbor?"

He thought for a moment about his interaction with the young boy and father just after he pulled into his driveway an hour ago. They were out walking, and likely dead if the pit in his stomach was correct. "They're a quarter-mile down the road. Hopefully not dead. I'm not liking this night."

Carmen shot him a look.

"You're the best part, but you always are."

She gave a half-smile. "What next?" She moved to the opposite side of the front window. "Ever heard about security lights?"

"Played the odds of my location being security enough. Plus, you had me looking for stolen mail when I bought the place. Not exactly the line of duty that has my location being compromised and us standing like *Mr. & Mrs. Smith* in the darkness."

Silence took over. Silver fog squeezed the house tight like a python, and mixed with the chilly mountain air, they heard the faint sound of the brakes squeak. No lights accompanied the vehicle this time through.

"Can you see anything?" Carmen whispered across the window. A shake of the head answered her query. She kept her eyes on him and followed along as he broke from looking out the front window to searching for something in the back of the house.

"Back of the kitchen," he said. Her eyes tracked. "See that dog door? On my 'go,' you make a break for it, and I'll be right behind you."

"The dog door? Why?" Carmen stammered in confusion.

"Got a feeling, and it's bad."

He moved back to the front window and pushed Carmen to head toward the kitchen. He studied the world outside. What should have been a residential pine forest was instead a barrier of swirling fog. Then the spark of a lighter. Then the red cherry glow of a lit cigarette.

"Go! Now! Go!" he shouted back at Carmen.

Carmen hurdled the coffee table and kicked over their glasses on her way. The front window shattered like a high school gym backboard, and the front of the house erupted in flames.

A searing heatwave pushed through the living room and into the kitchen as she drove her body out the dog door and into the chilly night air. She pushed herself back and away from the house to make room for Zane. He wasn't there. She grabbed the railing of the deck and pulled herself up. Smoke pushed out from every seam in the house. The hungry fire was spreading fast and back toward her. She moved along the railing until she found the stairs. A hand grabbed her arm and pulled her down.

Carmen's Kimber 1911's barrel quickly met the chin attached to the arm.

"It's me," Zane said. He braced for both of their weight along his back deck stairs. "I came through the bedroom door."

"Why'd you go that way after saying you'd be right behind me?"

They retreated into the woods and away from the burning house. Smoke plumed high and thick. Zane shielded his eyes with his hands as his house turned into a giant box of tinder.

"I was behind you. Then I remembered something in my room. Called 9-1-1 from the landline down there and then left. I always wondered when the door out of the bedroom would be handy."

"A keepsake, and called 9-1-1. Zane Bruce, you're my hero. What did you grab?"

"This," he unfolded his hand and revealed a matching USB thumb drive, like the one Alyssa had worked on finding the financial transactions that led them to TruProperties.

"Where'd you get that?"

"Fell out of my bag when I got home from the hospital."

"You're just telling me about this now?"

"Let's just say I wasn't fresh as a daisy when I discovered it, and it sort of slipped my mind. Took a barrage of Molotov cocktails through my front window to shake my memory. Could also be nothing."

"Yeah, could be nothing. Where did it come from?"

He shrugged. "I just know it wasn't mine, but somehow showed up."

The fog began mixing with the black smoke of the burning house, and the faint sound of fire department sirens wailed in the distance.

"Fuck, this is gonna be a long night. I liked that house too," he said. Fondness fell upon his face, and his eyes reflected the sight of the flames enveloping his home. The heat from the flames warmed his face, already flushed with adrenaline. "Got lucky with the weather. Should keep this from spreading into the forest. That would have been a problem."

"Does this mean you'll be crashing at my place?" Carmen asked. A concerned but excited expression on her face. Familiarity.

"Might complicate things at work."

"Yeah, my dog hasn't had a spooning partner quite like you."

"They say I'm the best. Damn, just when I thought I was out, I get pulled back in for one more job."

The sirens approached the front of the house, where the blaze was most intense. He cautiously led Carmen through the pine trees to greet Rimforest's bravest.

There were no signs of the perpetrator. No mysterious cars lingered on the street, and no strangers watched their handiwork from a distance. At least not that he could see through the fog and bright lights of the emergency vehicles. A hollow ache resonated in Zane's chest as he watched the fire crew, the acrid smoke stinging his eyes as his house turned to ash.

"I don't want to keep you here all night," he said. "Why don't you give your statement and then head home? I'll meet you once I'm wrapped up."

"I don't mind staying," she said. Her eyes were soft and inviting.

"I'll be okay. Gotta make sure these pervy firefighters don't snoop through my underwear drawer."

She laughed. "I'll see you at my place then. My pull-out couch should serve you well for a couple nights."

"My pull-out game is strong," he said.

"Gross." Her laughter faded. Silence ensued.

The feeling of a call too close washed over him before Carmen got into her vehicle. A small percentage of people have gone through it and understood the feeling. A chill snaked up his spine as they exchanged a look of wordless thanks, each breath a prayer in the suffocating moment of quiet.

CHAPTER 54

Zane pulled up at Carmen's house a few hours after saying goodbye. It was later than he'd hoped, but time was a vortex as firefighters drenched his burning house while he cleaned shards of glass out of his truck. He smelled as if he had bathed in a campfire and couldn't wait for a hot shower and a soft place to land.

Carmen's house was constructed in the 1930s and located off Euclid Avenue. Large oak shade trees, which had probably been here just as long, lined the street to create a canopy connecting one side to the other.

While a beautiful sight for the residents of the neighborhood, he considered the security concerns with the low visibility and lack of streetlights. Even with the city's update from high-intensity discharge lamps to LED light fixtures, the charm was gone without an increase in public safety. At least in this pocket of the Inland Empire. He preferred a 5,600 - foot elevation, and a curved highway as his security blanket. The thought made him laugh in defeat, knowing his home was still smoldering on the rim of the world.

Carmen's house was dark, which surprised him, but it was late. She was likely in bed, or close to it, after his delay. Motion-sensor lights triggered on as he approached the front door. He avoided stepping on the grass and stuck to the driveway before taking the walkway to the front door. The porch illuminated the area well, and he could easily see his truck parked on the curb.

He gave a quick knock and took a half step back to watch for interior lights to come on. There was nothing. He knocked once more, but this time with more emphasis. He checked his phone to see if he had a message from her, but there wasn't one. Putting his phone away, he knocked a third time. This time, a neighborhood dog barked in the distance.

He walked back to the front of the garage and jumped to see in through the little windows on the top row. It was a futile attempt. He checked down the street for Carmen's 4Runner, but the street looked like the sleepy suburban neighborhood it was.

A pit in his stomach twisted like hot acid. He jumped over the side gate and triggered every one of her backyard lights and cameras. He waved as they whistled to life. Every window was dark. He also found the backslider locked.

Where the hell are you? Zane's inner monologue turned negative in a hurry. He tried calling her again and again, but the call went straight to voicemail. Anxiety and fear gripped his insides like a vice as he bounced from window to window in search of Carmen. He made quick work back over the gate and to his truck, where he retrieved his Glock 17 and a window-breaking hammer from the glove box.

The dog's bark had dissipated, but Zane wondered how a broken window would liven things back up. He didn't care. Getting to Carmen was all that mattered. He sprang over the gate once more and moved to the back door. Pistol in one hand, glass breaker in the other. His adrenaline spiked for the second time in a handful of hours. His heart rate quickened. The pulse in his neck was like a bass drum at a rock concert.

Thump-thump. Thump-thump.

He banged on the door a final time. "Carmen. I'm coming in."

The light illuminated half of his body, while he tucked the other half tightly against the door. He didn't need to make a big swing, just enough to force entry. He'd cover the cost of any damage and then have lots of personal making up to do if Carmen was simply in the shower and he overreacted.

But what if she's in trouble? Act now, Bruce.

As he drew back to blast the door, his phone vibrated in his pocket, halting his motion.

Carmen?

No, his old man. He blinked as the screen vibrated in his palm, hoping the caller ID would change to Carmen's. He answered the call.

"Son," Sarge's voice was grainy and low. "Listen to me very carefully."

"What have you done?" Zane made a beeline for the gate and yanked it open with one hand, ripping the screws from the wooden post, as a chorus of dogs answered the noise.

Sarge said, "They paid us to pick her up."

"She's a cop. Where the fuck did you take her?" Zane was in his Ranger. He cranked over the engine and drove, not knowing his destination.

"I don't know. I lured her in, and then they took her. Can't be far, but I owed you the courtesy call."

"Courtesy? The courtesy would be remaining loyal to your family. To the badge you swore to protect and serve. Where the fuck is that courtesy?"

Zane ended the call. He jammed his phone into the center console, crushing an empty Diet Coke can. He had a limited amount of time.

Think Bruce.

He placed a call to Alyssa. He spoke like a machine gun, firing the moment the call connected. "I need a list of properties Truman has ever touched, bid on, stepped foot in, or gotten an HR complaint about. Anywhere in the area. Developers and real estate douchebags don't hang their hats on one property. They're always shopping. If he made an offer, I want that address. Check all the shell company files on that USB drive."

"You got it," Alyssa said.

"Alyssa."

"Yeah?"

"As fast as humanly possible, I need you to get back to me. Preferably ten minutes ago."

CHAPTER 55

The floors were dry, and the room smelled of body odor and decaying rodents. Graffiti riddled the walls like a court jester's funhouse. Tyler paced the room, his steps making a shuffling sound as he moved. This was his first ordered kidnapping. He had been there to see Russo's work, but this was different.

Was he ready to see a female in a similar condition to Josue? He needed a bathtub and a furnace. His surroundings provided neither. Only four walls, a floor, and a ceiling. Solid concrete, at least. Any required cleanup wouldn't be difficult, blending into the refuse of a long-abandoned building. Finally, regulatory delays that allowed properties to sit idle for years gave Tyler the opening he needed.

The room vibrated at a low frequency, then he heard the rumble of motorcycle engines. He bit down on his thumbnail and made quick work of getting over to the door. He slid the solid metal door to the side to welcome the party.

Two custom-looking chopper bikes flanked a black Sprinter van, which lacked its manufacturer's branding, likely stripped in a clubhouse garage. The engines stopped, and Tyler forced himself to avoid throwing up. A half-moon hung in the clear night sky, and the dull hum of traffic on Interstate-10 provided the ambiance for the reveal.

Grizzled bikers dismounted their steel horses like modern-day cowboys. Their leather vests and chaps absorbed any light, making their movements appear as if they glided on their feet. The men made their way around to the side of the van and yanked open the door. The men reached in and yanked a body out of the van. It was her.

Lieutenant Cruz's hair was messy and covered her face as she jostled to escape. She wasn't going anywhere. She grunted through the gag that someone had tied around her mouth. Her hands were bound behind her. She flailed and spat vitriol in every direction toward her captors.

Tyler concentrated. His mind worked deep in the recesses of possibility. *Overcome your weakness.*

He bit down on the inside of his cheek. Kidnapping a member of law enforcement was risky business. If Russo or Senior taught him anything, it's that you have to make your own bones in this business. Earned or taken, results were results.

"You made quick work of my request," Tyler said. "Bring her inside, and we can settle up your fee."

The grizzled bikers nodded. They were silent, which Tyler had no desire to understand. This was a transaction, nothing more.

He led the group into the building, and in the room, he stood awaiting their arrival. Holes in the roof provided enough soft light, but the bikers pulled out small flashlights and illuminated their way. The beams of light caught small rodents scurrying along the ground. The stench of mildew from a long-forgotten water ride came in waves.

An old office chair in the middle of the room would be the lieutenant's ultimate resting place. As long as Tyler got what he wanted.

Lieutenant Cruz was goon-handed into the chair, which almost tipped over without the support of all the wheels on the base. An MC member steadied her and turned to Tyler.

"That was the deal," the man said. Despite the low light, his goatee was an unnatural shade of black that created a stark contrast to his pale face. Gaunt cheekbones protruded like misshapen rocks.

Now Tyler was in charge. He'd hand over his fee and take the reins. His mind flashed to his hand shaking uncontrollably as he held the knife toward Josue. Russo, doing his best Tony Robbins impression, talking Tyler over the threshold. He couldn't do it. Russo's guys had to step in and finish the job.

Tyler grabbed the black duffel bag he had packed tightly with the MC's preference of twenty, ten, and fifty-dollar bills. He looked at the disheveled woman bound to the chair, then back to the two members of the MC. He didn't have Russo's guys anymore. He saw to that.

"How about this?" Tyler said. "I'll double your fee, and you handle this portion of the night." The gagged lieutenant grunted expletives in his direction. He threw the duffel at the feet of the two members of the MC. It landed with a thick thud. "Another bag, just as heavy, will be delivered first thing in the morning."

One man kneeled and unzipped the bag.

Tyler protested, "Right in front of me?"

The man next to the bag looked back at his partner and nodded.

"Take it to the van and get Randy," the man still standing said.

The lieutenant began bouncing in the chair. Hopping toward Tyler. The lone MC member walked up to her and hit her in the mouth with a backhand. She fell backward in the chair and tumbled over with it. The sound was dense and cold. Tyler shuddered and bit the inside of his cheek.

By the time the chair was upright again, the man who had left with the duffel had returned. This time with another man, Randy, and Randy carried a toolbox.

CHAPTER 56

Zane had his full weight on the gas pedal and pushed his truck back toward police HQ. Car horns blared as he weaved in and out of lanes. *Never drive when you're emotional.* A comment his old man used to say to him when he was first learning to drive on the hills of Chaffey College. This wasn't emotion. It was unfiltered rage.

He honked his own horn and swerved to avoid contact with a compact sedan. Air whirled around the truck's cabin through the non-existent side window, which brought his tires screeching into surround sound.

His breath fogged the windshield as he spat words into the ether, "Every. One. Get. The fuck. Out. Of. My way."

The steering wheel was being yanked and squeezed on stretching the capabilities of the late nineties model Ford Ranger to its limit. His phone lit up like a carnival in the center console's cup holder. He fumbled for it before answering.

"Alyssa. Talk to me."

Alyssa's voice fought for airtime with the stream of cars expressing their displeasure with Zane's driving. "I have three deposits going out. The Verge scores first and most obvious."

"He will not take her to an apartment complex. This guy is smarter than that. Though abducting Carmen may disprove that theory. What's next and quicker."

"You called me on the fly. I'm working through this as we speak."

"You're right. Please." Zane swung his truck toward the Interstate-215 interchange and pressed on. Instinct guided him toward the south side.

Alyssa breathed into the phone. "Next up, we have the TruCapital building."

"That's a zero-burger. Come on. There has to be something else."

"He hid these transactions better than my home equipment can decipher at the speeds we need. Wait. I'm still working. Give me a few."

"Carmen doesn't have a few. We can't miss this. I can't miss this." He slammed on the horn, and his tires screeched as he avoided another vehicle.

"Jesus Christ, Zane. Are you okay?"

"I'm fine. Late-night drivers leaving the Brandin' Iron should be rolled for two-three-one-five-two."

Headlights and brake lights blurred his vision. He blinked hard and shook his head like a wet dog. *Calm down. Find Carmen.* His mind fought a battle between poise and violent, negative thoughts.

Traffic thinned as he drove eastbound onto Interstate-10. "Anything? Alyssa, please tell me something is springing up?"

He could hear the clacking of keyboard strokes on the other end, but nothing from Alyssa's voice. Finally, she spoke. "I'm not seeing any ties."

Warehouse stores and legal marijuana stores passed along the interstate. Then, there were dark voids of empty dirt lots for sale that stretched for half a mile. He pulled off the exit at California and turned north. A knot twisted in his stomach. A lump formed in his throat the size of a Diet Coke can.

To his left was the dilapidated property of Pharaoh's Lost Kingdom.

"Alyssa, you there?" he asked with renewed spirit.

"I'm here. What do you have?"

"Let's reverse engineer this. Find every offer that's come in on the property that used to be Pharaoh's Lost Kingdom. Maybe Tyler Truman isn't the direct bidder. But if this pit in my stomach is telling me anything, it's that we'll find the connection."

"I'm on it. This could take more than a few seconds. Want to stay on the line, or should I call you back?"

"Call me back. I won't be far."

He idled at the intersection of California and Lugonia. The night sky was dark in this section of the city. Where many developmental lots sprang to life with construction the moment the FOR SALE sign went up, this one remained in rubble. Where graffiti ruled the design work and NO TRESPASSING signs were as useless as lipstick on a pig.

The arrow turned green, and he released the brake. Turning onto Lugonia, he crept along the avenue. It would be easy to lose somebody in the broken-down structure. Water slides that had run dry years ago, along with laser tag, arcades, go-karts, miniature golf, and party hosting facilities. An ideal environment for illegal activity. For kidnapping and torture. A place that only true locals would know about.

There was a delivery entrance off a small side street, so he opted for that approach instead of the main parking lot. A small homeless encampment had made refuge close to the freeway that caught Zane's headlights. He clicked them off and turned onto the property.

Come on, Carmen. Talk to me. Be here.

He followed the driveway as it reached deeper into the park as if it were a major artery supplying life. An incoming call rattled his phone in the cup holder. He answered the call.

"What do you have for me?" he said.

Alyssa's enthusiasm sparked through the receiver. "You were fucking right. Financial holdings are all over Lost Kingdom. Nothing obviously tied to TruCapital. However, another one stuck out, buried in the remarks line. SB-APN 0304-328-06 | TP-SF / BL-AT-EA."

"What is all that gibberish?" he asked as he eased down on the brake pedal.

"First part is standard county code. Next, we have the LLC connection. The last part, BL-AT-EA. That one I can't figure out."

The cabin of Zane's Ford Ranger felt like a box buried under the weight of the world. He cracked a window, listened, and thought. "What were those last letters again? BL-AT-EA?"

Alyssa repeated them back. "That's correct," she said.

He pulled a pen and a napkin out of the center console and wrote it down. "It's got to be some sort of code."

"Normally, this would be for zoning or sub-lots. But it matches nothing else associated with Lost Kingdom."

Zane circled a few letters, but a loud bang broke his concentration. He tossed the pen and paper into the cup holder next to his phone and stomped on the gas pedal. The Ranger's engine howled as he pressed the truck deeper onto the property.

He almost missed it, but as he rounded a building shaped like a Sphinx, a van and motorcycles caught his eye. He stopped the truck. Listened for more noise. Only the dull drone of vehicles moving along on the freeway. He parked to ensure he was facing the exit. *Always know your egress.*

Alyssa's voice broke over the phone. "Zane? You there?"

"I'm here. Carmen's here. I'm going in."

He ended the phone call, holstered his Glock, and headed for the mouth of the Sphinx.

CHAPTER 57

Zane kept his steps light as he moved closer to the Sphinx. The headdress, once painted blue and gold, and which had faded long ago in the intense Southern California sun, wrapped the face of a man. The missing goatee made it look like a poor shave.

He climbed over the outstretched leg of the lion's base and approached the main door. What were the odds of the front door being unlocked? He wasn't hopeful, but being the closest access point, he tried it anyway. Locked, as he suspected.

Silence engulfed him. His clothes squeezed his body like a python of anxiety. An abandoned park, once alive with families and people of all ages, had become nothing more than overgrown weeds and the occasional transient zombie.

Stay focused. Get to Carmen. You're running out of time.

He moved back toward the van and motorcycles, slowing his pace as he approached. There had to be a door closer to them; he couldn't see.

Pushing ahead, he hugged tight to the building in a crouch. With his pistol drawn, he moved closer. The panel van was all black with tinted windows. With heavy aftermarket modifications, the motorcycles were nearly identical. Bulging saddlebags hung off the rear fenders, explaining the common phrase, "steel horse."

Zane's throbbing pulse was certain to create enough noise to give him away. He checked the time on his Panerai watch. Thirty-three minutes had passed since his old man had called. That's thirty-three minutes of pain and suffering Carmen had endured. How much longer before the call had they taken her?

He found the side door directly in front of the van. Before he reached the handle, the door sprang open as if someone had kicked it. He leaped back, barely avoiding its impact. Two men emerged.

One in front carried a small metal toolbox. The other held the door halfway open.

"How much longer do you think she'll hold on?" the one holding the door said.

"She's one tough bitch," the man with the toolbox said. He slid open the side door of the van and tossed the toolbox in. "I'm going to need something heavier."

Zane couldn't wait.

He launched himself from behind the door and pistol-whipped the man holding it open. The biker dropped like an old tarp. The door propped open with the biker's ankle still between the doorjamb.

Zane didn't have time to inspect his work before a heavy thud landed between his shoulder blades. A thick chain came over his head and around his throat, quickly cutting off his air. His pistol dropped in surprise, and he pressed his fingers up between the chain and his neck, looking for any reprieve from the strangulation.

His feet skipped along the asphalt, a desperate attempt at traction. He was being pulled into the dark void. His light dimming.

Fight, dammit. Fight for Carmen.

"Who the fuck are you?" the biker spat over Zane's head.

He couldn't answer; only gurgling sounds of a losing fight came out.

His foot found the van's front tire, and he pushed off of it with all his might. They spilled backward and tumbled over one motorcycle. Zane's momentum carried his feet overhead, and he rolled to freedom. His lungs sucked in oxygen with such force that it burned his trachea. He scrambled upright and retrieved his Glock.

The Bigfoot biker backed himself into a seated position, his hands held up in defense.

Zane aimed his firearm at the man who had tried to end his life. The right words failed him, as if something was holding them back. All that came out was, "Where is she?"

The biker looked past Zane toward the door. Then, in a fast motion, he reached inside his leather vest and pulled out a gun.

Zane's Glock erupted to life with two rapid cracks that bit through the night air. There was a brief after-noise, a hiss of air, the ghost of shots fading away. No lingering thunder. No romance. Only the double-tap of impact, and then silence.

His hand trembled for a moment before he squeezed the adrenaline out of it. He had just taken a man's life. Turning, he looked at the man still lying motionless on the ground. Hopefully not two.

Going over to the man whose foot was still propping the door open, Zane kneeled and checked for a pulse. It was weak, but there. He made quick work of the side door to the van and looked through the toolbox to find zip ties. Fashioning a set of temporary handcuffs, he bound the unconscious man's hands behind his back.

Zane looked down at the two men. One dead, the other still holding on. "Now or never," he said. His breath was stale as the words pushed out from under his breath. He stepped over the man's foot and entered the building.

CHAPTER 58

Tyler's body convulsed into a dry heave as the rapid popping sounds were too close to be fireworks.

He looked over at Snake, who was the lone biker left with him, and said, "What happened to swift and silent?"

The beady-eyed biker made a hissing sound with his mouth and backhanded the lieutenant. Snake didn't look like much, but there was a violent and unpredictable nature about him. His feet slid across the dirty concrete floor with the smoothness of a serpent. A pair of bare, wiry shoulders poked out from his leather vest that may well have been nonexistent. Still, he was dangerous.

Deep yellow bruises formed around the lieutenant's eyes. Mixed in with blood, her face resembled a battered plum bound by a gag. The biker struck her again. This time from the other side. Spit and blood soaked through the gag and onto her sweat-stained shirt.

Tyler couldn't stomach it any longer. He bent at his waist and spread his feet. Acidic stomach bile projected out of his mouth and splashed between his shoes. He danced to keep the spray from reaching his pants. Before he could wipe his mouth, a quick and startling blow connected with his cheek. The snake-like biker was standing in front of him. A gloved finger pointed at his face.

"I'll tie you up next to her if you don't stop being a little bitch," Snake said. "Now's your time to shine." He pulled out a knife. The blade glinted in his eyes as the moonlight came through the broken roof.

Tyler held out a shaky palm. The biker slid the knife onto his open hand and gently closed his fingers around the handle. Tyler didn't have the stones to get the job done at the Dogpatch. Was this his redemption? Doing the work he had always paid others to carry out. His eyes scanned the room. His tongue ran over the raw side of his cheek. He had hired people not loyal to him, but loyal to the duffel bag full of cash. If he didn't follow through, he'd be next to die on this dirty floor.

He nodded to Snake. "Alright. Fuck it." He turned and made his way toward the battered lieutenant. The knife shook rapidly from side to side as his nerves raged war within.

Get it together, or you're going to stab yourself in the leg.

A broken face looked up at him. Half conscious. Eyes swollen as if they carried a disease. Snake hissed at him from behind. "Get on with it."

Sweat turned Tyler's palms into clammy oil slicks, and he nearly dropped the knife. Russo wouldn't make him go through with it. Russo was long gone. A ghost of protection from the dark elements of the business handed down by Senior.

He bit the inside of his cheek and raised the blade. The sharp edge moved closer to the lieutenant's face. She let out a defiant grunt through her gag. His hand trembled.

Another hiss from behind. "Do it already." The biker's boots stomped toward Tyler.

His eyes were wide with fear. With that final trace of humanity before the pit of despair drags you down into eternal darkness.

He placed the tip of the blade under her ear and pressed in. Blood formed a droplet before gliding down her slender neckline.

You can do this, Tyler. Press in and rip. You aren't designed for prison. This is the way of Senior. He lasted decades.

His eyes went from objecting his own reality to beady pinpoints of violence. He could sense his victim's body tense - an acceptance of her own fate.

See? Even she knows this is the way. Now.

His knee buckled beneath him before the popping sound reverberated off the concrete walls. He landed with a clattered thud. Looking sideways, he saw the face of death.

CHAPTER 59

Zane's throat was still inflamed, but seeing Carmen beaten, bound, and gagged ignited a far greater inferno of rage inside him.

He should have killed Mr. Pink. He still might. Night is young.

Scanning the vast room, he didn't see anyone else. The third biker still loomed somewhere in the shadows.

Get to Carmen.

Mr. Pink writhed on the ground. "How'd you find me?" he said. His voice trembled as he searched for his knife, which clattered to the ground.

Zane closed the distance and kicked the knife away. "First the pin in Johnson's apartment. Then your vanity plate—you couldn't resist. Last, your shell escrow company. All things coming up, beat LA." He stepped on Mr. Pink's wounded knee and leaned in. Mr. Pink screamed and howled for mercy. The agony the man was in only made Zane twist down and press harder. As he spun, he scanned the room.

Where's the third biker?

There was no movement in the shadows, so he focused on Carmen. He unclipped a pocketknife from his pants and cut the zip ties around her wrists. Her arms dangled at her sides like limp noodles.

A quick glance back into the shadows before he was back in front of Carmen. He untied the gag, and she collapsed off the chair into his chest. He put his hands on the sides of her face and pulled her back.

"I got you," he said. He wiped the matted hair away from her swollen eyes and bloody face. "Let's get you out of here and to the hospital."

Carmen nodded. She tried to say something, but no words came out. She gave up and spat blood onto the concrete.

The room vibrated, and the rumble of a motorcycle engine stopped them in their tracks. Biker number three slithered in from the exit in an S-pattern. With one hand on his belt buckle and the other holding a shotgun low at his side.

Zane bared his teeth. A wolf ready to protect and defend his pack.

Snake stopped a few feet inside the door and slithered to one side. Another figure emerged from the doorway. This unknown figure was twice as wide as Snake, with a long gray goatee. His seasoned hands hung at his sides like a gunfighter of the Old West. Except instead of Colt pistols, he wielded a long pipe in one and a rusted chain in the other.

Zane took a breath and eased Carmen back onto the chair.

"Fight's not with you, old man," he said. "But don't make me choose between her or you. You walked away long ago. I won't make the same mistake."

A puzzled look contorted Snake's face.

Zane continued, "Oh, he didn't tell you. That's my father."

Snake looked over at Sarge and tried to speak up.

Sarge stayed focused on Zane. "Zip it, prospect," he said. "Know your place. And your place is to finish the job you started. Wanna earn that bottom patch on your rocker? Better redirect your concern."

Mr. Pink's voice broke in from the dirty floor. "Doesn't anybody care about me?" he said.

"You'll be in handcuffs and facing a long prison sentence," Zane said. "Probably shouldn't speed up time." He checked in with Carmen's comfort level and faced Snake and his old man.

Snake racked the shotgun. The sound sent a chill through the room. Zane's arms formed goosebumps, and he held them up on display. Then, he pointed his Glock at the thin biker.

"I'd think twice before you raise that shotgun," he said. "I was careful with this one." He nodded his head toward Mr. Pink, who still cried. "For you, I'm aiming center mass for two, and then one between your eyes."

Snake stood frozen like a cobra propped up, eyeing its target to strike.

"I got an idea," Sarge said. "Lay down the guns. Each of you gets one of these." He held up the rusted chain and the pipe. "Winner gets the girl."

"I could just shoot you both," Zane said. Be a lot less to clean up.

Sarge shook his head. "We both know you can't shoot me."

Before Zane could answer, a sharp, fiery pain shot up from his calf. He looked back to see that the knife Zane had kicked away was sticking out of his pants. He dropped to a knee.

Didn't kick it far enough.

Mr. Pink laughed with a maniacal wheeze.

A guttural roar from Carmen stopped Zane when he reached to pull it out. Snake had dropped his shotgun and was sprinting toward him with a lead pipe held high overhead.

Snake swung. Zane rolled. The blow meant for his skull connected with his shoulder. He roared in pain and continued to roll as the lead pipe rained down upon him.

Ribs, shoulders, hips, and knees with every rotation caught a clubbing blow.

Get out of this, or you're certain never to see the sun again.

The wall stopped him when he ran out of space. He pivoted, placed his feet on the wall, and sprang like a panther from the shadows. He caught Snake in the midsection and drove him to the ground.

The lead pipe clattered and rolled away.

Zane mounted the slippery biker. The pain in his calf surged up his leg. He put one hand on Snake's throat, pinning his head in place, and wailed away punch after punch into the prospect's face. The sickening thuds ended as Snake went limp.

Before Zane could dismount, the rusted chain landed in a pile above Snake's head.

Sarge's boots entered the frame. "He's not done, son. It's time to finish him."

Zane looked at his father.

"He walks out of here," Sarge continued. "There'll be a bounty on your head. Won't be anything I can do to protect you from them." Sarge gathered the chain into a ball and presented it to Zane.

Zane took the offering. The weight forced him to reposition, and an explosion of shattered nerve endings reminded him of the knife still in his leg.

His father was right. MCs are just like any other gang that operates on retaliation. Eye for an Eye.

He lifted the chain overhead. One arm pushing harder than the other.

Carmen grunted again.

Zane paused.

"Do it now, son!" Sarge roared.

Zane looked over to Carmen. She was once again trying to say something. He leaned toward her as if a few extra inches would help her strain less.

She spoke. The words were almost inaudible.

"You're running out of time, Zane," Sarge said.

"Quiet," Zane said. "What are you saying, Carm?"

Her eyes were barely visible through the swollen slits. Her breathing labored. She took in as much air as she could, and then spoke. "I'm pregnant."

All the pain in Zane's body evaporated. He threw the chains down at the feet of his old man.

"I'm not like you," he said.

Distant sirens came through the exposed roof.

Sarge retreated toward the exit with a slight twinkle in his eyes and a devilish grin widening his goatee.

Zane got up and hobbled over to Carmen. He wrapped his arms around the woman carrying his baby. Then he looked back at his old man.

"You keep this up," Zane said. "You'll be the one I'm bringing to justice."

Sarge wiggled his fingers toward Zane and backed out of the door. The Harley's rumble vibrated the room again before fading, and then sirens approached.

CHAPTER 60

Zane used his good leg to do most of the work. Doctors instructed him to use a walking cane, and they bandaged his other leg. His movements were slow, but he could traverse the grounds at the cemetery with minimal hiccups.

He refused to say goodbye to Paul Duncan before he could bring those responsible to justice. With that finally behind him, the morning air lost its crispness as the sun steadily rose in the eastern sky.

Weeping willows and cypress trees surrounded the plaques with streaks of shade. His mind was clear as he approached Paul's plot.

He pulled the Saint Christopher necklace out from underneath his shirt. The words *Protect Us* etched in a circle around the image of the patron saint.

"Thank you, Duncan." He clutched the medallion. "You protected me and kept me in one piece. I'll never understand why, but I am grateful for your friendship and all the goofy bullshit times we shared. You lived your dash." He stood, retrieved a box of matchsticks from his pocket and placed them next to Duncan's name. "You were the law, and I became the cure for the disease that took you from us. Rest in peace, my friend."

He stepped back and locked onto the dates etched across the bronze plaque. A voice broke in from behind.

"Really going to say goodbye with a quote from Cobra?"

He slowly turned to find Carmen. Butterfly bandages outlined the corners of her eyes. The purple bruises were fading and turning yellow. The cuts on her lips had already scabbed over. She smiled at him and placed a gentle hand over the slight bump forming from her stomach.

"Wouldn't have it any other way," he said. "How much time do we have until our appointment?" He moved closer to her, placing his hand on top of hers.

"Appointment is in forty-five, and the drive will take thirty. Guessing we'll be late since it'll take you twenty just to get back to the car."

"Funny. Maybe I can get a little mirror for the bottom of my cane, so I'll know when the baby is coming."

"If you're still using a cane in seven months, you're not the specimen you think you are."

"Please. DCs and cold showers will have me back in no time."

"I'm going back to the car. Take another minute or two, and then it's time to go."

"Yes, ma'am." He saluted. "You know. I hate to see you go, but love watching you walk away."

She playfully flipped him off over her shoulder as she went to the car.

Zane breathed in the freshly manicured lawn, which he always thought smelled a bit like watermelon. The breeze blew in his face, and all was calm. He planted his cane and limped toward the car.

The familiar rumble of a motorcycle engine caught his attention. A few hundred yards away, a man with a long gray goatee sat atop a black Harley-Davidson. The biker revved the throttle a few times, making the engine roar, drowning out the peaceful ambiance before pulling out and driving in the opposite direction.

ACKOWLEDGMENTS

Foremost, to my wife, Courtney. Thank you for being my first reader and supporting this passion of mine. You push me every day to be a better man. To our four kids, Sophia, Spencer, Cora, and Jo, for showing me what truly matters.

To my parents, Mike and Fran, for being the constant example of dedication and commitment. You live an inspiring and motivating life from which I'm still learning lessons forty-six years in.

My sister, Julie, ain't no party like a Dawson party. Thanks for being an incredible big sister. Brock, Brooklyn, Hayley, Sweet T, Jakob, and the rest of your crew out in East Texas, you are missed every day. I look forward to our next visit.

Carmel and Hank, your help with our kids is invaluable. Thank you for always being there. Taquito night to celebrate?

Patrick and Meaghan, living so close has been the gift I didn't know we needed. Mentone bar crawl still needs to happen.

To my friends in law enforcement, who live the stakes I only get to write about, thank you for your service, your candor, and the perspective you trusted me with.

All the guys of The Ranch. You've kept me humble, driven, and always laughing. Your loyalty over the years is remarkable.

My family, all my aunts, uncles, cousins, and spouses, your support means the world. Steven, David, Michael, and Ronnie, let's keep battling for those chips.

To the great VNGCE trainer, Truman Barrett, for graciously allowing me to borrow the Truman name for my villains under one condition—they had to go out in style. I hope you enjoyed their ride. You are the exact opposite of these scumbags. I'll see you at the gym.

Nina Bruhns for your incredible eye for editing and shining a light on areas that needed work. You were instrumental in getting this book where it needed to be. I learned so much working with you.

Lastly, the crime-writing community. You are second to none and have welcomed me with open arms.

David Putnam, your generosity in sharing your wisdom and knowledge of the craft is unmatched. Thank you for welcoming me into the De Luz Writers' Group and teaching me so much. If you ever have time to hear Dave give his lesson on writing, he will not disappoint you.

Chris Mullen, John Stamp, Paul "Roscoe" White, and J.A. Adams, thank you for all your encouragement and shenanigans on our text chain.

The Writers' Dossier creator, Jeff Circle, you are the man. What you do for this community is truly special. Now, I can finally move from the Watchlist to a full Dossier.

L.S. Goozdich, Nathanael Hummel, and the entire Veritas Team. You gave me my first published writing credit for my short story, *The Tongue Collector*, as part of *Western Tales Vol. 1*. I am forever grateful.

Steve Stratton, Terrance Layhew, T.G. Brown, Traci Abramson, Marcy McCreary, Parker Jameson (Ox Devere), Jeff Clark, Claire Istenthal, Dustin Carter, T.R. Hendricks, Steve Urszenyi, Scott McCrea, Eric P. Bishop, and Ryan Pote you all have reached out and helped me along on this journey. Thank you.

Those who have invited me onto their podcasts and helped me believe in myself as a genuine writer and member of this community. I'm honored. This is only the beginning.

www.ingramcontent.com/pod-product-compliance
Lightning Source LLC
LaVergne TN
LVHW041919070526
838199LV00051BA/2671